ALIEN HUNTER

HUNTER

THE WHITE HOUSE

ALIEN HUNTER

THE WHITE HOUSE

WHITLEY STRIEBER

TOR

A TOM DOHERTY ASSOCIATES BOOK

NEW YORK

ALIEN HUNTER: THE WHITE HOUSE

Copyright © 2016 by Walker & Collier, Inc.

A Tor Book
Published by Tom Doherty Associates, LLC
175 Fifth Avenue
New York, NY 10010

www.tor-forge.com

Tor® is a registered trademark of Tom Doherty Associates, LLC.

The Library of Congress Cataloging-in-Publication Data is available upon request.

ISBN 978-0-7653-7869-9 (hardcover)
ISBN 978-1-4668-6329-3 (e-book)

Our books may be purchased in bulk for promotional, educational, or business use. Please contact your local bookseller or the Macmillan Corporate and Premium Sales Department at 1-800-221-7945, extension 5442, or by e-mail at MacmillanSpecialMarkets@macmillan.com.

First Edition: April 2016

Printed in the United States of America

0 9 8 7 6 5 4 3 2 1

Alien Hunter: The White House *is dedicated to the memory of my beloved wife, Anne Strieber, who was my dear friend and companion for forty-five years.*

What survives of us is the love we have made in the world.

—ANNE STRIEBER

I would like to acknowledge the help of historians of the White House, its public relations department, and the U.S. Air Force for advice regarding White House protocols and daily life, and the organization of U.S. missile defense systems.

ALIEN HUNTER

HUNTER

THE WHITE HOUSE

CHAPTER ONE

MELANIE HOLLISTER, a member of the White House secretarial pool for thirty years, was the first to see the dark liquid oozing out from under the door of Albert Doxy's office. She stared down at it. Could it be blood? That's what it looked like.

She tapped on the door, but softly, tentatively. Doxy was just a kid, but there was something about him that made her uneasy. He didn't belong in the West Wing, surely, or, for that matter, even in government, not at twenty-four.

"Mr. Doxy?"

No answer. She reached down, but hesitated. Maybe she should inform somebody. She walked on, her heels tapping smartly as she hurried back to Legislative Affairs.

She sat down at her very polished desk and at once dialed the Secret Service duty officer. Then she stopped. She should have examined it more closely. What if it was floor cleaner, or paint; she'd look like a fool.

When she returned to the corridor, she found that the gleaming, dark red pool had spread almost across to the other side of the hall. It was blood, no question, and a lot of it.

Fisting the scream that the sight of it drew from her, she went to the nearest inside phone and said to the duty officer, "I believe we have blood on the floor here."

Moments later, two Secret Service agents appeared, guns drawn.

Confirming that it was blood and that there was nobody responding from behind the door, they initiated a "possible intruder" alarm.

Under such an alarm, the first thing that happens is that the president, First Lady, and family members are evacuated from the building. If possible, they will be escorted aboard Marine One on the South Lawn and flown to a place of safety.

In this case, though, the helicopter was not present, so they were hustled into a car and driven away. The nondescript emergency sedan, its existence known only to a few security personnel and the first family, was heavily armored. It was balanced in such a way that its exterior—the body of a Chrysler 300—revealed no hint of either its great weight or its powerful engine. Normally, no escort accompanied it, just the agent driving. It was meant to be incognito, this car. Still, its every movement was tracked, both via a GPS unit built into its onboard computer and by satellite. Unmarked cars shadowed it, ready to pounce at the least sign of trouble.

As the First Family left, a staff evacuation took place and all tourists were escorted to the street. Just as in a fire drill, the staff members moved calmly to their assigned staging points, identified themselves to their group heads, and waited. As always, they were given only necessary information. They had no idea if this was a drill or the real thing. Some of the most powerful people in the world stood in the Rose Garden and on the South Lawn, shielding their eyes from the bright sun and staring back at the building's dark windows.

Within four minutes of the emergency being declared, the agents on scene received word that the building was clear and that POTUS was on his way to a safe house. This could be the vice president's mansion; 716 Jackson place, the ex-presidents' "clubhouse" across the street from the White House; or any number of other locations in Washington, kept ready for the president in the event he needed to evacuate but not to leave the city, and so far that did not appear to be necessary.

After a series of double and triple checks of the complex building, the staff was allowed to return to all areas except the second floor of the West Wing, which was now sealed, all stairways and the elevator guarded by Secret Service agents.

It was to the ex-presidents' clubhouse that the Secret Service took President "Wild" Bill Greene, his wife Lorna, and their daughter, the tightly self-contained Annette, known to her few close friends by her childhood nickname of Cissy. Privately, the staff called her Snow, for her flowing blond hair and her coldness. She was twenty and as desirable as a woman could be, tall, smooth, and slender. She had gray eyes that watched the world around her with a vigilance that all who met her found disconcerting. She had a difficult past, Cissy, hidden even from her parents. Something had been revealed to her when she was all of seventeen that should never have been revealed to anyone without the skills necessary to cope with secrets, and this was not just any secret. It was the most toxic secret in the world.

It was illegal for her to tell even her father, despite the fact that he was now president. The secret had transformed her from a hell-raising, fun-loving teenager, every bit as wild in reality as her father was by reputation, to an old woman in a shimmering young body, her once-innocent face now wrapped in shadows.

The First Family's Secret Service code names were Rover, Silver, and Tea, all chosen at random, so it was claimed. But Wild Bill had many girlfriends, Lorna—understandably—had silver hair, and Cissy would have looked very appropriate behind a formal tea service.

Back at the White House, the teams that now filled the corridor outside of Doxy's much-coveted office prepared to enter. These people were all in shock, but only the Secret Service understood this. The agents were watching closely for the sorts of fumbling mistakes and emotional outbursts that come with these situations, ready to pull anybody out of their task at the first sign of trouble.

Al Doxy's having a West Wing office had been deeply resented by everybody in the administration who thought they deserved one, which was everybody who indeed did, who might have, and who absolutely didn't.

If you're anywhere in administration in the Executive Branch, you need that West Wing address. It doesn't matter that many of the second-floor offices are closets, crammed in under the roof so that all you might see from your window is the inner view of the parapet and, above it, a little slice of sky.

The office of Albert Doxy didn't have even that. It was windowless, located next door to the National Economic Council's suite. It was identified only by its number and a small placard that said A. DOXY.

He reported to the Assistant to the President for National Security Affairs, Maynard Peebles, who had not wanted him anywhere near the National Security Council, let alone in an important supporting role. Peebles had been career Foreign Service until he had been tapped by Wild Bill's secretary of state, Tom John Costigan, for the NSC position.

Costigan was a protégé of Robert Calhoun Doxy, Al Doxy's father. The elder Doxy was a close friend of the president and his most important contributor. They'd grown up together in Midland, Texas, both of them privileged sons of wealthy oilmen. When he'd been tapped for the NSC job, Costigan had been president of the TR Corporation, a defense contractor owned by Doxy.

Was he capable? He was loyal, and that was what was crucial to the president. First and foremost, he wanted loyalty at the top. Ability could show up among the underlings.

Truth to tell, young Albert Doxy was not entirely unqualified. He had excelled in college. He was University of Texas Plan II Honors, *Texas Law Review,* then briefly with Adams, Walker, Price and Smith, the Doxy Companies' captive law firm. He'd gone from there to the White House, appointed at the insistence of the president to the job of coordinator on the staff of the National Security Council's senior director for intelligence programs. He'd read his le Carré and David Ignatius, so he considered himself ready for the job.

He was in a position that saw substantial memo traffic, and that was just where President Greene wanted him. Loyalty at the top, ability in the middle, loyalty again among supporting staff. Call him a crook, as many did, a fool as many more did, you could not fault Bill Greene's management skills.

The boy's death—for he was quite likely in there dead—was going to cause a major upheaval, and everybody working the case knew that. The least mistake, and you were off to the farthest, most miserable, most thankless post that could be found for you.

Among the thousands of contingency plans that the Secret Service had run over the years was one known as Host Element, which was to be applied in the event that somebody was behind a locked door in the White House, holding hostages, carrying a bomb, or in some other hostile or extreme state.

Host Element had been activated, and therefore, before opening the door, the agents swept the room with portable sonar. The image that came back showed a figure slumped over a desk.

"Suicide?" the operator muttered.

They sent a camera in on a flexible cable, working it under the door, through the blood.

There were now six agents in the corridor, not enough to compromise security elsewhere, but enough to raise the odds that an unexpected event could be handled.

There is no door in the White House to which the Secret Service does not possess a key, and that includes even the bathrooms in the residence. The lives of presidents are not private lives—they are protected lives. The difference is profound, and tests men to their core. Weak men succumb to the disease that the presidency can so easily become. Anything you request is yours, and at once. President wants a Coke, it's there. An omelet, it's there. An attractive intern, nine or ten of them are there. Life in the beautiful trap.

The door to the wunderkind's office was about to be opened, and when it was, William Robert E. Lee Greene was going to be subjected to a great test.

The agents who popped the door did three things: They stepped in, they sucked in their shock when they saw the boy, then they forced themselves to do the work they were trained to do.

They sent the emergency medical team that was waiting outside away, and called for a collection crew from the D.C. Medical Examiner's Office.

There was an immediate response from the Joint Operations Center: "Nix that. Get all nonessentials out of that corridor and nobody comes in."

Outside, somebody—a fireman—began vomiting from the reek of blood, which with the door open now filled the hall.

"Get 'em out," Jim Allendale said over his shoulder. He had been in the Secret Service for twelve years, White House detail for four. With him was Elizabeth Cruze, also twelve years in, five in the White House.

"What are you looking at," the chief crisis officer asked over the secure phone.

"Albert Doxy was beheaded, sir. His head is on his desk."

The response was a cry, instantly choked off.

Nobody at the scene had ever encountered anything like this. Not a single person involved had ever seen a severed head. There had never been a murder in the White House, nor any violence that came close to this, not even an accident.

The firemen were escorted out, along with the White House uniforms. This was Secret Service officers only, and the fewer the better. From long experience, they all understood that, while their first job was to control this crime scene, a close second was to keep the president's options open, and that meant slamming the lid down hard and fast.

They worked silently, carefully, almost robotically, each member of each team trying to avoid vomiting, fainting, or doing anything except the best job they could.

The forensics team photographed the scene, with special attention to the neck, its severing incision so neat that, now that the blood had drained, it looked like the work of a surgeon or a skilled anatomist.

It would later be determined that the cut had been done with a blade less than a centimeter wide, and that would remain a mystery to all now working in this room, because none of them had a security clearance high enough to know the probable source of such a remarkable tool—or, in this case, weapon.

At Secret Service Headquarters on Murray Drive, something close to a riot was unfolding. But it was a controlled riot, as agents moved quickly to do what they could to contain the threat.

The first order of business was to locate and identify the perpetrator. As the White House corridors are all covered by surveillance cameras, this should not have been difficult.

But it was. The only person seen to have entered Doxy's office was Doxy himself. His movements were traced back to a point when he had been picked up returning to the White House on foot, which in and of itself was highly unusual.

He'd left empty-handed, but come back with a file.

The surveillance system was ultrahigh-resolution, precisely so that details like type could be read, and this file was from the National Security Council Historical Record. The tongue of the folder said, NSC 13220-543 CL 14. It was not a standard designator, and the agent placed on the detail determined within minutes that it was either highly classified or a fake.

The Greenes remained under guard at 716 Jackson Place. Chief of Staff Matthew Finch was the only outsider with them when Bill finally accepted the fact that he had to call Bob Doxy despite having no explanation for what had happened to young Al.

First he made another call to the director of the Secret Service, Simon Forde. "Sim, is there anything I can tell Bob Doxy? Anything at all?"

"Mr. President, we have moved the body to cold storage."

"That wasn't my question."

"He died due to criminal activity and his body will be returned to the family as soon as possible."

"Where is it?"

"Sir, at the moment it's in the meat locker."

"Our meat locker? The White House meat locker?"

"Yes sir, I'm sorry. We'll move it as soon as possible."

"I want to ask about sanitation here. And legality. Don't we have legal obligations?"

"It's in a sealed body bag."

"That's not something I can tell him! I want information I can use. What in hell happened? Tell me exactly."

"Mr. President, he was—"

"Yes, he was beheaded. But that's damn well classified, you hear me? National security. That gets leaked—well, it can't. Flat out cannot."

There was a silence. It extended.

"All right, Sim, do your work." He hung up. "Lorna, what do I do? What do I say to him?"

"You're the president, you figure it out."

Cissy said, "Just tell him. What else is there?"

"So I call and go, 'Hiya, Bob! Al got his head cut off in his office.' Is that your suggestion?"

"Come on, Dad! You tell him what you have to tell him. Al's been killed, it's a national security matter, he died in service to his country; you can't say more."

"And the public is going to be told it was an accident," Lorna added.

"Then in a few days I pick up the *Post* and read that he was beheaded by an outraged lover or some damn thing like that."

"He didn't have any lovers," Cissy said.

"You can guarantee this?"

"Dad, I can't guarantee anything. Nobody can. But he was arrogant and fat and oily and not social. His thing was, he was brilliant."

Lorna said, "An accident. Fell downstairs, whatever."

The president, from his seat at the end of the long mahogany dining table, looked at each of them. "So what in hell really did happen to him?"

Nobody spoke.

"WHAT HAPPENED?"

Lorna looked down into her lap. Matthew Finch took out his phone and began texting. Cissy got up and left the table.

"Where are you going?"

She stopped. She turned back. The pain in her was so great that it was like being burned alive from within. "Daddy," she said, "if you must know, I am going to the bathroom."

CHAPTER TWO

TEHRAN WAS choked with dust, the Alborz Mountains invisible from the city center, but just visible from the campus of the College of Aburaihan in the northern suburbs.

The college was devoted to the study of agriculture. Animal genetics, biotechnology, even silkworm husbandry were taught here. For this reason, foreign intelligence agencies left it alone. The worrisome ones—the CIA, MI6, the French DGSE, Mossad—were nowhere in evidence, which was why the brain biology faculty had been relocated here.

Dr. Ibrahim Josefi did not teach about silkworms or cattle genetics. Unfortunately for him, Western intelligence had recently identified him as an important nuclear engineer who was probably working outside the treaty. They would on this day kill him for that. The identification had happen for two reasons. The first was the new car the regime had awarded him. Such things were watched. A genetics researcher did not merit a priceless reward like that. So it was presumed that he was a nuclear engineer who had been hidden away in an obscure institution because his work was secret.

He knew nothing about nuclear weapons. He taught something far more sinister, which was the poetry of the mind: how to manipulate moods and change ideas, and how to gain control over the seat of consciousness. His work was against Moslem belief, but it was also useful to the Islamic

Republic, so it was not only tolerated, but lavishly rewarded—to his cost, as would shortly become apparent.

He looked out across the small lecture hall. Only half of its seats were filled by this extremely important group of attendees. There were guards on all the doors. The hall itself had been swept for surveillance devices just minutes before he was to begin this critical talk.

One group of attendees were skilled police officers and organizational experts, the men who would one day soon govern the West, what might be left of it. The others were medical personnel who would manage the mind control program that was going to place the Islamic Republic and the Persian nation where it belonged: at the center of the world.

To wet his parched throat, Ibrahim took a sip of water. Meanwhile, a satellite overhead watched his car. In four different safe houses, four men waited, preparing, cleaning their guns, watching their encrypted cell phones for instructions.

Ibrahim began the speech of a lifetime—in fact, the last speech of his lifetime.

"We have learned how to control the human being by controlling his consciousness. Understand, please, what a mind is—nothing more than the dance of electrons among the neurons, refereed, if you will, by the chemical bath that surrounds them and modulates their behavior. To an extent, it's possible to change the mind chemically. Introduce a tranquilizer, the subject becomes more calm. A stimulant does the opposite. There are many quite powerful drugs, with profound effects."

Some of these people used such drugs every day. Davood Ghorbani of the Revolutionary Guard, for example, was an interrogator with a great mastery of the mind-altering pharmacopoeia.

"But drugs have their definite limitations. They can alter the way the brain functions, but they cannot add an idea to a man's mind." He paused. He spoke what he believed were the two most important words ever uttered by a human being. Lowering his voice, leaning into the microphone, he said, "We can."

Again, he paused. He looked out across his audience. They were rapt, sitting forward, eager.

"It isn't a matter of whispering thoughts into the mind, not precisely that, but rather to make it appear to the target that the fulfillment of our policy and his own wishes are the same thing." He took a couple of breaths, then continued. "We have discovered that by altering the electrical currents in a certain part of the brain called the claustrum, we can change thought, and very profoundly."

He did not speak of the true origin of the knowledge, and certainly not of the fact that the Americans had gotten it first and were also developing it, or that it involved the implantation of magnetically sensitive microchips into the brain. But how far along were the U.S. experts? Could they be ready to implant the Iranian leadership?

He had just received word that an example of an American implant was on its way to Tehran right now, removed from the head of a White House flunky by a master espionage agent.

The great difficulty was that Iran's new and very secret ally was reluctant to simply give them the technology. The reason for this was unclear, but then again, so was almost everything about this strange ally.

He completed his explanation of how the devices worked. It wasn't only that tiny pulses were delivered to the claustrum, but that they were programmed in complex patterns that would entrain the neurons in such a way that the subject would react to outside signals as if they were his own thoughts.

"So, in conclusion, I think that you can see the great power of this technology. It is the future of the Persian people and of our republic, and it is also the future of the world."

It was time to ask for questions, always an uneasy moment. Some of the people here were connected to very high levels of the leadership, even the Supreme Leader, and it was never entirely clear where questions might be coming from or what they might actually mean. He smiled, and requested them.

At once, hands were raised. Ghorbani was first.

Politely, he came to his feet.

"How can the changing of one mind lead to the changing of the world?"

Of course, it was *the* question. He had wondered himself, until the explanation of just what to do had come from the hidden ally. Not even these people, among the highest of the high, knew of it—only he himself, the Supreme Leader, and Mohammed Wahidi of MISIRI—the acronym for the Iranian Ministry of Intelligence—and he knew only the outlines, not the details of how it would be executed.

He took a breath. "We have made a thorough study of both the American and Russian land-based missile systems. Both are fully operational, and both have significant safeguards against accidental or unapproved firing of the missiles."

Ghorbani frowned. "I don't understand. Why does this matter?"

"If the great powers engaged in a nuclear exchange, they would no longer be great powers."

The silence was absolute.

"Let me show you a tape." He turned on his projector. The test subject, a prisoner of the revolution, lay strapped to a table. A neurosurgeon masked in white inserted a long silver probe into an opening that had been drilled in his skull.

"This is an electromagnetic pulser. It works like an implant, but obviously it's more crude. The tape was made last year, before we had implantable devices. Like an implant, this device can deliver very slight streams of electrons to different areas of the brain. In this case, it is going to deliver to the claustrum a very specific pulse that will cause the subject to believe something that he knows for certain to be true is not true."

He was also the neurosurgeon on the film. He watched himself say, "Ali, can you hear me?"

The prisoner responded in the affirmative.

He said to his audience, "On the film I will shortly apply current to the claustrum. First, I will use another instrument, a sonic hammer, to knock him out." He chuckled. "It is a very gentle hammer. It turns out that there are sounds that can induce unconsciousness. Really, more than that—they can turn off the claustrum. To the subject, it is as if time itself ceases to exist."

Ali didn't close his eyes, but they began to stare fixedly. On the film,

Ibrahim said, "Ali?" There was no response. "Ali!" Nothing. He took a needle and slid it into the subject's cheek. There was no reaction.

"He is not asleep. Instead, his entire self—all he knows of himself—has been turned off. He is completely unaware. Except for the claustrum, though, his brain is fully functional. Now, watch what happens."

On the film, he saw himself manipulating the probe. "What I am doing is adjusting the various frequencies to deliver a very specific thought into Ali's brain."

"But how is this possible? How do you know these frequencies?"

The question came from one of the police officials. Of the people in this room, only Ghorbani might know the answer to that question. How he longed to tell them of Aeon, of the Wire, and of the power that this marvelous new alliance was conferring on the Islamic Republic. Instead, he said, "There has been a long study, and it's still continuing. Actually, it's most of what I do. We analyze the thoughts of test subjects, then create frequencies that will duplicate these patterns in other brains. For example, the thought that I am going to introduce into Ali's brain was originally derived from my own. I was the test subject, lying for hours in a functional magnetic resonance imaging machine until we had recorded every electronic nuance of the thought that my brain was producing." He watched the film for a moment longer. "Here," he said, stopping the action for a moment. "The pulser is now operative. Ali is receiving the thought that his wife is not in America anymore. That she is in Iran, in custody. That unless he declares support for the revolution, she will be executed at once. Now, he knows for certain that this cannot be true. He spoke with her on a secure line in the American embassy just a short time before we picked him up. She is in America, and he knows this for certain. But watch."

On the film, he withdrew the probe. Ali blinked. At first, he was confused. Then an expression of horror crossed his face. He sat up and cried out, "The Islamic Republic is the will of God! God is great, God is great!" Then he burst into tears and covered his face with his hands.

Ibrahim turned off the tape.

The silence in the room was again profound. All of these people were advanced in their understanding of his work, but they had never seen this. Until now, nobody had. But they understood the implications; he could see that from their rapt attention. The slight smile that had appeared on Ghorbani's face particularly pleased him. One day, this ferocious revolutionary, an expert in the arts of secrecy and government by compulsion, would be the head of the American Protectorate, governor of the United States.

One of the women present, Nadja Parandi, raised a hand. She was a skilled neurologist and, since the recent advances, an expert on brain implants.

"Professor, thank you for taking my question."

"I am honored, Dr. Parandi. God willing, you won't stump me."

There was a ripple of laughter. In the West, Iran was portrayed as a slave state for women. Ask this one, though. An able, loyal, and brilliant woman had a place in the modern Iran.

"I understand that most here will be government officials in the West after we have taken over. What I don't understand is how in practical fact this will be done. It's all well and good to show us how a man can be controlled under ideal conditions. But the Kremlin and the White House are hardly ideal conditions."

She sat down and folded her arms.

Ibrahim was concerned by her question. If he appeared to be holding anything back, these powerful people would be furious. But he could not tell the whole truth. In fact, he did not know the whole truth.

He drew his thoughts together very carefully. If he said too much, Wahidi would be on him like a tiger. If he said too little, these people would come to distrust him. Someone, at some point, would have his head.

"The weak links in both missile systems are the national leaders. I think we all know that."

"Respectfully, Professor, I submit that Vladimir Putin cannot be successfully subjected to this mind control technique, or any such technique."

"I would agree, but we only need one of them, not both. The American is our target." He was careful not to say "President Greene," because the situation was more complex than that.

"Very well—so I thought. What of the practicalities? How do we implant him?"

She had assumed that it was Greene, which was what he had hoped would happen. Even among these trusted people, there had to be a level of concealment.

"We do have a program in place. It will lead in the direction we desire."

"Which is?"

"The Islamic Republic, may Allah defend it, will become the most powerful nation in the world."

"Thank you, Doctor. May I know when?"

She took her seat. Her face was totally devoid of expression. Unreadable. Before the treaty, the West had believed that Iran intended to build a vast nuclear arsenal, but Iran already had all the nuclear weapons that it needed—enough to destroy Israel once the United States could no longer defend it. The strike would be so quick and unexpected that Israel would not be able to return fire.

After he was done, he strolled across the campus, enjoying the stillness beneath the yew trees. It was a familiar sort of afternoon in Tehran—airless, the campus possessed of a silence that always seemed to him to reflect his own deep loneliness.

On the surface, he was a devout man, careful in his observances—but that was only the surface. Truthfully, like most educated people, he was an atheist. But he was also a patriot, deeply in love with Persia, its poetry and art and ideas, and the grandeur of its long journey across time. How little the English understood of a civilization so ancient, and the Americans, those grinning, immeasurably powerful children, bullies of the world—they understood, quite simply, nothing.

He reached the car park and went to his Toyota Avalon, sparkling blue and still smelling crisply inside of its newness. The revolution spared no expense for him, and he enjoyed the material advantages that came with his work. As he walked, alerts went to four cell phones in different parts of Tehran, and four operatives checked their weapons, put on their helmets, and went to their motorcycles. But Ibrahim knew nothing of them.

When he had first heard of the new technology and how it might be used, in the large office of Mohammed Wahidi of MISIRI, he had almost laughed aloud, it seemed so impossible.

"You cannot," he had said. "To get in there—the White House—it would be difficult even if you weren't brown."

Wahidi had simply stared at him in silence, which was most disconcerting.

"You are a loyal man," he finally said. "Loyal and, from your papers we have read, one of the best-informed neuroscientists in Persia."

"Thank you."

"So you do the neuroscience and let us do the tradecraft. Best that you not even ask about it."

"No, I can understand that."

Wahidi had then leaned forward, radiating menace. If ever there existed a predator in human form, it was this man.

Wahidi had told him, then, the greatest secret of all, the one that he must never reveal. The awesome secret that, to any Persian, would have been profoundly inspiring: *They* had in their wisdom—in their infinite wisdom, the wisdom of gods—surveyed the nations of the world. *They* had seen and rejected them all, but for one: beloved Persia. *They* had seen that the Persians should be masters of the world.

They.

He got in the car and turned it on, listening to the quiet hum of the engine coming to life. Such a car as this could not be built in Iran—not yet, but that would come. It would all come.

As he drove toward the city center, the four motorcycles converged on his route, moving through the traffic with easy efficiency.

This evening, Ibrahim planned to attend a reading of new poetry. The revolution watched the poetry movement very carefully. There was protest in it, but it was also true that the very soul of the revolution—of Persia herself—was there.

He turned on the radio, then lit up one of the wonderful American cigarettes it was his privilege to smoke: a Camel, richly flavored and powerful. Iranian cigarettes were much milder, and being steadily made more so by the government, in the interest of health, he assumed.

But health was for tomorrow. Either he would live or he wouldn't. In any case, this was his last carton. Next week, he would stop.

The narrow streets of the old city were, as always, choked with traffic. Thus it was that he failed to notice the fact that motorcycles had come up on both sides of his car. Perhaps it was also a bit of arrogance, his having been educated at MIT and Cambridge. He'd had the chance to stay in the West, but the revolution had drawn him home, that and the call of Persia herself, the sorrowing, glorious nation that was the true center not only of the human past, but of mankind's future.

These thoughts, half-formed, were drifting through his mind when the snarl of a motorcycle engine finally intruded into the cool, quiet interior of the Avalon.

Many people in Tehran had bodyguards. Many had armored cars. On the theory that such things would only draw attention to him, he'd been given neither.

Seeing the two motorcycles, he knew at once that he was in peril. Frantically, he hunted for the button on the steering wheel that would activate his cell phone.

Then he saw the motorcyclist on the driver's side, anonymous in his gleaming black helmet, slip a hand into his leather jacket. Ibrahim jammed on the gas. The car burst forward—but struck a lorry, causing its cargo of onions to come cascading out over his hood.

His desperate attempt to get out of the trap hadn't mattered, though. He had been dead before his car struck the truck. His body remained behind the wheel, sitting stiffly, eyes open, face strangely rapt. He looked like a judge officiating at a complicated trial.

In the driver's-side window there was a neat hole, and on his temple a steady runnel of blood. By the time the furious driver of the truck had come storming back to confront the fool who had rammed him, Dr. Josefi's collar and the arm of his shirt had turned dark red. The soaked sleeve clung to his skin, outlining his muscular arm. He had been trained in martial arts. He had been trained in defensive driving. He had been trained to drop down below the line of the window at the first sign of trouble.

He had not, however, been trained to never be surprised.

The motorcyclists were gone, absorbed in the twisting streets and the unending stream of traffic. They would go on about their business as soldiers in the enormous Western espionage system that wound through Tehran, an ever-changing tangle of suspicions and discoveries.

From Paris to Berlin to London to Langley, Virginia, the news had already been flashed: Dr. Ibrahim Josefi, an important nuclear engineer with an as-yet-unknown brief, was dead. The Iranian nuclear program—the one running off treaty—had been set back yet again—how far they would determine as soon as Josefi's exact role became known.

They would never find out, would never understand the breathtaking peril he had represented—which was greater than even he knew. In fact, his work was part of a much larger plan, one that no human being would support, no matter how extreme his or her views. Not Josefi, not Ghorbani—none of them.

Iran's new ally was like that—far more clever than any human being could ever be.

A fool had completed his fool's errand, as had the fools who had killed him. The real plan, terrible beyond human understanding, now began to unfold in earnest.

CHAPTER THREE

SECRET SERVICE director Forde arrived at 716 Jackson at four in the afternoon. He found the president, Mrs. Greene, and Cissy in the parlor. The president was drinking and pulling on a cigar. He was dressed in what he had been wearing when they'd been evacuated: jeans and a white polo shirt. Cissy wore a tan and rust sweater and Lorna a green silk suit. They sat close together, huddling like people in a storm.

"Sir," Forde said, speaking softly, "the situation is under control."

"Meaning?"

"The entire house has been searched. There is nobody in it who might pose a threat. It's safe to return."

"So you caught the perp?"

"No sir, not yet."

"Then it's not safe to return, so don't tell me that."

"The White House is safe—I'll stake my reputation on it."

"You've got a lot of guts, then, or you're a moron, because what you've just told me is that a murderer got in and out undetected. Until you can come to me with an identified criminal, I'm not going back there. I hate all that old stuff, anyway. 'Don't sit in this chair, don't drop crumbs on that rug'—Jesus, give me a break. I sat through a Dolly Madison chair just yesterday. I'm sick of the place, I hate it and I'm not going back." He flashed a big smile. Not a nice one, though. "Let's turn it into a museum."

As he railed, Forde glanced at Lorna. She called the shots, wore the pants, ran the country, however you wanted to put it. But she did it from behind the mask of the southern belle. Her smile was sweet, but her stick struck hard. You most definitely did not want it to connect with you.

"If we suddenly leave the White House," she said, "it calls attention. Right now, that's the last thing we want."

"There's been a murder, Lore, there's gonna be attention!"

"We're not calling it a murder and we're not calling it a suicide, Bill. As far as the world is concerned, it was an accident, nothing more. There will be some attention, but nothing we can't handle. As long as we don't do an Eisenhower, this will hang in the news cycle for six hours tops."

"What's an Eisenhower?"

"He went out to some airbase in California and disappeared for a few hours. It was international news for a week. If we leave the White House, it's international news for a week. If we do it because of a suicide, we're in trouble for a month. Inevitably, it comes out that the suicide was really a murder and we go down in flames. It was an accident; the building clearance was a routine precaution. So let's get our tails back where we belong."

"Where did he go?"

"Who, Bill?"

"Eisenhower."

"He went to the dentist." She turned to Forde. "Can we move now?"

"Any time. We're ready when you are."

She stood up. "Let's go, honey, we have dinner with Justice Reinhardt and Justice Fuller tonight. We've just got time to change."

"Oh, God, those fossils." He stood up, then thrust his face into Forde's. "Serve and protect, eh? Except for the son of my best friend."

"Sir, the Secret Service is charged with the protection of the First Family."

Greene shoved him aside and strode out to the waiting Chrysler, Cissy and Lorna following.

In the car, Bill again asked his daughter if she felt safe returning. She still didn't, but she also didn't want to contradict Lorna. You didn't mess with Mom. She kept count, and she did not forget.

"Daddy, I feel like Mom does. That we have to be there."

"Yeah, and Henry the Eighth had to stay at Versailles, and look what happened to him."

Lorna shook her head. Cissy swallowed her guffaw. Daddy had been studying history, God help the United States of America. He was not a genius with facts. Now that he had Henry the Eighth at Versailles, heaven only knew what else he might come up with.

On the way back, Cissy reflected that she needed to get to her room as soon as possible. She needed a private moment to call the secure number she'd been given. There was no way to be sure that the murder would interest the people on the other end of the line. But it was an "extremely unusual event," no question there, and she'd been told to inform them of anything like that.

A few years before, she'd witnessed some very strange things on a ranch in Texas. The people in control had made her sign a security document. Flynn Carroll of the ice-gray eyes had popped up out of nowhere in a bar and thrust the paper at her. He was the coldest, most unsmiling human being she'd ever met, and the most thrilling. Even more so than his friend Mac, with whom she'd fallen in love back in those days. Innocent days, shacked up with that wonderful crook. Mac was dangerous and delicious. He wasn't like Flynn, though, a man so hard you could believe he had a soul of steel. He also wasn't limitlessly wealthy like Flynn, a child of the great Permian oil boom that had transformed West Texas, starting way back at the beginning of the twentieth century. Flynn's was the same sort of Texas story as her own: hardworking ranchers ending up sitting on millions of dollars' worth of oil.

He wasn't flashy like her dad, though. He had a charitable foundation so hidden that its name wasn't even publicly known. God only knew how much money he gave away. Or had, for that matter. Certainly, he was among the richest men in Texas, and yet he lived modestly, so much so that, when he was a cop in Menard, only his old friends even knew he had money.

Strange guy, all the way around. And appealing as hell, damn him.

Fourteen years her senior, just enough to be too old for her, at least in her crazy parents' book. The Greenes were schlocky new money. The Carrolls were old Texas, deeply rooted. Dad and Mom just hated that.

When they got back to the White House, Cissy went upstairs at once. She had selected the East Bedroom, the same room that Tricia Nixon, Susan Ford, Amy Carter, and Chelsea Clinton had used. It was OK. Livable. But she always wondered, every second she was in it, who might be watching or listening. Supposedly, it was private. Like, really? Since the days of her, shall we say, youthful indiscretions, Mamacita had hired hackers to invade her Internet space and detectives to bug her rooms. Lorna despised Mac and distrusted Flynn. She'd known and loathed them both in college, too, for that matter. Mom was tame, Mac was wild. Mom was greedy, Flynn was noble.

Cissy played with her cell phone. Use it, or use the landline? No, she had to use the cell, otherwise she couldn't get on the virtual private network Flynn's people had installed on it.

If you had a secure device or what you believed was a private space, long tall Lorna was liable to be in there somewhere, and now she had the Secret Service to amplify her snooping.

She'd just have to risk being overheard. The First Daughter couldn't exactly take a walk. Because she was pretty, she was hyped silly in the media. Everybody knew this face of hers and everybody assumed that she had time for them. "Hey, Annette, take a picture with me, sign my napkin, sign my face"—it started the moment she so much as stepped out of a car.

As she had been taught, she logged her iPhone into the VPN. She punched in the number Flynn had made her memorize.

The phone rang at the other end. It was picked up in the middle of the second ring. As she'd been told would happen, nobody said anything.

"Two four four," she said. It meant that she needed a meeting with Flynn.

The line went dead.

A moment later, her phone rang. She was given the address of an exclusive restaurant in Georgetown, the Pennington. It was very small, very quiet. There was a bar with high-backed booths. Many an affair had unfolded at the Pennington in one of those infamous booths.

She called Marty Skinner, her current Secret Service detail, and told him she was going for cocktails at the Pennington. Then she went down to the private entrance to wait for the car.

As she waited, one of the ushers came discreetly up behind her. "Your mother wants to know where you're going," he said. She could hear the embarrassment in his voice, which softened her a little toward him. She'd been about to bite his head off.

"Tell her I'm going to a hookah club to smoke a little hash with some cat from the *New Republic*. Liberal transgender cat. Black. Atheistic. Muslim."

"OK, you're going to Madame Sally's."

Madame Sally was a dressmaker expert in alterations, and Cissy had been dieting. Mom would be pleased. "That'll do."

The car came up, and she got in and told Marty to take her to the Pennington.

"Date?"

"No, I'm gonna sit in the bar and hope for a pickup. Maybe some post-sixty'll come along and offer to take me to his place and show me his Lawrence Welk DVDs."

"You should be so lucky."

"Funny guy, Marty."

"I try."

"Well, don't."

It was five forty when she reached the Pennington. The restaurant, which would be full in an hour, contained only a single ancient customer, apparently a man, gumming away at what looked like a pile of mashed potatoes. The bar was completely empty. Cissy took a booth and waited.

FLYNN CARROLL used the Pennington because it had a little-known side entrance that led directly into the bar. The place had been designed a hundred years ago specifically for discreet meetings. During the Cold War, every booth had been bugged by CIA, but now there was only one

hot spot, booth three—and sure enough, there was Cissy Greene, all 128 svelte, shimmering pounds of her, sitting well back in booth three.

An accident? Flynn couldn't know that, but he could get her to change booths.

"Come on."

"Flynn!"

He nodded to his left, and Cissy obediently got up and moved to the corner booth he had indicated.

She had grown up since he'd last seen her. Her skin was as soft as smoke, and when she moved, she flowed.

He took a seat across from her, and immediately saw in her eyes something he wished had not been there. She was afraid of him. Terrified, in fact. He watched her tongue touch her dry lips. Her eyes never stopped darting, as if she was also afraid she'd been followed. As well she might have been.

"Give me your phone," he said.

He powered it down and removed the SIM card.

"What are you doing?"

"Taking precautions. You act like a person who suspects that they're under surveillance."

"I am under surveillance."

A waiter came. She ordered a vodka martini, he a bourbon on the rocks.

"Are you already twenty-one, Cissy? Has it been that long?"

"No, but who's going to card me? Nobody, Mr. Carroll."

"Flynn."

"No, it's Mr. Carroll. You're far too frightening for first names."

"You've changed, Cissy."

"Keeping secrets is hell. It makes you old inside, Flynn."

"I've noticed."

She took a deep breath. 'Here it came,' he thought. Small talk was done.

"There was a murder at the White House today."

He contained both his shock at this unprecedented crime and his confusion about why she had reached out to him.

"A wunderkind called Al Doxy."

"The Doxys of Plainview?"

"Yep."

"Where do I come in, Cissy?"

"He was beheaded."

"And this brings me in how?"

"Flynn, I overheard my father on the phone with the Secret Service. They told him that the head had been severed with something that left a wound under a centimeter wide."

Flynn was not often shocked, not given what he'd seen in this life and what he knew, but he felt shock now, an unfamiliar coldness creeping over him, accompanied by ultraheightened awareness of his surroundings. He noted the whisper of the bartender's cloth as he polished a glass, the faint drone of traffic on the street outside, a faraway clink and clatter coming from the kitchen as the evening service got under way.

He said, "Are you back in the White House?"

"Mom insisted."

Lorna Greene had been student body president at UT when he was a junior, a classic example of the steel magnolia. "Sounds like her."

"Should we have gone back?"

"I'm going to need to go over there. I'm going to need to look into this."

"Mom and Dad are out of the loop, you know that. They have no idea about you."

"Cissy, the entire government's out of the loop."

"All I know is you're weird and scary and I can't talk about what I saw."

He reached toward her, then stopped. But she slid her hand into his. She wanted to be reassured, but he couldn't tell her not to be afraid. He was no liar, and she had good reason to be afraid.

"I thought of trying to get them to go up to Camp David."

"No!"

She blinked, startled. He realized that he shouldn't have been so intense, but going to an isolated place like that would be incredibly dangerous, far more so than Cissy could possibly know.

He didn't think that they should stay in the White House, either, but he could see the political storm that would erupt if they left. "The murder's a secret, I assume?"

"Al Doxy was an NSC aide. So it's all classified. National security. The press will be told it was a freak accident."

"What kind of an accident?"

"Don't know. Deflated, maybe."

"Deflated?"

"He was a roly-poly. I knew him in college. Math genius, very over-weight, incredibly boring."

"What was he working on in the West Wing?"

She shook her head. "No idea."

He made a decision. "I'll stick close," he said. "I'll be in the Residence tonight."

"How? Do you need my help?"

He considered. Could he penetrate the White House? He called its security precautions to mind. He considered his skills, and Diana's skills. He said, "I'll be OK."

"The place is a prison. You can't exactly ring the doorbell."

"I'll look over the West Wing, then spend the night in the Closet Hall."

She was frowning. He thought she was probably trying to under-stand how he'd get past the many layers of defense that protected the president.

"I'll be in the Secret Service contingent," he said.

She nodded. "Can you tell me anything more?"

He considered the horror that had descended on his unit since the revolution on Aeon. The brutal battles with marauding alien bands had not only continued, but without the support of police from Aeon, the situation had deteriorated. And now there was the constant threat of state-sponsored escalation, which this could be. "You don't want to know anything more."

"Are they demons?"

"They might as well be, but this isn't supernatural."

"Then it's aliens."

"Maybe. Maybe something a whole lot stranger."

"What could be stranger, Flynn?"

"It's a big universe. It's very, very old. There's just so much out there. Truthfully, we don't know even yet what we're dealing with."

Frowning, she absorbed that. She leaned forward, washing him in her clean, soft scent. "What happened to your wife—is it connected with all this stuff?"

Abby had disappeared four years ago. She had been taken by a ferocious alien criminal who was here stealing DNA and probably things about us that we don't yet understand.

She'd been asleep in bed at home in Menard. He'd been a detective on the Menard City Police at the time. He'd woken up one morning and she'd been gone. The police, the Texas Rangers, and the FBI had all searched, but to no avail.

Even after the case had died, Flynn had not stopped searching. He'd been in love with Abby since they were kids. She'd been pregnant when she'd disappeared. He had continued on with a stubbornness so great that his efforts had eventually come to the attention of Diana Glass, who was running the highly classified special FBI unit that had eventually been transferred to the CIA and was now known as Detail 242.

There had been no closure for Flynn. He still did not know if Abby was dead or in some awful way still alive. She lived in his mind and heart, all the time. He knew he should move on, but it was just very damn hard to do that. Loyalty ran deep in his blood. He did not give up. That was deep in his blood, too.

"I don't know what happened, not exactly," he said.

"Yes you do."

Maybe that was true, and maybe it was something he just didn't want to admit to himself. He suspected that there were slaveries beyond human understanding, and captivities that made hell seem a blessing.

Again, her hand came to his. He let it remain there. "I won't let that happen to you or your family," he said.

She leaned closer. Now she was right in his face. "What about getting beheaded, Flynn? Will you protect us from that, too?"

Diners were entering—congressmen, a boisterous senator, some Chinese

Embassy personnel, and a couple of high-end whores who sat together and whispered.

"I'll be there," he told Cissy. "Don't let your mom and dad know, obviously."

"Obviously."

He stood up. She raised her eyes. He saw that they were swimming with the wetness of fear. He left her, then, a golden child behind a vodka martini in the comfortable, wood-paneled safety of the discreet old bar.

Would he see her alive again?

Maybe.

CHAPTER FOUR

DIANA LAY naked in the dark. He could see her form on the bed, and as always, his first reaction was desire, followed at once by loneliness. He stepped across the room and looked down at her.

While you were sleeping . . .

"I've got to get into the White House."

She sighed, then snorted. Her eyes opened. For a moment, she stared. Then she leaped out of bed.

"Holy shit, Flynn, how did you get in *here*?"

"I live here."

"Sort of. When you feel like sneaking up on me. Have you ever knocked on a door?"

"My razor's in the bathroom, dear. I don't have to knock."

"Well, stop sneaking around. Find a less annoying compulsion." She fumbled for her bedside clock. "What time is it?"

"Six in the evening. What're you doing asleep, anyway?"

She gave him a puzzled look. "You know I'm up all night just like you."

"Yeah, but I don't sleep all day."

"I was taking a brief nap. Anyway, you don't sleep at all."

"When I have Abby back in my bed, I'll sleep." He saw the tightening around her eyes, the downcurling of her mouth. Why did he say things like that? Did he want to hurt her? "Meaning that I'll never sleep . . . except with you." He leaned down and kissed her cheek.

She drew away.

He sat down on the foot of the bed. "A twenty-three-year-old kid named Albert Doxy—yes, that Doxy—was killed in his West Wing office today."

"Jesus."

"He was decapitated. Clean cut, precision."

"Them?"

"That's why I need access."

She was silent. They were considering the same question: how to get him into the loop of the murder investigation without breaking secrecy.

The public believes that presidents know all the secrets. The truth is that they are told as little as possible. Nobody in intelligence wants attention from the executive level unless it's a legal requirement, least of all people like Flynn and Diana and their colleagues in Detail 242. The group of them were keeping the most dangerous secret in human history. Flynn could not imagine what somebody like Bill Greene might do with knowledge of the alien presence, especially since it was hostile. When he came to understand how dangerous this all was, and how helpless we really were, he might do any damn thing.

The revolution on Aeon had put the criminal class in power. The decent people who had been trying to stop them were now either fugitives or dead. Exploitation of Earth had ceased to be illegal. Now it was the law. Previously, they'd been dealing with isolated criminals. Now Aeon itself was the criminal.

If the public found out what it really meant when people disappeared, as they were doing at an ever-increasing rate worldwide, there would be absolute panic. With the entire world in an uproar, Aeon's game would get harder. Right now, all Aeon had to deal with was the careful pushback of the detail, protecting one individual or another, stopping an incursion here and there, doing enough to preserve at least a semblance of human safety, but not enough to make Aeon lash out.

Public panic would definitely make Aeon lash out, and what that might involve nobody could tell, except that it would certainly be extremely dangerous.

"Can we trust Cissy with anything beyond what she knows already?" Diana asked. "We may have to."

"She's got Lorna's toughness and brains."

"And Bill's unpredictability, from what I've seen. What if she showed up on *60 Minutes* with this?"

Flynn knew where this was going, and he didn't like it. Diana could have Cissy killed. Contrary to popular belief, the president is not the only American official with the legal power to cut such orders.

"She's reliable."

Diana's ice-crusted eyes met his. "So you say."

"If we ever get this thing under control, there's history as yet unwritten, and you're in it. So how do you want to be remembered, as a kid killer? You need to get me in there, D. Tonight. And leave Cissy to me."

"I can do that, but you're gonna have to avoid Lorna and Bill on your own."

"Assuming they live out the night."

"You protect them!"

She walked into the sitting room adjacent to her bedroom, her long legs flashing in the last light slanting in the window.

She was his commanding officer. Officially.

They lived together here in Georgetown. Unofficially. Sometimes.

When the nights wore on them, they brought each other comfort.

They were and were not in love.

He could not imagine life without her, but he wanted to. He wanted to continue to be loyal to Abby.

Diana was already on the phone in her adjacent office, speaking softly and intently. Had he wished, he could have picked up every word; he had that kind of hearing. There was no point, though. She would succeed in what she was doing. Her clearance was literally higher than the president's, and her authority was very extensive. In the end, it emerged out of a level of government so deep and so powerful that not even the most off-the-wall conspiracy theorists would believe that it was there. Or that it was as small as it was, just a few experts in things like genetics and neuroscience, exobiology and esoteric communications devices. And a supervisor to whom Diana reported, but whose name and place in the tangled web of government was kept from her underlings, which included Flynn—at least officially.

It had not always been this way. They had started out as part of the FBI. An alien cop had been attached to the unit.

Now Aeon was hostile and the lid was on.

Diana hung up and came back into the bedroom. "Go over to H Street. They'll orient you and send you to the White House." She paused. "The director's strung, Flynn. He sounded like a scared child."

"Did he have any idea what he's actually dealing with? I mean, given a weapon like that, it's not a stretch to think aliens might be involved."

"You'll need to determine that."

Flynn drove through the evening streets of Washington, passing along H Street. Across Lafayette Square he could see the White House. There were figures on the roof, barely visible, but there. Every light that could be turned on was blazing away. Understandable.

Secret Service HQ is a nondescript building on a nondescript street, in keeping with the low profile that the agency considers important to its mission.

Flynn entered and was quickly passed by the challenge desk. He was using his real identity. There had been no time for anything else.

He was taken up to the crisis center by an agent armed with a small pistol in an ankle holster and a Sig Sauer under his arm, probably with one of the new DAK triggers. In Flynn's opinion, it wasn't the best Sig Sauer and they should never have moved to it. The SA/DA version has only one trigger reset point, not the two of the DAK trigger. In heat, who's going to remember which reset to use?

The agent was left-handed, as Flynn could see from the positioning of the shoulder holster. As they ascended in the elevator, Flynn watched him in the reflection in the door. Carefully.

The crisis center was smaller than he had expected, centered by a long oak conference table. There were five people present, all males, all armed.

He recognized only one of them, the director, Simon Forde. He'd never met him, but he'd seen him on television.

As he entered, nobody reacted, let alone uttered a greeting. In fact, nobody spoke at all. Their eyes were mean pins, ten of them.

"I realize that this is an intrusion," he said, "but I have no choice but to be here, just as you have no choice but to accept that."

"This is Flynn Carroll," Forde said. "He's deep alphabet and he wants to sniff under our tails."

Flynn looked from man to man. "What I need now is access to the body. I need to see the remains."

"No press," Forde said. "You'll be looking at a felony. Know that."

Flynn let his contempt live in his eyes. Forde glanced down at his notepad and moved his pen. In the privacy of his mind, Flynn identified him as the sort of person who can waste the lives of others in service to the rules. He would not forget this.

"We need to know something from you," one of the other men said, this one young, his face civil-service bland. He had his job, he was good, he was marking off the years until retirement.

"Sure thing. Shoot."

"Take a look." He threw an image of a young man strolling, seemingly casually, down a corridor with a file in his hand. It was the first time Flynn had seen Al Doxy, and his immediate response was that the puffy kid's body language was a lie. The tight shoulders, the head thrust forward, the quick, stiff movements: This was a frightened walk.

Then Flynn recognized the file identifier, and when he did he had to fight back any visible trace of the surge of surprise that swept over him.

"Did you recover that file?" he asked, his voice carefully modulated to conceal his inner horror.

"We did not, and the identifier isn't recognizable."

It wouldn't be, not to them. There was no way he would tell them anything about it, nor reveal that files with that identifier were only stored physically, rather than being scanned into the electronic system. Electronic files are open doors. Paper files locked in underground storage facilities are far harder to access.

"I need to see the body."

"Who are you, Mr. Carroll?"

The inevitable power play. "You have my ID."

"Who do you work for?"

"Freelance."

"We're not stupid," Forde said. "We're thinking, with the resources you probably command, you can help us."

Flynn said nothing.

"Look, you're talking about the most incredible security breach in history. It's the White House, for God's sake! Tell us what you know."

Flynn said nothing.

The room crackled with tension. Flynn had identified the positions of all the guns. He could take these men out before they could get off a shot, all of them, even the ones with decent pistols.

"DIA? No, too low-level. NSA? No, too operational. NRO? Not a techie. So where are you from, Mr. Carroll?"

What he knew about that file was that its loss was the most serious problem he could imagine, not only for him personally, but for his entire operation.

"I need to see the body," he repeated, his voice carefully modulated, expressing a calmness that he did not feel.

Forde glared back at him.

"I need to see it now."

Silence.

"Director Forde, I have the authority."

His face was stone. His eyes bored into Flynn's. "The body's been moved to the Navy Yard. There's a coroner's facility there. We'll let them know you're coming."

"Thank you." He stood up. "I'll want the coroner's office cleared of personnel. I don't want anybody to observe me."

"What about the doctor? To explain the wounds?"

"Nobody's to be in the facility." He tossed Forde a cell phone. "When you've got me included on your White House detail for tonight, call me. All you have to do is press talk. The phone will do the rest."

"On the White House detail? Are you serious?"

"Not really. Jacking people like you up is my hobby."

"We can't put you on the White House detail. You have no idea how things work."

"Nobody will see me."

"What if they do? The president wanders at night."

"Nope. Bill Green sleeps like a hibernating grizzly and Lorna wakes up at five, so I won't worry about him and I'll avoid her."

"I can't let you impersonate one of my officers."

"OK, then, let's be clear: If I'm not in there, there's a reasonable possibility that they'll be murdered in their sleep. You will bear responsibility for that." He pointed from man to man. "You. You. You. You. Your responsibility."

There was an uneasy stirring around the table.

Simon Forde looked down at the phone. "I've never seen one of these."

"It's from the future."

CHAPTER FIVE

HE LEFT Forde staring at the small instrument in his hand. It was GSMK CryptoPhone modified to support quantum encryption. The phones had been especially created for the detail by a high-end Russian hacker who called himself "Dimitri Kronos." He thought the work he did was for the Russian mafia, and so was afraid to provide anything but his best. If he'd known that his real client was an American intelligence unit, he would have provided his worst.

Back in his car, he called Diana. "We have a problem. This kid was walking into the White House with our paperwork in his hands."

"*What?*"

"Our core file. No question. Organizational structure, identities, all the fundamentals. I saw the file identifier on the folder he was carrying. And it's gone. No sign of it."

"Aeon has our core file?"

"So it seems," he said.

The Navy Yard is a big place, but its coroner's unit a very small one, with facilities for three cadavers. It's not refrigerated, because it's intended only for temporary use, if somebody in the facility dies suddenly. But in 2013 there had been a mass shooting here. Twelve people had died very damn suddenly on that occasion, and as he pulled up to the low gray building where the unit was located, he wondered if it had been put to use then.

He'd been waved onto the facility when the security police identified his license number. They had instructions not to approach the car and to allow him to park anywhere he wished. Diana's usual excellent work.

He turned off the car and opened his jacket in order to expose his pistol. He entered the building. At the end of a narrow corridor was a small sign on a door: CORONER.

He had been unusually effective when it came to cleaning up criminal elements from Aeon. In fact, he was the only cop who was effective, at least in the field. Diana was good at deskwork and planning, but he was the one who could go out into the forests or down into the caves where Aeon's biorobots lurked and actually get kills. When the biorobots had been run by a few criminals, he had been a constant target. Now that the criminals were the government of the planet, the danger he was in had escalated even further.

They were capable of fielding bios that appeared to be human, but when you shot them, the skin sank against the metal frame in such a way that made it immediately apparent that they were anything but. When they were functional, though, they were very, very good.

So, were such things behind that door waiting for him? He had no reason to think so, but nevertheless his pistol slipped into his right hand. It happened so quickly that it would have seemed to an observer like a magic trick, as if the gun had appeared out of nowhere. As he drew, he simultaneously threw the door open. He determined that the room was empty except for a stainless steel double sink along one wall and an examining table at its center, its surface scuffed dull from many years of use. On the wall opposite the sink were three cabinets held closed by heavy-duty handles.

He could see by the fact that the handle had no dust on it that they had used the center drawer. He grasped it, felt a click, and stopped. Another pull and the door would swing wide.

Again, he braced the pistol. Only then did he open the door.

Darkness within. The odor of raw, dead blood. Total silence, no movement.

He released the handle, drew a small flashlight out of his pocket, and trained it on the dark.

What he saw was a corpse, and only that. He pulled at the gurney it was on, and it rattled forward on old rails.

The body was naked and headless. Tucked in between the legs was a black plastic bag.

Carefully, he ran a hand over the gray skin of the corpse. He next opened the bag and drew out the head. A human head weighs about three pounds, and he didn't notice anything unusual about the weight of this one. The young face was intent, the lips parted in a way that suggested pleasure. Pleasure in death? Why? Was it relief, or had whoever killed him somehow deceived him about what was happening?

He looked a long time into those eyes. Given the weapon used, he probably hadn't even realized that he was being killed. It had been strung from wall to wall where his throat would connect with it when he sat down and bent to his work. There would have been a sharp stab of pain as it slid through his neck but his head would have fallen off before he could so much as cringe.

"Why did you have our dossier, Albert Doxy?" he asked, speaking to himself, his soft words sinking into the quiet. "Where did you get it?"

Over the past year, their unit's files had been moved to the Iron Mountain facility in Rosendale, New York, one of the most secure such operations on the planet. And yet, here was a twenty-something with arguably its most sensitive file in his hands, walking into the White House from an unknown destination.

He called Diana. "The cadaver's ready to move. I'll wait here with it until the mortuary team shows up. Where are we taking it?"

"The coroner's facility at Langley," she replied. "It's been cleared for you. Nobody will stop the wagon, nobody will do any ID checks. Just be sure you're directly behind. They're expecting a caravan of two vehicles—you and the coroner's vehicle, that's it."

"Got it."

While he waited, he examined the wound. When he set the head back on the neck, it appeared that the boy was wearing a thin red string.

He called Diana again. "I'm going to want you to start examining the

Secret Service video, and also find out if they had any surveillance in the kid's office. Go over it frame by frame, layer by layer."

"I'm doing it now."

"Inform me the moment you get a hit. If you do."

The coroner's team appeared in the doorway, three men and a woman.

"We're ready," the team leader said.

As they moved toward him, Flynn held up his hand. "Slow down. I want your units and your names. I need to do some clearances."

They traded glances. This wouldn't be a familiar procedure to them, but they had never encountered this level of security before. Once they were back out in the hall, he ran their names through the CARAT system, which addresses all accessible information databases on the planet, including many that are believed by their owners to be encrypted. In two minutes, he had all their records. They were all Air Force personnel, which was good. The USAF had a good security system and a good relationship with his own unit. Seeing nothing unusual in the records, he continued with his work.

He put both the body and head in a single body bag that he pulled from the supply closet beside the sink. He zipped the bag and put yellow plastic tape over the head of the zipper. Under no circumstances could these people be allowed to see the headless corpse. Media types would pay a fortune for a shot of somebody who'd been beheaded, and when it was discovered that the crime had been committed in the White House, six figures would be in play.

Safest way to prevent leaks: Don't tempt.

He opened the door to the team. "OK, kids, it's yours. There's a classified seal on the bag, though, and the tape is tamper-proof. Any sign of entry, and you're in a world of hurt." In his car, he reported to Diana again. "Following on. There's four USAFs in there. They all have straight records."

"Got it. Let 'em do their job. Back off."

He disconnected and waited, watching as the body was brought out and put in the federal meatwagon for its journey to Langley.

As it left the Navy Yard, Flynn drove just behind. He called Diana again. "You find anything on those tapes?"

"We pick him up on the surveillance as he comes up the driveway. He enters via the main entrance, then goes straight to the West Wing."

"Anybody engage with him?"

"A busboy exited his office five minutes before he arrived, carrying a food tray."

"Show me."

"Flynn, you're behind the wheel of a car."

"Show me!" He turned on his iPad, which was on the seat beside him. An instant later, an image appeared. Flynn glanced down at it, looked more closely. Then he returned his eyes to the road. "It'll interest you to know that the busboy who cleared up after his lunch is now driving the meat-wagon. In other words, he has Doxy's remains."

"I'll dump SWATS on the meatwagon right now," she said, her voice crisp with urgency.

"No, not yet. Let's play it out a little."

There wasn't a single country in the world that wouldn't want to acquire the experimental implant that was in Doxy's head. It was also true, though, that few of them would go to these lengths to get it.

In his mind, he inventoried the possibilities. Russia? Maybe, but they'd gone broke over Ukraine and Syria and now needed Western friends again. China? They didn't kill, and certainly not in the White House. Iran, then?

"I think it's Misery," he said. The acronym of the Iranian Ministry of Intelligence was MISIRI, universally referred to as "Misery."

"Misery is getting more sophisticated, then."

He cut the connection. No matter how secure the line, safety meant keeping conversation to the minimum. The great problem with their work was that there were plenty of people on the other side who were smarter than humans. Not natively, but Aeon was thousands of years ahead of us technologically. How much they were machines and how much biology it was hard to know. You were not, however, dealing with human logic. What they did made sense, but it was their own kind, so that generally it was hard to grasp until after the fact.

Once, the detail had been linked to Aeon by a communications device we called "the Wire." Through the use of quantum entanglement, it was able to transmit across interstellar space instantaneously. But when the revolution reached the campus of Aeon's exobiology staff, the Wire had been shut down. Now it was just a hulk in Detail 242's small headquarters deep in the CIA building at Langley, a dark unseeing eye. It wasn't alone, though. A back-engineered system was installed in some ships and submarines, in Air Force One, and in spy planes.

He punched up Diana. "Meatwagon's not slowing," he said into his phone. They'd crossed the gray darkness of the Potomac and were heading up Memorial. The Dolley exit that led into Langley was just ahead.

"I've got eyes on it," Diana responded.

"OK, if they're gonna be bad boys, I'll let them lose me, then move in on them when they've stopped."

The old ambulance passed the exit.

"Stay with them. I'm hanging back."

It accelerated through 70, through 80.

"They're shaking tails. Keep the cops off it, let it happen."

"On to the highway patrol now."

Ninety. One hundred. The purpose of such a maneuver was to force anyone tailing them to show his hand.

Flynn let himself drop back, then a little more. The truck was now doing something close to 110.

It flew up to the Beltway, weaving through traffic. The taillights disappeared into the winking mass ahead.

"They're slowing," Diana said. "Taking the Beltway north. You're two miles behind them."

How naive could they be, thinking that speed would shake a tail?

The most probable answer was that they weren't naive at all. They knew that the ambulance was under surveillance that it couldn't shake.

So, why were they playing it like this?

"They're exiting onto Bear Island. Taking the underpass right now."

"You still have visual?"

"Infrared. Too dark over there for visual."

Flynn hung out his blue light and flipped on his siren. The car leaped ahead, engine growling. Infrared wasn't much use. Games can be played with it: All you need is a foil blanket and you're invisible from above. Meat-wagons carry such blankets.

When he came to the exit, he drove into Carderock Recreation Area, but not far. "What's their position now?"

"A half mile ahead of you. No movement on the truck."

He got out of his car. He could cover a half mile on foot faster than they probably realized. If they realized that the tail had not been shaken, he hoped, they would expect him to come up in his vehicle, but maybe not.

"You see me?" he asked Diana.

"I have your position, you're too close."

"I have eyes on them. There's movement. They're pulling out the body."

"Back off, they're going to see you."

He could hear birds settling in for the night, beetles moving through the leafy forest floor, a squirrel scratching its way up a tree.

"Flynn," came Diana's voice from the earpiece.

He took it out and turned it off. He needed both his ears. He hardly breathed. He needed to see and hear these people. If they had something to do with Aeon, this strange behavior might be explained. If not, then what in the world was Iran up to? Why had they stolen the detail's file, or even known that such a file existed?

Aeon and Iran?

There were now more sounds ahead. The crunch of tires. No engine noise, though. A huge splash, followed by gurgling. What in hell were they doing?

He reinserted the earpiece.

"Flynn! Flynn!" She was hoarse. She'd been screaming at him.

He popped the mike to indicate that he could hear her.

"He rolled the ambulance into the Potomac!"

"He?"

"The other two are in it—they have to be."

As it sank, the old ambulance began making louder splashing and gur-gling noises. A truck going into a river is a loud business.

The idea of trying to help the people in it was out; it was too late for them. He would concentrate on just one thing now: the identity of the last man standing.

He popped the mike again. She reported, "Nobody got out of the meat-wagon, so the two other kids are indeed still in there. The body's in it, too."

"The head?"

"Not clear. He may have it."

He pulled the earpiece out again, and at once heard a stealthy sound, cloth slipping softly against the trunk of a tree. With it came footsteps on damp leaves. He could stop him right here, but that would freeze the trail.

Now he could hear breathing, unsteady, afraid. The kid passed close, then the sound of his movement faded. Flynn returned his earbud to his ear. "See him?"

"He's emerging onto the road. There's a car coming."

Flynn took off after him, angling toward the road, keeping well out of sight.

"He's getting in the vehicle. It's a late-model Mercedes. It's pulling out. Tracking."

He didn't care where it went; that was no longer important. "Get the river dredged. See what can be found. And do you have any good face shots of the perp?"

"Working on it. Gotta reconstruct off the infrared."

He reached his car. "Where are they now?"

"In heavy traffic, moving north. I'm still tight, though."

The police would locate the truck, perhaps the bodies, or parts of them. If he was lucky, the head. The river was swift and deep, and finding things in murky, tricky water like that was likely to be much a matter of chance. Flynn did not like chance.

As he drove, he analyzed the situation, but his thoughts led in no definite direction.

"I've got the kid," Diana said. "Misery op, definite ID."

"OK." Now he had something useful. "The Iranians possess a weapon from Aeon and they're interested in our unit. And in the White House."

Dots were connecting. He broke off the chase. This was a sideshow, nothing more. Aeon had created this garish mystery as a distraction. "I'm heading for the White House," he said.

"You're breaking off the pursuit?"

"Doesn't matter."

"I don't get it, but OK. Be careful."

"If I can."

CHAPTER SIX

THE WHITE House is divided into three sections: the West Wing, the East Wing, and the familiar old mansion that stands between them, the Residence. It is the Residence that tourists enter, passing through elegant rooms on the ground floor while the presidential family's life unfolds upstairs. It's not a home, really, the White House, but more an intimate version of Versailles, where a relentlessly public person carries out a rigidly constrained existence under ceaselessly watching eyes.

The domestic staff and the Secret Service personnel assigned to it know essentially everything that happens in it, including the private areas. Even so, the tradition of discretion is rarely broken. For example, most presidents have entertained a continual succession of women—interns, secretaries, social acquaintances—who have brought momentary comfort to what is, invariably, a fraught existence. The presidency of the United States is not quite powerful enough to succeed, but too important to fail. They enter young and confident and leave it old and useful. When they leave, they all take a secret with them: All that power is an illusion. The presidency is about compromise, frustration, and broken promises. It is also about fear, constant and ever-increasing, escalated each morning by the first terror trip of the day: the intelligence briefing.

Flynn was not naive. He'd seen presidents come and go. Bill Clinton, the amateur with a taste for bimbos; George W. Bush, with his strange and very private vulnerabilities and needs; Barack Obama, who like Ronald Reagan, had a wife too domineering to allow him to get into female trouble.

And now Bill Greene. Back in Texas, Lorna had hired Manny the Torch to burn down the Governor's Mansion after she'd found him in bed with his secretary of state, Will Shifley. It was whispered that rent boys slipped into press conferences and stayed the night.

How in the world had he ended up as a governor, and now in the White House? What can the American people have been thinking, to believe for even a moment that he could run the country, he who could not even begin to run his own life? But the American people were ever ready to be led, and the money behind him—money that knew his secrets—had led them very well.

Flynn knew all of these things and more, and reflected on them as he drew up to the private entrance. The uniforms let him through, but not without glares of pure steel. He was an invader. He didn't belong here, not in this most exclusive few acres in the world, the White House, where slept the most important human being on the planet and her husband, the president.

The elevators in the White House are small and not new, and they don't give the impression that they'll necessarily get you where you're going. More than that, as far as Flynn was concerned, they were liable to be turned off by vindictive Secret Service agents. He could easily be left in one all night, so he took the back stairs to the second floor. He was met there by an agent and a butler.

"I need to see them," he said.

The agent looked at the butler. Then they both turned their eyes to Flynn. "The doors are closed," the butler said. "We can't enter unless called, not at night."

"You two do your thing," he said. "I have to have eyes on them, all three of them. I'm going to expect free use of the building for the rest of the night. I don't want to be followed, watched, spoken to, or disturbed in any way whatsoever. Is that clear?"

The agent's face was basalt. He looked like he belonged on Easter Island. The butler said, "Of course, sir, that's our understanding."

In recent years, the president and First Lady had slept together in the master bedroom. That was not the case now. Lorna had the master. Bill was in the living room, which had been converted into a bedroom with a narrow single bed and a bookcase containing the thrillers that he loved. There was a big-screen TV and a PlayStation. He'd spend hours plugging away at tactical military games, then settle into a thriller of the kind he could count on: not too much gore, not too many complications, and the outcome never in doubt. Lorna was a student of history. She spent her time with Machiavelli and Churchill, studying power and past conflict to find present insight.

Flynn crossed the center hall in a few steps, then silently indicated to the Secret Service agent outside that he was going in the president's door.

The agent jumped up from his chair and blocked it.

"Don't do this. Let's just cooperate for a few minutes. It's not hard."

"You can't enter that room."

"And if we find him dead in there in the morning, what then?"

"We can protect our people."

Flynn said nothing. He didn't need to. The agent stepped aside.

Inside, the insulated windows meant that the only sound was the air-conditioning, a faint hiss. The room was larger than one would expect, with a high ceiling and walls painted blue. There was a desk, spotless, and six TVs built into a large wall unit. The president was a serious sports fan. Officially, he was a golfer. He wanted to appear presidential at all times, and golf was a powerful tradition. But in the case of Bill Greene his handicap was, well, a handicap.

A second sound joined that of the air conditioner: the president's steady breathing. He lay on his side, so buried in blankets that only his face was visible.

Flynn approached the bed. He looked down at Bill, now a grizzled man of fifty-five. He'd been elected, basically, on the strength of two factors: the glasses he'd started wearing, which made him look presidential, and the fact that he had the best grin. Looking back across history, most presidents since FDR had been elected because they had better grins. Roosevelt's jaunty cigarette-holder smile was hard to beat. Truman had grinned like an undertaker, but his opponent, Thomas Dewey, had the terrifying rictus of a corpse.

Dubya had grinned like a Weimeraner having a gas attack, but when Gore smiled, you thought "card shark." Kennedy had outshone Nixon as heaven outshines the Black Hole of Calcutta. Even so, Nixon's grimace, deadly as it was, had made Hubert Humphrey look like an even shiftier used car salesman. Obama's smile was devastating, a commercial for teeth. McCain smiled like a shark, Romney like a priest. Thus Obama's two terms. Ronald Reagan, same deal.

Right now, Greene's postcard smile was locked away behind the frank truth of his dry, sunken face. He snored like a rhino. But he was very definitely alive and the room was otherwise empty, so Flynn left him and did the harder part, which was to enter the main bedroom and make sure that Lorna was still undead.

In college, she'd been a Delta Gamma Epsilon. Their house had been accessible after hours, but you had to be damn careful of the housemother, a perpetually infuriated Junior Leaguer who was far from junior, and who'd years back renounced her vows and laicized from the Sisters of the Holy Sepulcher. Laicized maybe, but Ietta Swiney had remained a Sepulcher at heart. Still, unlike their housemother, though, some of the girls welcomed company in their rooms. Others didn't. Lorna was one of the others. Worse, she slept so lightly that she always seemed to some degree awake. She'd apparently been on the prowl for a rich boy she could control, and had hit on Bill when she'd seen the difficulty he had outthinking Bevo, the university football team's mascot, who was known to be unusually dim even for a steer. Bill's first success in politics was to get elected Bevo Wrangler by the honorary organization that maintained the creature. But Bevo had wrangled him. Seeing this, Lorna had decided that she could not only push Bill into politics, but also control him. And he had the finances to make that work.

Flynn tried the door between the rooms. It was locked from Lorna's side. She sure as hell wasn't interested in any midnight calls from Bill, as if that would ever happen. They probably linked up only rarely, every few years perhaps, when they both happened to be full of booze and memories at the same time.

Flynn examined the lock. It was an ordinary pin/tumbler mechanism, all brass. He took out his pick kit and dipped a snake rake into the slit. He bounced the pins, but not by simply putting pressure on the rake and hoping for the best. He had a practiced touch, and the pins were soon all on the shear line.

As he drew the door open, he heard the beginnings of a slight creak. He froze, listening for stirring from either room. Bill continued to rumble, but there came from Lorna's room the sounds of two people, and neither of them was asleep. There were faint, pleasured sighs, all female.

Like Eleanor Roosevelt in her time, Lorna Greene kept girls. Flynn didn't judge one way or the other, but he did open the door far enough to get a look at her, so that he could do the visual check he felt was necessary.

For a dizzying moment, he thought Cissy was in bed with her, but then he saw that the fan of blond hair belonged to Ginny Bowers, Lorna's young secretary.

He drew the door closed, relocked it with the rake, then slipped out into the softly lit corridor, closing the president's door behind him.

His Secret Service buddy was right there, right in his face. "Seven minutes," he said. "I was about to hit the alarm."

"I didn't realize that you were planning to resign."

"I'm not."

"If you'd tripped that alarm, you would have."

He glared at Flynn. Flynn didn't glare back. He just looked at the guy and waited until he'd looked away and dropped his shoulders.

"I'm gonna be in the Closet Hall for most of the night. I'll be patrolling at random. You're not to address me again, and sure as hell not to interfere, not if you want to keep working here and avoid criminal charges."

The man's lips turned up with contempt. "Criminal charges?"

"This is a national security matter. It's way above your clearance level. If you impede me or fail to obey my orders, you're going to be looking not only at getting your ass torched, you'll be facing a treason charge."

The smile went away. So did the agent.

Flynn crossed into the Closet Hall and tried Cissy's bedroom door. Also locked, which was good. Because this door opened into a common area, it had a better lock on it, electronic. Using his Slagel pick, he was through it in under a minute. The room was lit by two night-lights, one near the bed and another glowing from the bathroom.

Cissy's canopied bed from their Texas ranch stood against the wall opposite the windows. In fact, now that he looked around, he saw that the room was an exact duplicate of the one from the ranch, right down to the Kit-Cat clock on the wall with its swinging tail and phosphorescent cat eyes.

She lay very still, on her back. Her breathing was shallow. She wasn't asleep and she was armed. The weapon was under the covers, in her right hand.

"Cissy, release the gun."

"Flynn!"

"Hey there." He stepped over to the bed.

A smile lit her face. She sat up and patted the covers. He dropped down into the grace of her perfume. When his old buddy Mac had romanced her, she'd been underage. She wasn't underage now.

"How's Di?" she asked.

"Good."

"Oh, God, Flynn, what happened?"

"We're working on it."

"Flynn, I need to know or I'm going to go insane here."

"There's a lot of legal issues."

"I signed the form!"

"That's a confidentiality agreement, not a clearance document. You've never been cleared."

"Flynn, we're going to be killed, aren't we? Or worse—like Abby."

The words hung between them. She knew that Flynn's wife Abby had disappeared, and that it had had to do with the aliens, but very little more. She did not know of his relentless search for her, or the fact that he'd originally been recruited into the detail by Diana because of his tireless determination to find her.

"Abby was kidnapped," he said evenly.

"By them!"

"Who?"

"Come *on,* I'm not stupid! The aliens, and now they're here, they're in the White House and they killed Al Doxy." She shuddered, her voice dropping to a whisper. "Beheaded him."

"We don't know who was responsible. Not exactly."

She threw herself on Flynn. A bitter rack of sobs engulfed her. He held her shaking body. Soon he felt himself stirring. He wished it down. But wishes don't always come true, and this one definitely did not. His arousal made her feel more in control, and she leaned against his chest. The smell of her hair—fresh, sweet straw—filled his nostrils.

"Flynn, I don't want to die."

"I'm here to protect you, and I'm going to do that."

She leaned away from his chest so that she could look up at him. "For how long? One night? Two?"

"As long as it takes."

Her eyes were darting indicators of panic.

"Are they in here now? Right now?"

He wanted to be truthful, but if he told her the truth, which was that he didn't know, she was only going to get into a worse state.

"Why not go back to Austin? It's a city, so it's fairly safe. Stay in a big condo, lower floor. There's no public reason for you to remain here. Or your mother, for that matter."

"Mom's President of the United States. She can't take off and leave the alky in charge."

"Is your dad hitting the bottle again?" Bill was known to binge.

"He's been quoting Ecclesiastes and smoking cigars."

"Not good." That was his first phase, when he had about half a pint of bourbon in him. If he kept going, in a couple more days he'd be so drunk he couldn't move, collapsed on a floor somewhere and wallowing in his vomit. Years ago, when that had happened in the old Faust Hotel in Menard, Flynn had been the one to clean him off with a garden hose, pour him into the bed of a pickup, and drive him back to the Governor's Mansion. (Lorna's revenge fire had taken place later.)

Cissy went to the sitting area across the room. He wished—he dearly wished—that she wasn't completely naked.

She had inherited her mother's brains, though, and this was, he knew, a carefully crafted effort to determine if there were any seduction possibilities. She'd been expecting him in her web tonight, pretty spider.

Part of him thought, "Oh good." Another part thought, "Oh God."

Diana would say to him, "It's not a big deal, we're not a thing. I don't mind." Then she'd tear up, and that would hurt. He surprised himself, realizing how much she mattered to him. More and more, Di's feelings mattered.

He went to the closet and found a fluffy, flimsy robe. As he strode to the sitting area, he tossed it to her.

She gave him a too-bright smile, experience playing at innocence. As she got comfortable in the cushiony chair, her legs opened. She was not one to give up easily.

She hadn't picked up the robe. He laid it across her shoulders.

"Really?"

He sat opposite her.

"I'm not a kid anymore."

"Neither am I, Cissy. But you're real stressed."

"I want you. I think about you all the time."

"That's the fear talking. You think you want me, but what you really want is what I'm already here to give you, which is protection."

"He was my age, Flynn. So is this about kids? Am I next?"

"I don't know exactly how much you understand about what's happening, but I have reason to take you into my confidence. You might be able to help us in some important ways."

"I know that there were aliens on that ranch near Austin, and I know that you killed them all, you and Mac and Diana. There was some kind of an underground thing there." She paused. "When it burned . . ." She stopped herself.

"Go on."

She shook her head. He heard her murmur, "I smelled meat."

He hadn't known that she was there, not until a few months ago when the newly minted First Daughter had showed up at Diana's town house and demanded to know what was going on. She had naively imagined that her father's election had given her some authority. Talk about a loose cannon. It was a miracle that she hadn't told her parents or her younger sister, Lorna, Jr., who was presently burning up the base paths at Sul Ross University in Alpine, Texas.

Fortunately, Cissy had been afraid to do any whispering, afraid she'd get Flynn in trouble and Mac in more. The detail had done voice analysis and a lie detector test on her, then an fMRI interview. She'd passed everything, so they'd hit her with the confidentiality agreement and let her go.

"What we're looking at is what we believe to be an alien presence that has negative intent toward mankind." He didn't mention Aeon by name. "Put simply, they want Earth."

"Why?"

"Same reason we would, I'd assume. Expand to a new planet, enrich themselves."

"You'd think they'd be more spiritual. Ethical. Given that they're more advanced."

"The Nazis were far more technologically advanced than any previous generation of Germans, but Bach and Beethoven were far more civilized."

"Why just you, Flynn? Where's the air force, where's the army?"

"What do you know about Al Doxy?"

"We used to call him Dorksy in school. He was a geek whose glasses steamed up if you so much as blew on his ear. But he was—you know—a meatball."

"Rich, though."

"Nobody cared. We were all rich in our crowd. We didn't mingle with the toads. They, like, didn't exist."

"So he showed up here. Did he say hello?"

"He took me to dinner. Told me how important his job was. He must've said 'West Wing' fifty times before dessert came. Totally boring, and he'd gotten even more enormous. He looked like a big, droopy elephant who'd lost his trunk."

"Did he tell you what he did?"

"Wouldn't that have been illegal?"

"Yes, but he's dead. We can't put ghosts in jail."

"He told me he was working on some kind of microwave project. Managing it."

"Did he ever mention any names? Mine, for example? Anything about aliens?"

Her eyes widened. "Will you tell me what's going on?"

"He died because of something he knew. I'm trying to figure out what that was."

"There was something on his iPad in his office. 'The United States is in danger of being destroyed, and along with it the whole of mankind.'"

"That was there? You're certain?"

"I heard Dad talking on the phone about it. Trying to figure out what it might mean."

He laid a hand on her cheek, then drew it away. "I need to do a round."

"No you don't, not really. If they come, you'll know. Mac said you always know. You're uncanny, he said. Also that you won't share your secrets, or how you do your work."

"We've got people in training. To share my work."

She chuckled. "Not you, Mr. Huge Ego. This is your baby. Only you and nobody else." She tossed her hair out of her eyes. "The hero's journey, and you're the only one on it, and that is your weakness."

Her voice was a melody, but the words scorched him. Was ego really why he couldn't train anybody, and why the only person who could actually give him meaningful support in the field was Mac, a professional criminal so compromised that he'd never dare to take any credit for anything?

"I have to go," he said. "You will not be harmed."

She leaned back in the chair, exposing her perfect breasts to the room's night glow. "Slay the dragon," she said. "Save the damsel." A grin spread across her face, gleaming with fear. "Save the world." She pitched forward, stuffed her fist into her mouth, and screamed, forcing the sound back into her throat. In a house without privacy, it was what you did.

He went to her and touched her heaving shoulders. She looked up at him and all the smiles were gone, there was nothing here but a woman in raw dread.

"Get out of here," she said.

"I won't let them hurt you."

"Get out! OUT! GET OUT OF HERE!"

He spent the rest of the night in the Closet Hall. When he heard Lorna and her friend stirring, he slipped out, walking quickly off into the thin, cold light of dawn.

CHAPTER SEVEN

FLYNN WAS becoming clearer and clearer about what he had to do. The autopsy he was about to witness would tell him more. If he was right, his plan couldn't be revealed to anybody, not even Diana. If Aeon was watching, they were watching very closely, and the least word could reveal his plan to them.

She would need to figure it out on her own, and he planned to leave as many hints as he dared. If she failed to understand his signals, he was heading for a hard death.

This coroner's facility was far better equipped than the one in the Navy Yard and, because its use would be so unexpected by Aeon's surveillance experts, safer than Langley.

The bodies of Al Doxy and the two medical service personnel lay on gleaming metal slabs in the freezing cold. Doxy's head was where it ought to be, except for the fact that it wasn't attached to the neck. One of the two kids had something in his face that Flynn had often seen in the faces of the dead, a kind of sad peace. The other one was not at peace at all. Her glazed eyes were filled with horror. Her mouth was opened as if in a terrible sort of rapture. One fist was clenched, the other a bloody mess.

She'd been in the back of the wagon with the body, and had hammered with all her might on the doors as the vehicle filled, but hadn't been able to prevail against the pressure of the water that was flooding in.

She had drowned in full consciousness, slowly, breathing her last against a tilting ceiling. Had she seen her life pass before her eyes? What sort of a life had it been? Like all lives, hers was at once of little consequence to the world and, to her, a vast ocean of consequence. She mattered, if only to herself. Parents? Maybe. Boyfriend? Could be.

She also mattered to Flynn Carroll. She mattered a very great deal, just as did all his dead. These kids now added to the tally.

"I need an MRI of the severed head," he said.

"Sure, Officer."

Flynn wasn't surprised at the assumption. He looked so much like a cop that even plain clothes didn't help. When he walked down a street, perps and wanteds just faded away. And, in fact, they were right to do so. He'd started as a street cop, then a small-city detective working meth labs and car boosts, the occasional murder. His current job was still cop work, and their unit was listed under policing organizations.

They did Doxy first, confirming that he had died of a severed spine. The massive blood loss that followed had not been a cause of death. Cut the head off, and both parts are dead within a minute, blood or no blood.

Because this was a forensic autopsy, primary attention was paid to the cause of death, which was the cut that had severed the head. The pathologist spoke quietly and crisply, but Flynn could hear the puzzlement in his voice. The cut was about a micrometer thick. It would have been made by a garróte so thin that it could not be seen, but so sharp that it could cut a brick in half and slide through steel as if it were butter.

"Officer, do you have any information about the weapon?"

"We do not."

The pathologist straightened up. He was a young man, maybe thirty, wearing jeans and a T-shirt. He said, "I don't know of a blade thin enough to do this."

Flynn said nothing.

"I'm going to list the cause as severing of the head by unknown means. Because what I'm seeing here doesn't make sense. It's impossible." He turned to Flynn. "Who are you, anyway? Can you shed any light on this?"

"Let's get that MRI, take it from there."

With the head in a medical transport chest, they took a coroner's vehicle to George Washington University Hospital. Flynn rode in the back with the chest. He didn't need questions.

Fifteen minutes of light traffic brought them to an ambulance entrance. The two attendants got out and took the chest between them. Flynn followed them into the Radiology Department, then down into the subbasement where the radiation facilities were located.

There were prints on the walls of the waiting area, an attempt to make the place seem cheerful and alive. They didn't work. All the landscapes did was remind you that you were here, not there.

The MRI operator came out of his control room as soon as they arrived, and took them back into the facility, through a door marked with a large yellow DANGER sign and a warning that metal objects must not be taken beyond this point.

Flynn didn't need to ask the technician whether or not he'd ever scanned a detached head before, because he hadn't.

"OK, we need to get this done. I want the thinnest slices; I want to see as much detail as I can."

The two coroners lifted the head out of its container, and the MRI operator promptly bent double and vomited. "I'm sorry," he said, "I am so sorry."

Flynn put his hand on his shoulder. "Get it back together, get it done. Time is of the essence."

"But what—what the hell? What in HELL happened to this man?"

He'd doubtless see a picture of Doxy somewhere at some point, and be left to wonder, because the story of the kid's death wouldn't exactly square with his head's being separated from his body. Flynn would need a confidentiality agreement brought over here.

He sat in the dark operator's room watching the scan take place. For the first few passes, there was nothing. Then there was.

"Jesus," the technician said.

The third pass had revealed a small pit deep in the brain. It was just above the claustrum.

He said to the young medical examiner, "Something's there."

"Could be. Can't be sure." He was silent for a moment. Flynn looked at the image. He wasn't sure, either. They would need to dissect.

In the interest of time, Flynn would have liked to have had it done here, but if he did, the story would be all over the hospital in an hour. He said, "We're going to move to the ME's office. Gentlemen, I'd like to thank you for your work. Another officer will be along shortly with confidentiality agreements for you to sign. This is a national security matter, and discussing it even among yourselves is illegal. Remember that."

The two staffers stared at him wide-eyed.

Flynn left, followed by the young ME, who insisted on coming into the back of the truck.

"I need to know how to document this," the kid asked.

"Death by murder."

"This wound in the brain." He paused. "It's not a tumor, and the MRI guy didn't know jack shit about it. Do you mind if I ask you something?"

"Go ahead."

"Does this have to do with aliens? Because it looks like something was in there and it got pulled out."

Flynn chuckled. "Are you a professional asshole or just an advanced amateur?"

"It's a reasonable question."

"It's a ridiculous question. But don't document the dissection."

"You do realize that we'll be on video."

"Turn it off."

"I don't have the authority."

He called Diana. "I need you to get the video turned off in—" He addressed the young man. "What room?"

"Four. We'll use four."

He said, "Dissection room four at the ME's office," and hung up. "No video, so no report." He didn't say this, but this kid and everybody involved at the medical examiner's office were also going to sign confidentiality agreements.

"I have just one other question."

"No you don't."

"Not even one?"

Flynn did not reply.

The dissection took two hours. First the skull was opened and the brain extracted. "I am seeing a puncture wound in the surface of the cerebellum. Rather than begin at the Lewy Body landmark, I will dissect following this wound. I note that there is a postmortem point of incision in the skull above the wound that extends through the derma, indicating that an instrument was inserted into this brain after death."

"Son, I need you—"

"Doctor. I'm a doctor."

"Sorry, Doc. I'm just nervous as hell right now. I need you to forget the entire dissection routine and get down to where that opening ends and see if there's anything left there, any scrap of material."

"This is the most curious thing I've ever encountered in my career. Just for my own peace of mind, can you give me some idea here?"

"He died in the service of his country. These are the remains of an American hero."

The young doctor was silent for a moment, his head bowed. "May God receive his soul." Carefully, he did his dissection, using a delicate brain knife, working until he had spread a dozen slices across the worktable. "Nothing," he said.

"Microscope. Can you do that?"

"Absolutely."

Flynn watched as he made an ultrathin slice that centered on the spot where the now-removed implant had rested. He slid it into the microscope and they both watched the screen as it focused.

"There's material there."

As Flynn had hoped, the implant had been seated long enough to have begun growing in. "Get that," he said. "I need that."

"What the hell—it's a metal base with cilia growing out of it. What is that thing?"

There was no legal way for Flynn to explain. He said, "Please mount it on a slide that I can carry with me."

Silently, the doctor did as he was ordered, and as silently Flynn left, taking all of the biologicals with him. In the end, they would be cremated and returned to the family, but they would not be left in hospital mortuaries or coroner's offices. The body itself was at this moment on its way to a specialized facility at Wright-Patterson Air Force Base, where extremely sensitive materials were destroyed in a superheated furnace. The family would be given the ashes in a nice urn, and the Intelligence Medal to bury with them. The ashes would not be their son's, of course. The specialized burn was necessary because there could be something else in the body, some other piece of high-level technology, that normal cremation would leave exposed, and still dangerous.

Flynn put most of the remains in the trunk of his car, but the slide with the implant fragment on it he laid on the seat beside him. It looked like nothing, hardly visible at all, but he knew how powerful it actually was. These things did not die, and a small part of one was just as potent as an intact object. It would take it longer to grow back to full size and full strength, that was all.

It was now afternoon, hard sun, the trees whipped by a brisk north wind, leaves rushing along the street, the old Federal houses of Georgetown seeming to watch him, their windows eyes. He'd been working for something close to twenty hours at this point. Not good, even for him. But typical.

He shook off the exhaustion. There would be no sleep tonight, and maybe not for a while. He didn't really sleep, anyway. He waited. "Guarded sleep," the doctors called it. It wasn't good, but it was better than ending up wherever Abby had gone.

He and Diana had Zone 2 permits for their cars, but they used Colonial Parking across the street; best to keep their vehicles out of sight. After he pulled into his space, he wondered if he should take the thing into the house at all. But the wall safe had been specially designed to hold "extremely mobile" objects. It had been created by their scientific team after they'd come to understand that Aeon could deploy implants that were capable of homing in on their victims from a distance, entering the body without leaving a scar, and seating themselves.

He got out of the car and went quickly across the street to the yellow three-story house, carrying the implant in his pocket and feeling like a damn fool for doing it.

He loved this house. It had been built in 1817, in the building boom that followed the American defeat of the British in the War of 1812, and the subsequent opening of more trade in the region.

He waited for a moment before the facial recognition system identified him. The door clicked faintly, and he opened it. There were cameras hidden in every room, covering the entire structure, even the four feet of crawl space above the top floor, and the roof as well. A hand-clap sequence could drop steel doors between all the rooms and seal the entire structure off from the outside. If somebody was let in whom the facial recognition system didn't recognize, they couldn't enter any rooms but the kitchen, parlor, dining room, and guest bathroom without being coded. Should they go into a restricted room without the system getting the proper clearance code, the room would be instantly sealed by its steel doors and window coverings.

"I called Emmett," Diana said as he entered her office.

He hardly heard her. He wished that he could tell her what he was about to do, but it was too dangerous. As hard as they worked to keep this house free of hostile surveillance devices, it was never possible to be entirely sure.

She was going to suffer like hell, poor damn woman. She cared too much, was her problem, and caring about people like Flynn was never a good idea.

She was sitting at her desk, which was lined with screens on which various images danced—of street corners, of the interior of the White House, and of Flynn's car. The image of the car was frozen in a close-up of the implant, which had been on the front seat.

There was a heavy scent of cigarette smoke in the room.

"You're smoking again."

"Don't like it, leave."

He didn't like it, but if he wanted her in his life, the cigarettes were going to come, too. She used them only when she was apprehensive—or, to put it more accurately, sick with fear.

"Put that damn thing in the safe," she said, her voice so tense that it sounded as if she were being choked.

The wall safe was open. He put the evidence bag inside and closed it.

"Why the hell did you move it in an evidence bag? What were you thinking?"

"That I had no other container."

"Should've called me. Should've waited."

The screens showed a dozen different images of the interior of the White House—all the public rooms, some parts of the Residence and the West Wing.

"I see you're in the White House."

"Some. Most of the official spaces are clean, unfortunately. Not the Oval, though." She tapped a square on her iPad and one of the screens changed to a familiar scene. The Oval Office was empty. "He spends his working hours either in his office in the Residence or in the study. He probably knows that the Oval is covered."

She next picked him up in the Rose Garden.

"I don't like that, him outside alone," Flynn said.

"No."

"How often is he out there?"

"He plays tennis, Flynn."

Diana put up a new video clip. Lorna was in bed. Ginny was walking around the room naked, looking for something.

"I thought you said the bedrooms were clear of surveillance."

"This is an old system installed by German intelligence. After Obama pissed them off by bugging Merkel's cell phone, they retaliated. The Secret Service found it in a sweep about four days after it was installed. Now it's mine."

Their doorbell rang downstairs and the system put Emmett's face up on the screen. Diana buzzed him in. He was cleared for the downstairs, the stairway, and this room. He showed himself up.

Emmett had been among the first to be recruited into their scientific team. By training, he was a biologist. He was a tall man with long, careful hands and quick, uneasy eyes. If he hadn't looked so much like a spy, he could have been one. He came into the room almost furtively, moving, as he always did, like a man who was going into hiding. He carried the portable containment, fifty pounds of woven carbon fiber and tempered steel.

"Get the damn thing in there," Diana snarled. "I want it out of my house pronto."

"Hello, you two, it's good to see you again."

"Do it!"

Emmett unlocked the containment. "Ready."

Flynn opened the safe and took out the evidence bag. He gave it to Emmett, who stared down at it.

"Get it sealed!" Diana shouted. "For God's sake!"

"No. No, wait." Emmett looked from one of them to the other. He still held the evidence bag in his hand. He said, "This isn't alien manufacture. This is one of ours."

"Did you know this, Flynn?"

"I thought it was possible."

Emmett took the object out of the evidence bag and held it in the palm of his hand. "This is dead. Ours don't reconstitute or penetrate. I worked on the encapsulation for these, actually."

Ordinary people worried about Facebook and Google invading their privacy, or the NSA listening in on their calls. But that was primitive stuff. The brain is accessible to very deep invasion, and this was an example of what our own intelligence community, back-engineering from Aeon's crumbs, now had at its disposal. Using a small microwave transmitter, the implant could be used to turn off the host's consciousness without shutting down the rest of his mind. He could then be interrogated, and he would have no memory of it at all. People like Doxy, placed in positions of extreme sensitivity but judged to be not reliable, were implanted like this so that they could be routinely questioned without their knowing it.

"I need to file a report," Emmett said. "Most of this thing is in the wild now. Do you guys know who took it?"

They couldn't tell him that. His job was cataloging and maintaining objects like this, not tracking them down when they were stolen.

"Guess not. I get that. Whoever it came out of, that person is now dead."

"He is," Flynn said.

Emmett left, his footsteps pounding on the stairs and shaking the house. He wasn't a particularly big man, but it was an old house and he was in a hurry.

Diana lit another cigarette off the first one. Flynn took them both and put them out.

"Do that again and I'll beat you up."

"Sounds like fun."

She laughed. "So Iran assassinates Doxy and harvests one of our implants. I get that. They'd lust after a low-tech implant like the ones we create. They'll never manage to duplicate one of Aeon's beauties, but they might be able to manufacture ones like ours. But why was he carrying the detail's core file, which Iran now also has?"

"This was about the implant, but it was also about our file. Aeon wants it, and this was the only way to obtain it. Or the most reliable way. Iranian agent. Perfect surrogate."

"Aeon and Iran working together?"

"Looking more and more possible."

"The detail has no assets in Iran, and we can't ask CIA covert to work on it, not without blowing hell out of our internal cover."

"Then it's up to us."

"Yeah, well—no! Oh, no, Flynn! Don't even think about that." She was silent for a long time.

"Speaking of assassinations," she finally said, "there was one in Iran. One of their nuclear experts was gunned down by motorcyclists in Tehran. The proximity of the two events suggests they could be related."

"I think the first step is to find out just exactly what in holy hell the Iranians are doing in the middle of this."

"Agreed. How?" She lit another cigarette, puffed it once, then held it away when he tried to grab it. "No."

"I love you, I—" He stopped, shocked at his words. A nervous smile flashed in her eyes. They were colleagues who sometimes bedded together, but that described half of the intelligence community. Love was not part of it. Not supposed to be.

As if she could hear his thoughts, the joy that had flickered in her face like heat lightning faded quickly away.

She put out the cigarette. He saw a flush rise up her neck and set her cheeks aglow, just like when she was mad. Was she mad? She said, "Let's reach for that damn kid, pull him in and shake him."

"Sure. Might help."

Over the next half hour, they tracked the Iranian kid, reconstructing his movements of the previous night, watching on satellite footage as he threaded his way through the park, then out onto the highway. They watched him get picked up by a blue SUV. As it pulled away, Diana got a clear look at the license plate. It took the computer a few seconds to correlate with the make and model of the car, then to display the title and the owner's driver's license.

"Sure enough, Persian community," Diana said. "Went to a MISIRI safe house."

"I could pay them a call." He wouldn't, he didn't care, but he needed an excuse to get out of here without uttering a word about what he was actually planning to do.

"What about the president? What about the White House? You need to go back there."

"Either I sit over there and wait for something to happen, or we find out what this is about and stop it before it goes any further. Our choice. Or yours, actually—you're the boss."

She scrawled something and held out the paper. "It's near Embassy Row."

He took the paper, crumpled it up, and tossed it in a trash can. "I know where it is."

"But you couldn't?" She paused, frowned slightly. "You're telegraphing that the kid's location doesn't actually matter. You're not really after—" She clamped her jaw shut.

He nodded.

"OK. I get it. I think."

Not a word of what he was about to do could be said aloud. If Aeon was involved in all this, then they were being watched right now. Iran couldn't bug a place this secure, but Aeon certainly could.

She needed to realize what he was actually doing. If she did, he'd have the backup he needed where he was going, and he had little doubt that it would be *very* needed. If not, then he was going to be putting his head into the jaws of the lion, and doing it alone. You don't escape that.

He left, but did not go across to the parking garage. Instead he headed into the freshening north wind. He was looking for a taxi, and after a block or so, he found one. He took it first to his apartment.

"Wait for me."

"You got it."

He went up in the elevator, walked down a long corridor lined with black doors, and stopped before his own. This was hard. It was always very hard. So he hesitated, and at a moment when seconds might count. He smelled the odor of steak cooking in a nearby apartment, heard people laughing, music, then the shouts of children, faint and poignant.

He entered the darkness of his foyer. He didn't turn on any lights. He didn't need to, and showing light in here right now would be a bad idea.

He went into his bedroom and opened the wall safe in the closet. He pulled out nine thousand "cured" dollars—cured in the sense that they had been gotten from his bank in return for a cashier's check, and had now been out of circulation for more than a year. He kept a hundred grand in cash handy, and twenty thousand in gold coins. You didn't need gold in Iran; dollars there were as desirable and easier to use. Despite the treaty, Western credit cards didn't work, and the ATMs would be useless to what to all appearances he would be: a Swiss arms dealer. But it didn't matter. The Iranians were famished for hard currency, and the nine grand—as much as he could carry without questions being asked—would go more than far enough.

He hadn't been planning to go into the second bedroom. In fact, he'd told himself he would not, absolutely not, do that.

He crossed it, drew the drapes, and then turned on a single lamp, but not enough to reveal any light through an unnoticed gap in the curtains.

Not even Diana was invited here, and had she come, she would have been horrified by the number of pictures of Abby on the walls. He'd taken down the "Abby Room" in his house back in Texas, telling Mac and his other friends that he was putting her behind him. But it wasn't true. He had moved her here. He had tried and tried to leave her behind, but nothing worked. When he needed her so badly that he could bear it no longer, he would come to this room, which was his secret home.

"I love you," he'd said to Diana. He wanted to love her, that was the truth of it. He wanted to accept his grief for Abby and the baby. He looked from one photo to another, Abby on her front porch back in the depths of time and happiness, Abby on Serena, her hilarious, wonderful horse with the improbable Roman nose, he and Abby drinking at Scholz Beer Garten in Austin. Then the harder one: their wedding picture—two nervous Texas kids grinning hard, hand in hand, knuckles white. Then the worst one of all, the one he told himself never to look at again every time he did: the sonogram. Tiny image, hands fisted, eyes open, the sense of amazement that lives in the faces of babies.

He changed into a business suit, grabbed a pouch with the deepest, most solid identity he possessed in it, and got the hell out of there.

He got into the cab and slammed the door. "Reagan," he said. The driver responded with a grunt.

He was going to the one place on Earth that mattered the most in all this, the place that was the unexpected and most certainly deadly center of the operation. He was going to Tehran.

CHAPTER EIGHT

AS FAR as the world was concerned, Flynn was now Stephan Grauerholtz, a Swiss citizen. The alias was deep enough to stand up to all but the most intensive analysis, right down to Stephan's boyhood years at the exclusive Le Rosey prep school in Rolle, Switzerland. He'd been a decent kid and now he was a decent arms dealer, unless that's an oxymoron. Swiss arms dealers are among the most welcome of all travelers in countries like Iran. He had read that their visa on arrival system could be difficult to use, but he expected that Mr. Grauerholtz would sail through.

The identity was far deeper than most he'd used in the past. For example, social media was thoroughly covered and kept up to date by CIA specialists who managed such identities—without, of course, having any idea who was using them. At least in theory. Stephan's Facebook page went back three years, chronicling his life of travels and his appreciation of beautiful women, cultural events, and fine dining. His Twitter feed, mostly sports (he was a Man United fan), went back a year and a half. A search further into his background would reveal the reason that a Swiss would be the fan of an English football team. His mother had been born and raised in Manchester, and was a lifelong follower of the team. His father, a professor of linguistics, was indifferent to sports.

Rather than go to Dulles, Flynn—or now, Grauerholtz—took the Delta shuttle from Reagan to LaGuardia, then grabbed a cab over to JFK. At Reagan, he'd bought only the ticket to LaGuardia, using cash.

Riding through Queens on his way from LaGuardia to JFK, he watched the surge of the city around him, glimpsed the lights of Manhattan and the vast Mount Zion graveyard, a huge gray shadow at their feet.

Should he really do this? Should he leave the White House behind? If Cissy was hurt, he'd never forgive himself—hurt, or worse, taken like Abby. It would be all but unbearable. More than that, though, he should be protecting the president.

And yet, wasn't that what this was? Until he understood what was happening, the truth was that he couldn't really protect anybody. All he could do was stand guard, and that was not going to be enough. He had to do this and get back as fast as possible. A quick, clean penetration, gather the needed information, return. Three days, four at the most.

What information, though? And how did he gather it? His only real plan was to bull his way into the foreign ministry on a pretext and take it from there.

Even buried in a new identity and with his plans known only to his own mind, he kept watch, but not in such a way that it would be obvious to the cabdriver that he was uneasy about being followed. When cabbies noticed such things, they remembered. He needed to be just another uninteresting, commonplace fare. He used the rearview and outside mirrors to watch for lights, and leaned against the window as if tired. From this position he could scan the sky for trouble from above. Over the long battle that was his career, there had been many times that menace had dropped down on him out of the sky. He was very good at spotting the star that should not be there, or was too bright, or moving strangely. This time, though he didn't see anything, it didn't mean that he was in the clear. At no time, under no circumstances, would anybody experienced in this particular conflict ever assume that Aeon wasn't nearby. Drop your guard and die.

A flock of European flights took off between nine and eleven at night, so Terminal 7 was reassuringly busy. Flynn, buried in the crowd, moved with the assurance of a businessman who flew a lot. He crossed to the ticket counter, and got in the first-class line, behind an elderly couple speaking brisk, annoyed German. He was decent in the language but hadn't spoken it in some time, so listening to them was useful.

He got a first-class ticket at the British Airways counter. Rather than pay cash, which would raise flags, he used one of the Grauerholtz credit cards. Should MISIRI become suspicious at some point, their investigation would begin with his route into the country. If it turned out that his tickets were cash purchases, they would probably arrest him first and investigate later. It wasn't a place where you wanted to be arrested, Iran.

Through the large window overlooking the flight line, he watched operations, looking for anything that struck him as unusual, just letting his instincts work. Nothing stood out, though, nobody seemed out of place, and operations continued with fluid precision.

There were storms muttering to the north, and as he sat in the first-class lounge waiting for the flight to be called, he watched blue flickers of lightning reflected on runways where planes moved like ghostly sea creatures, coming and going in the dark.

His flight was called on time, and he filed on with the other first- and business-class passengers. He was now deep in the character of Grauerholtz, right down to the German accent and the courtly manners of an upper-class Swiss.

The plane was an older 747 with a recently refurbished interior. If Aeon knew he was on it, they would cause it to crash, but not before coming aboard and capturing him. His fellow passengers would find a great secret revealed to them . . . as they died.

They went after him when he was at his most vulnerable, on lonely roads sometimes, but more often in planes, where he was, essentially, trapped. They didn't try for public places like airports and train stations or, usually, city streets. They knew from experience that he would elude them unless he had no place to go. And even then, he had escaped—so far.

Once the meal service was over, he turned out his light and flattened the bed, not to sleep but to think through events in microscopic detail. It was this method that had, in the past, enabled him to overcome impossible odds, and he was convinced that this situation was no different. A weapon was pointed at the White House, but who was going to pull the trigger? Above all, when that was done, what would happen?

He slept, then, an uneasy sleep, although never deep enough for dream.

It took him into the glow of dawn over the Irish Sea. He woke up and drank coffee and worried. Had the thing—whatever it was—already happened?

The flight landed at eleven. His next plane left Gatwick at one forty-five, and he spent most of the time between airports getting through customs, finding a cab, and sitting out the London traffic.

Another seven-hour flight, this time on Emirates, then a five-hour lay-over in Dubai. Most of his work was done in the U.S., so he wasn't all that familiar with places like this. The airport was a gleaming extravaganza, as luxurious as first class had been on the Emirates plane. On the flight, he'd had what amounted to a private room. He'd even been able to take a shower in a small bathroom reserved for first class.

A U.S. agent masquerading as an arms dealer might give himself away by flying coach. Arms dealers didn't fly coach. In fact, the big ones used their own planes. By traveling commercial, Grauerholtz was saying that he was prosperous, but not yet a major player.

Not knowing how long it might be until his next meal, he ate again in the airport, at an Indian place called Gazebo. He ate everything—the melt-ingly tender *paya yakhni shorba,* lamb trotters simmered in curry; a fluffy saffroned *biryani tikka bahar;* vegetables grilled on a skewer with pine-apple. He could have used a beer, but not in Dubai.

He noticed, on boarding the Tehran flight, that the general atmosphere of the airport was far less tense than what one found in the United States. And why not? It was doubtful that terrorists would target Arab airlines.

He watched the world from the window, first the bright blue of the Persian Gulf, then the brown emptiness of the Iranian hinterland.

He reviewed his approach to the foreign ministry. He would be seeking an end-user certificate for imports from the European Union. The goods he intended to offer would be of the most intense interest.

As they had never seen him before, they would be suspicious. He trusted that his curriculum vitae would be convincing. If it wasn't, he was in trouble, because he couldn't arrange to carry his weapons on international flights without drawing official attention to himself. The result was that he was unarmed. He wouldn't try to buy a gun in Iran, and in any case, he'd never attempt to enter the foreign ministry heavy.

Khomeini International Airport was a mixture of sparkling new and what appeared to be abandoned construction. Flynn immediately noticed the odor of the air, which was a mix of burning coal, engine exhaust, grease, and dust. Even inside the terminal, the air was dense.

The passport control line moved slowly. Very slowly. Ahead of him there was a woman dressed in a Chanel original worth easily five thousand dollars, her head covered by a scarf of sheer, floating silk. She was perhaps forty-five. Her face, with its large, questing eyes and tight-set lips, expressed a regal calm that reminded Flynn that you don't approach customs looking uneasy, or, for that matter, too relaxed.

She spoke Farsi, so he was able to pick up only a few words, but it soon became clear that she expected to get an on-arrival visa. The customs officer appeared for a moment concerned, then indifferent. He picked up a telephone, spoke a few words, and put it down. A moment later, another man appeared, this one in the weary business suit of a police official, and began escorting the woman away. He stopped, then turned back. His face opened into a smile that lifted his broad mustache almost comically.

He said, "Oh, and Mr. Grauerholtz, too, right here. Come, also, please." He gestured grandly, like a pretentious maître' d.

As Flynn followed the woman's sweeping silks, he thought that Iran's foreign ministry must be very damned efficient to not only expect him, but to send somebody who knew him by sight. As he walked, another man fell in beside them, this one in an expensive Italian suit. Ahead of them, the woman was drawn into a hallway. The door closed and she disappeared.

The man said, in German, "I am Davood Ghorbani, vice minister of armaments in charge of acquisitions. We'll pass the formalities and go directly to the ministry."

"Yes, I think that's best." Flynn's German had better be as serviceable as he imagined it to be.

Ghorbani's suit was an excellent cut, which put him far up in the ministerial hierarchy. Flynn had signaled almost nothing about the purpose of his visit, but Grauerholtz's manufactured reputation must have preceded him. His specialty was rocket parts, most specifically highly machined nozzles for rocket engines—in other words, one of the items highest on the Iranian wish list.

The engine was not just the power source of an intercontinental missile, it was the basis of its accuracy. Without an engine capable of producing a clean burn, no guidance system could achieve enough accuracy to hit a city at a distance of five thousand kilometers. In addition, the engine had to have far more lifting power than anything presently in Iran's arsenal. The current state-of-Iranian-art missile was the Saji-3, which was capable of throwing a modest payload as far as four thousand miles. But to make a nuclear warhead small enough to be lifted by that system was going to take a major technological effort on Iran's part. And so far, anybody who was working in that direction was almost certain to be assassinated by the Israelis and the West. No doubt that was what had happened to Dr. Josefi.

The car passed quickly through Tehran's traffic in a protected official lane. Flynn noted that the traffic was extremely heavy—in fact, the heaviest and most chaotic he had seen in any city. He would not forget this.

As they moved into the governmental area, Ghorbani said, "We won't be going to the ministry."

"Oh?"

"To a home."

So they assumed that their ministry was bugged and under observation by the West. And they were probably right.

Five minutes later, they were in a quiet, leafy neighborhood, with houses set back from the wide, empty streets. They passed the Canadian, then the French embassies. As they drove on, ascending into higher, even quieter precincts, Flynn drew a map in his head. In case he had to do a runner, he needed to know where these embassies were. Diplomatic refuge would likely be his only escape.

The car turned into a park rioting with flowers and centered by a large house, a Spanish colonial dressed with Persian touches.

"A Shah House," Ghorbani commented. He chuckled. "But not recently."

As they pulled up to the tall front door beaded with large studs, a man in a white soutane appeared. Silently, he opened Flynn's door. Flynn noted a pistol on his left hip, and that there was a specially tailored slit in the soutane that would enable him to reach the gun quickly.

An older man, the left side of his face immobilized by a stroke, came out and hurried down the steps. He wore a western suit, Saville Row. "Welcome, Herr Grauerholtz." His mustache and eyebrows were curly and white. His toupee, as black and slick as a polished shoe, hung low over his face. His left hand was clenched, his right extended.

Flynn got out of the car, noting that this man, also, was armed. He carried a very small pistol in a shoulder holster, no more than a .32. Flynn wished to hell he had a pistol of his own right now.

As he entered the house, he gauged the accessibility of each weapon. He could remove the larger pistol, the one under the arm of the man in the soutane, before either armed man could react. If the older one had a very fast draw, he might be able to get a shot off before Flynn killed him, although this was not likely.

So Flynn was safe from a direct assault. At the moment.

They entered a library that must have been constructed by a Westerner. Although the volumes in it were Persian, the design, with two tiers of bookcases around three walls, was something out of an English country house.

"This was the residence of the last president of Aramco," the older man said. He sat heavily in a wing chair and motioned to Flynn to sit opposite. "A man of impeccable taste."

Flynn took the seat, noting that the guard in the soutane was now standing behind him. Ghorbani was behind the minister. They had formed a defensive box, and Flynn was no longer safe from assault. If they were going to try to subdue somebody very fast and very dangerous, this was the sort of positioning they might choose. Flynn hadn't seen a weapon on Ghorbani, but he must be carrying one.

"And now, my dear Mr. Flynn Carroll," Ghorbani said, smiling, "why do you imagine that we have brought you here?"

Flynn froze any and all reactions.

"Calculating the odds, are you, my dear superman? You will find that they are against you."

He heard the faint sound of movement behind him as the guard readied himself.

Flynn's heart rarely raced, but it did so now. The boyish unease had left Ghorbani's smile. In fact, he wasn't smiling at all, and probably never had been. He was showing teeth. To the "minister," he said, "You may go now, Habib." The old man dutifully got up and left the room—fast. He knew very well what might be about to happen here. For some time, Ghorbani regarded Flynn. "Your cover was, I am sorry to say, puerile," he finally said.

Flynn estimated that he could get to the Canadian Embassy in six minutes running flat out.

"Ah, my friend, you are still calculating." He stood up and came around the desk, put his hands on Flynn's shoulders, and looked up at him. "A human war machine," he said. "How magnificent you are." He stepped back. "I feel that I know you better than I do my own son. Oh, I must show you—" He took out his smartphone and put his arm around Flynn's shoulder. At the same time, Flynn felt the barrel of a pistol touch, ever so gently, the small of his back. If it was fired, it would sever his spine but not kill him. He'd be left helpless, but still available for interrogation.

"Now look." On the phone's screen was a photo of Flynn with Diana. They were in their office at CIA headquarters. "We have eyes on you." Ghorbani's face was now blankly reptilian. He snapped a command in Farsi, then extended a hand to Flynn. "Come, my treasure. I think you'll find what I'm about to show you quite interesting."

The pistol barrel in Flynn's back pressed a little harder.

Ghorbani opened a door at the far end of the room. It led into an office, windowless, lit by blue neon. There was a digital map on one wall that revealed every detail of Flynn's journey, right down to his meal in Dubai.

Lying on a steel desk were dossiers on him, Diana, and a number of other individuals in Detail 242. Dozens of stills of them were tacked up on corkboards in one area of the crowded room. There were also pictures of Abby taken from the newspapers, pictures of Mac, of Cissy, of the president and the First Lady, of Mac's ranch in West Texas and Flynn's own house in Menard.

Flynn scanned them, noting that only the pictures of Abby dated from prior to Bill Greene's inauguration. So Iran's interest had been sparked by the arrival of the Greenes in the White House.

He filed that information away.

"My Flynn Carroll Room. Modeled after your Abby Room. Not as tragic an outcome, though. Must be very hard for you, not knowing." His voice all but sang. This was a very happy man. Flynn could have killed him with a blow, but even he was not fast enough to escape the bullet that would immediately follow.

"I've learned so much about you, Flynn, I feel as if we are, in quite a profound sense, brothers." The man's liquid face was now projecting menace of startling intensity. "Of course," he added, "you must have had the same knowledge of Dr. Josefi."

"Who?"

He threw back his head and laughed. "You were very foolish to try spycraft, soldier. You lie like a stammering child. Now come, there's somebody waiting to meet you." He gave him a wink. "She's *very* eager."

He stepped through to another, more austere room. Flynn followed.

In the center of this room, made dim by what appeared to be blackout curtains, there sat a woman of perhaps forty in a black head scarf and a gown. Beside her were a solemn preadolescent boy and a little girl. The three regarded him with buzzing, hate-tight eyes.

"Now, Mrs. Josefi, I promised you that I would bring you the man who killed Ibrahim. This is Flynn Carroll of America. This is the man who planned your husband's murder, and whose life you may either spare or take."

Slowly, she looked from one of her children to the other. Each gave a slight nod. She said, "Execute him."

"Very well, then that's decided, Flynn. You see, here in Persia we are very civilized, not like you Westerners. The West buries its savagery in a flood of procedures and technicalities. Here, we are plain about sin and retribution."

"I have no idea what you're talking about."

"Ah, you disappoint me. Spies lie, but not soldiers. I thought you a soldier."

One of the guards hustled the family out a side door, through which Flynn glimpsed a courtyard filled with yet more flowers, and heard bird-song. Then the door slammed and there was a flash behind his eyes, the result of a terrific blow to the head.

He knew that he was falling, and that was all he knew.

CHAPTER NINE

THE PAIN started in his groin, pulsing upward into his gut, bringing with it waves of nausea, while also burning down along his legs, as if his skin were being sanded.

"What an embarrassment, Flynn. You've been weeping like a baby. And here I thought you such a wonder. Brilliance, courage, and strength. That's what I thought, yes."

Hands turned his head roughly to one side, and he found himself looking at a TV screen. On it was an image of a naked man. His mouth lolled open. A nurse in a white uniform was placing electrodes on his penis and scrotum, her fingers working with practiced dexterity, her face reflecting the concentration of a professional doing a familiar job.

She stood aside, and a man in a black uniform picked up an old-fashioned rheostatic control, which was wired to the electrodes. He turned the control knob, and the man on the table writhed and shrieked. Flynn had never heard himself sound like that, so abject. In his unconscious state, he had reacted like a terrified child.

They were really very skilled, to think to undermine a victim's will in such a diabolical way.

The screen went blank and the man in the black uniform approached the table. "You may call me Ishmael," he said. "And now we try again, just to adjust and test the current."

"I'll answer your questions."

"You will indeed, and not with lies. But not just now."

As he twisted the controller, Flynn's genitals seemed to catch fire. He forced his screams deep into his throat. Straps too thick even for him to snap bound him.

The pain rose until it was a seething, red-hot wave surging up and down his body.

Then it was gone. Flynn gagged, gasped, tried to fight down vomit, failed. He lay there choking in his own sour bile.

Ghorbani moved into his field of vision. "So embarrassing, Flynn. I'm really disappointed."

"You and me both."

"Oh, a quip, just like James Bond." He clapped his hands. "Not a very good one, though. In fact, Flynn, quite lame. Now, let's get started with our questions." He picked up an iPad, a rarity in Iran. "My goodness, so many questions we have! Every house on our intelligence street has added a few. We are so very curious about you, you may be flattered."

"Go to hell."

"As indeed I may. But you certainly will, you devil." The words were full of hate, but the voice still contained not a trace of anger. This man expressed his anger through his work.

It had taken Flynn far too long to understand that he wasn't in the hands of the foreign ministry or even the Iranian intelligence service. These people were Revolutionary Guard, and when it came to torture, he could expect the worst from them. His life was also over; he understood that. Unless he could find some tiny sliver of inattention or miscalculation, he was going to die here.

In other words, he was going to lose this thing, and with it maybe a great deal more would be lost, maybe all the freedom in this world, and maybe the world itself.

He needed time, so he decided to cooperate. If he wasn't under torture, he would have a better chance of finding that one microscopic chink in their armor that he needed. He would answer every question they had.

"Oh, incidentally, throughout our time together, I'll be waiting to hear you tell me why you came here, given that the Josefi assassination had already succeeded." He sat down on the table and laid a soft hand on Flynn's forehead. "Such nice skin. When we cut through it—we will be inserting electrodes into your brain—we'll have to leave a scar." Stroking Flynn's hair, he added, "It's so unfortunate. But then again, that poor Mrs. Josefi and those two lovely children. Also unfortunate."

"Who is this person?"

"No, Flynn, it's not you who ask the questions."

Red, flaming haze, from his groin in flooding pain, the sense of fire within. Somebody screaming from far away, a memory of the ocean—a flash of peace—then back and plunging into greater pain.

It stopped. Flynn found himself gagging and gasping, his body heaving against the straps.

Silence fell. Extended. Sunlight crossed the room, lazy gold with the smoke of the nurse's cigarette curling through it. She got up from her chair, came and listened to his chest with a stethoscope. She put a blood pressure cuff on his arm and pumped it up. After a moment, it sighed and she nodded curtly to the torturers. She returned to her chair and continued watching, her young face as impassive as a sculpture. Iranian culture supposedly reverenced and protected women. But not this one, apparently. She obviously saw a lot of this, otherwise there would be some expression there, some emotion, but he saw only the mild indifference of somebody waiting for her coffee break.

"What do you know of Dr. Ibrahim's project?"

Flynn understood that he was in the worst possible situation. He was being tortured to extract information he genuinely did not know. He couldn't just deny, not if he expected to live through this, and he couldn't tell them anything useful about something they knew more about than he did.

Nevertheless, if he was to buy even a little time, he had to try. He took a flier. "He was run by Albert Doxy."

"Run? How run?"

"Doxy was his controller."

Ghorbani smiled. He came to the edge of the table and gazed down at Flynn. "Don't you understand how practiced we are at this? What we can do?"

"Doxy was his controller!"

He shook his head. "Flynn, Flynn, Flynn. There are worse ways to die than even you know." He spoke in Farsi, and the nurse, sighing like a child forced to do a chore, came over and began loosening his straps.

His heart soared. Surely there would be a chance here. She was weak, inattentive. She would give him an opening.

"Now," Ghorbani said, "turn onto your side."

The barrel of a pistol was once again thrust into the small of his back.

He felt something very unpleasant being done to him, and knew that an electrode had been inserted into his anus.

"Flynn, please be reasonable. That thing will burn you from inside. The pain is so great, Flynn, that you will tell us everything to make it stop. We will remove it, for we are honorable that way, but you will die in any case, burned like that. It is a lingering death, too awful to tempt." He lowered his voice. "We put them in a cell and return when the screaming stops."

"I'll tell you everything right now!"

"Very well, then let's shift our approach a little. What is the name of your operation? Its code name, Flynn?"

"Oilman. It's Oilman." He'd made that up, too.

"Is it?"

His rectum began to sting. He thrust and struggled, but he could not make the penetrator move. "Yes! For the love of God!" Always express more suffering than you're feeling. That's the key to surviving torture.

"What does the implant in Albert Doxy's head do?"

"It's a tracking device. Everybody in sensitive positions has one."

The pain rose. "Too deep in the brain for that. Who knew the truth about what he was doing? You, Flynn, did you know? Were you observing him?"

"I don't know how to answer."

The room swept away until it was a dot of light. The nurse made a sharp statement in Farsi and Ghorbani laughed. The others in the room—and there were now quite a few—followed suit.

"Oh, Flynn," he said, "please face that you're a soldier, not a spy. You should give up this charade and just tell us what we want to know. You can't hide anything anyway." He then spoke in Farsi and there was a murmur of chuckles. "I am telling them what I said to you." He and the nurse then conversed in Farsi for a moment. "I am asking her if the next phase will kill you. It's Mrs. Josefi's right to carry out the actual execution, and I would be embarrassed if I deprived her of her right. Now Nurse Dilara wishes to practice her English."

She said, "I explain we now cause angina attack."

"No, no, my dear. Remember your verbs. English verbs are very exact. 'I will explain.'"

"Thank you, sir. I will explain this. It will be great agony and it is dangerous. It will continue for some time. If we must keep repeating this procedure, it will damage your heart, transforming you into a ghost of yourself who can never get a breath."

"Yes, 'will.' Very good, Dilara."

"Thank you, Colonel."

Flynn hardly heard them. They had now revealed a second fact to him. Not only were they interested in the president, they'd had an agent on the inside. It must have been Doxy. Who had killed him, though? The mystery was still very deep.

Nurse Dilara placed electrodes on his chest, circling his heart. Then she slid a metal plate under his back. She nodded to Ghorbani.

"Now we talk about Aeon."

"Which is?"

"Don't be a child. We have your file."

"Then you know everything."

"We know enough to ask more."

If they weren't already in an alliance with Aeon, Flynn now believed, they soon would be. At any cost, he had to get this information back to Washington, but that meant doing the impossible. Escaping. Surviving.

Once such an alliance was in force, Iran would be the most powerful country in the world.

He said, "I don't know what you're talking about."

"A year ago, a police officer from Aeon was detailed to your unit."

"No idea about that."

Flynn's chest exploded, his throat seemed to collapse as if a wire were being twisted around it, and the world sank away into a vague and terrifying gray.

The agony went on.

At last, silence came, broken only by the sound of his raw, gagging breath.

"Please understand that I can use all of these implements at once, Flynn. As you know, you're not like most men. Such extraordinary pain will not render you unconscious. You'll suffer and suffer and suffer, Flynn."

Flynn did not respond. He fixed his mind on a happy moment from long ago, riding out with Abby, their horses' hooves thundering across the Llano Estacado.

Agony swarmed him from every direction, the heat of it, the searing, ripping torment of it, the burning of his guts, the fire in his genitals, the cruel squeezing of his heart.

Then it stopped.

"That was a taste, Flynn. I know for certain who you are and what you do. Understand this. We have all Aeon's records about you and Delta 242. Al got them for us as his last act of courage, and we were able to remove them from his office before he, unfortunately, had to give his life for the revolution. That's why we lured you here. We were taught just how to handle you psychologically. We set our trap just as Aeon's intelligence service instructed us and, soon enough, here you came."

They had killed Doxy. The Alliance with Aeon was, therefore, active. But they hadn't broken the encrypted parts of the core file or he would not be here and this would not be happening. Aeon must certainly have broken it, which meant that, while they might indeed be in touch, the alliance wasn't yet deep.

They might have a Wire, though, the same sort of direct connection to Aeon that Flynn's unit had once had. It would have been over such a device that they would have received instructions about how to capture Flynn.

Ghorbani moved away from the table. Across the room, he quietly consulted with a colleague. Flynn took the moment to go deep into himself, to embrace his pain as tenderly as his mother would have, and to wait empty, without thought or expectation. This, he knew, was the only way to endure torture, with a surrendered body and a mind emptied of hope.

As slow sunlight crossed the floor, the nurse methodically smoked, her face turned away from him. There was shame in her somewhere, or she would have watched.

He could now see that she despised her work, and so began to think that she might be a key to freedom.

He had more than once escaped from horrendous alien captivities, and so had come to trust his skills. What concerned him was that the torture was eroding those skills fast. The longer it went on, the more likely he was to miss whatever tiny chance might present itself.

The nurse would never consciously betray her masters, but an unconscious expression of her hatred for them was possible, and it was this he had to watch for.

"Flynn, I want to warn you, the next round is going to do some permanent damage to your heart. Understand this."

"I understand."

"Gail—you remember Gail—is she still here on Earth?"

"She went home."

"No, she did not. Where is she, Flynn?"

She was the lone police officer Aeon had sent to give them support after the death of Oltisis, their previous representative. They called her "Gail" because her real name was unpronounceable.

"I haven't seen her since the night she left."

"You know that it's impossible to hide on Aeon."

"I'm sure." Given what the NSA could do on Earth, he could well imagine how total the invasion of privacy must be on Aeon.

"Then she must be here. It follows, no?"

"Maybe her ship blew up on the way home. All I know is, I saw her leave."

The torture resumed. From some distant, heavenly place, he heard through his agony Ghorbani saying, "Let's get a tea."

Everyone except the nurse left the room. Flynn was left with electricity burning in his genitals and a cloth over his face that made it necessary to relax completely in order not to smother. If he was going to live, he had to let the pain possess him. He had to accept it. Only then could he relax enough to take sufficient breath.

His beloved first horse Twenty-Kay was standing across by the fence. His dad had her reins in his hand. He said, 'Come on, Errol, she's yours now.' Dad and Mom had called him by his real name. He'd come up with Flynn in high school. It beat Erroll Carroll all to hell.

It was his ninth birthday. A Texas kid's best birthday was his horse birthday. Twenty-Kay was blindingly quick in the quarter mile. Within a day, they were deeply in love, horse and boy, and that love lasted.

They were crossing the prairie in the springtime, the air sweet with flowers and new grass.

But then why this agony? He had to get this off him! Why this agony?

Mom said, "Just relax, honey, open yourself to it, relax into it."

The air was thick with cigarette smoke and the stink of shit. His shit.

The end of the pain was like falling into infinity. He was left gulping air, his heart thrusting like a pile driver, his breath hardly working.

The world blurred, but breathing became easier.

The nurse had removed the cloth and covered his face with an oxygen mask.

They knew about Aeon, Oltisis, Gail, him, Abby—the whole sordid tale.

Aeon had changed sides, and with that act, had changed the balance of power on Earth. Iran, not the United States, was now the most powerful nation in the world.

He had to find out all he could, then get out of here. Except for one problem: Escape appeared to be a pipe dream.

She was gazing down into his face, her brown eyes ridged with concern. She removed the mask. "Breathe," she said in her heavily accented English.

"The chest strap—it's too tight."

Using her long, delicate hands, the hands of an artist or a surgeon, she loosened it a little. In that moment, he could have snapped it, but it would only have been an act of bravado. The wrist and ankle straps would have prevented him from escaping.

He said no more. This was not the moment to attempt to get her to release one of his wrists. But that was all he needed, just one hand, and he'd be off this table in four seconds flat.

A barking, spitting fusillade of Farsi invective caused the nurse to at first widen her eyes, then spit back like a cornered wildcat. Davood Ghorbani had returned and, Flynn guessed, been outraged that she had turned off the torture devices on her own.

He strode over to the table. "You're lucky—that one has a soft heart. We'd hoped that the nurses wouldn't be as soft as the damn doctors. Women usually aren't. Plus this is a double-pay posting for them. But it doesn't matter—they're all soft and they all hate it." He lit a cigarette, inhaled, and blew smoke out of his nostrils. Flynn saw a dragon breathing fire. Ghorbani smiled. "Hallucinating, Flynn? Good, we're getting some-where, despite the foolishness of Miss Softy. Where is Gail?"

Torment blasted through him from all directions at once.

It stopped.

"Where, Flynn?"

"Texas! She's in Texas. A ranch north of Marfa. The Bar K Bar, ranch of MacAdoo Terrell."

"That one; yes, he's interesting, too. So the creature is there, protected by his gun collection and his radar fence." He smiled a boy's cruel smile. "That won't do, Flynn."

"Aeon must know where she is."

"Then why did they ask us?"

"To get you to torture me to answer a question I can't."

"Why would they do that?"

Aeon wanted him dead and had failed time and again to kill him, but he chose not to say that. "Ask them."

Ghorbani's crew had now also returned, some of them carrying paper cups of tea and coffee, and the smell of it was wonderful to Flynn.

"Yes, the closeness of death intensifies all smells and tastes. I suppose it's why the condemned so relish their final meals. But whether you have that opportunity will be Mrs. Josefi's decision—and perhaps she will relent. They so often do, the Persians. We are such a kind people."

This caused Flynn to laugh.

"You're the strong one, I'll grant you that. But do you know that you have been answering my questions truthfully from the beginning? Here, let me show you what I mean." He turned to the assembly of officers. "Please bring the tape."

A young man came up with an iPad.

"Human beings cannot lie, Flynn." He did something that Flynn could not see. Then he heard his own agonized shrieking. "Now—this is interesting—we slow it down." The shriek dropped to a lower register. "Again." The iPad now emitted a low, long growl. "And compress."

A ghostly, hollow voice, clipped and tight, said, "Mind control."

"You see, that was when we were asking you about the implant. Your conscious mind informed me that it was a tracking device. Believable enough, but it was not the truth. Your unconscious wanted so badly for the pain to end that it inserted the truth into your scream. So Al Doxy was under mind control. Why was that, Flynn?"

Flynn stiffened, waiting.

"Another jolt to your heart could kill you, so listen carefully. What did Doxy's implant give you?"

Flynn knew his body well, and now sensed that it had come to the end of its ability to resist. But he also didn't know the answer to the question. He decided to take another wild flier; there was nothing to lose. "We knew he was turned, that he belonged to somebody, but we didn't know who." A lie, of course, but one, based on what he had heard so far, that they might believe.

"Did you build that implant, or was it stolen from Aeon?"

He couldn't reveal that the U.S. had this capability. He tried to change the rules. "What do you know about Aeon?"

"You and I both know what'll happen if we have to repeat the treatment. Best never to ask me another question." He raised his eyebrows. "It's not your place, really."

"We didn't know exactly what it was, just that it was there. We found a fragment. Whoever killed him took the rest."

"You are not capable of making such things? Back-engineering?"

"We cannot."

Ghorbani once again laid a hand on his forehead. He stroked it gently. A soft, very slight smile flitted across his face. "You know, I'm actually fascinated by how profoundly I despise you. I try not to enjoy hurting you. It's not healthy. But I do, Flynn, very much."

The whisper of his touch made Flynn's stomach churn with acid.

"You must understand that I have some other tricks up my sleeve. Do you know anything about the past of this place? Persia? Probably not—you're an American. They're ignorant; they can afford to be. We Persians cannot afford to disrespect history." He patted Flynn's cheek. "Let me show you a picture."

It was a line drawing. Two men held the naked body of a third. Blood dripped from his throat. His captors were working on his back with knives.

"This is a drawing of an ancient bas-relief, found in an old Hittite ruin. Four thousand years old. They're flaying him alive." He held out a small, ugly knife, curved with a nasty hooked end. "They would open the throat first, because otherwise the screams were rather annoying. Then"—he touched the hooked end to Flynn's chest, pressing just hard enough for him to know that it was there—"you slip the blade in and lift the skin." He drew it back. "Let's talk. Really talk."

Flynn said nothing.

"Here's a question for you. Very important. Which company manufactures these?" He held out a silver object. It was the implant taken from Doxy's head, and Flynn thought again that these people were really very good at what they did.

"I'm not sure. What is it?"

Ghorbani smiled a little. "Did you ever read anything about medieval methods of torture?"

"Not my area of interest."

"There was something called slow fire, where the subject is cooked over a low flame. Roasted alive." His hand came back, gently stroking Flynn's forehead. "There are people in this room who will eat the meat of a victim while he still cooks. Eat it, and force the victim to do the same."

"I don't know any more than I've told you."

They had recruited Doxy, then intentionally raised enough suspicion about him to get CIA to implant him. Then they stole the implant, killing him in the process. Brilliant. Ruthless. More Aeon than Iran, too.

"We'll come back to the implant at a later time. Perhaps next week or the week after."

A common ploy, to face the victim with an unthinkable amount of time. No man being tortured at this level of intensity was going to last anything close to a week, not even him.

"We've seen video of you fighting some of Aeon's biological entities. You're extremely fast. Inhumanly fast. When did this start with you?"

"Two years ago."

"Did you notice any change prior to this happening?"

"Over a period of a week, I began to draw my pistol faster and faster. Finally I could pull my trigger faster than my gun's mechanicals could respond. I had to have it modified."

"The Casull Raging Bull?"

"Both Casulls. All my guns."

"And your accuracy is also perfect."

"It is."

"Now, a question that may save your life. Can you teach this?"

This was a chance, a very serious one. He had something they wanted. "I can."

"Will you teach it to Revolutionary Guards?"

"I want to live."

"Your eyes are moist, Flynn," Ghorbani said as he withdrew a handkerchief from his pocket.

"Like I said, I want to live."

"And now you think you have a chance."

When he wiped Flynn's face, Flynn felt a gratitude so overwhelming that a choking sob escaped his throat.

After they left, music began to play, and it was familiar music: "Plaisir d'amour," the old French love song that Abby used to sing with her guitar long ago.

How had they known that?

"The pleasure of love lasts only a moment, the grief of love lasts a lifetime."

Once again, he was left to watch the sunlight crawl across the floor of the smoky, empty room. Pain assailed him from every muscle, from his still-hammering heart, from his captured soul.

CHAPTER TEN

HE AWOKE in the night cold and thirsty. The moon shone down through the high windows, sailing in fast silver clouds. He strained against his bonds, contracting the muscles of his arms and legs until the table itself groaned. He expanded his chest until he was ready to break a rib, but the thick leather strap gave not at all. He writhed, he shook like a wet dog, he twisted and turned.

His itching, burning skin tormented him, sour acid rose in his stomach, and his heart seemed to be skipping beats.

So this was it; this was how it ended. How ironic. He'd been hounded by aliens using highly exotic weapons and technology, but he was going to die here, in the basement of a house in Tehran, tortured to death by people he could have killed with a flick of his wrist if the right moment had presented itself.

"Flynn?"

Oh, God, Abby's voice—even that. He'd heard it often at home in Menard, but it never was her, and it wasn't her now; it couldn't be.

"Are my brown eyes bright?" She laughed a little.

"Are my brown eyes bright? Is my nose on right?" had been something between them when they were kids.

She stepped into view and his heart, already hurting, began to hammer. His mind was simply blanked by the incredible, perfect physicality of the apparition. She could not be here, not really, but here she was.

She wore a crisp white jumpsuit. Her hair was as it had been in the days of their happiness, flowing around her face, framing that delicate shape. She laid a hand on his chest, and it felt as if his heart was being touched by light.

"Abby?"

"Listen up, because I can't stay long. I'm going to release you. The guard on this corridor is one of ours; he'll let you pass. When you leave the house, turn right. You'll see a blue Corolla. Get in—you're going to the airport. But hurry, Flynn, there's very little time."

With that, she reached down and unbuckled the strap that was stretched across his chest, then the one binding his right wrist. At once, he opened the other one, sat up, and unbuckled the ones that held his ankles. He got off the table. "They have eyes in here—they must."

"At the moment, a loop is running. They're not seeing this."

He went to her, he embraced her, and it felt so incredibly, deeply good, as if the sweetest water in the world were being poured on the deepest pain in his heart. But he knew—he *knew*—that this was not really Abby, that it was just another trick of some kind.

"Go," she said. "There's no time."

He remembered that look, soft and stern at the same time. "Flynn, you can do it"; "Flynn, I have faith in you."

He met her eyes, and that really, really hurt.

"Go, Flynn."

"I have to see you again. I have to be with you."

"Yes."

"What about our baby?"

She shook her head, lowered her eyes. Then she put a plastic bag on the table. In it was a Revolutionary Guard uniform. She helped him get it on. It was sweaty and still warm. He wondered if somebody had been killed for it. It was a question he didn't intend to ask.

"Come with me, Abby."

Silence. He whirled around, but the room was empty. He bent double, such was the sorrow, as powerful as a blow to the gut.

Gone.

If he hadn't been off the table and actually wearing the uniform she'd given him, he'd have thought she was a hallucination. He thought that nobody could disappear that quickly and quietly, not even him.

In three steps he was at the door and through it. The corridor outside was lit by a couple of bare bulbs. At its end, as she had said, sat a guard behind a small table. He was nodding over a Persian comic book.

Flynn passed him and all but flew up the stairs.

Voices. He froze.

They came from the back of the house. He smelled something hot and spicy, and cigar smoke. There was another guard on the front door, this one smiling and nodding like a fun-house clown. Flynn realized that he was high. As Flynn approached, the guard reached up and pulled back the dead bolt that locked the door.

The outside air was still thick with pollution, the moon now almost directly overhead. To the right along the quiet street, he saw the Corolla. A couple came toward him, the woman behind the man with her head down, a child tagging along on each of her hands.

He was appalled to recognize the nurse, and to see in her face an eerie, haunting echo of Abby. He drew the bill of the uniform cap down over his eyes and walked quickly past the couple.

As he approached the Corolla, he saw that there was someone in the driver's seat, a man who turned his face away.

"Don't look at me," he said. "Safer for both of us."

It was true, he couldn't deny it. "Agreed."

The question of whether or not to trust him was not an option. He didn't know Tehran at all. It would have taken him hours to find the airport.

He got in and the driver pulled away from the curb. As he drove, he handed Flynn his Grauerholtz passport and a boarding pass. He'd be flying to Amman aboard Royal Jordanian Airlines.

"You're sure I can get out on this?"

"The Guard plays its hand close to its chest, so customs is unlikely to know about you, at least not yet. We're stopping for another change of clothes, then we're moving out."

Ten minutes of hurtling traffic and confusing side streets later, they were in another neighborhood, a much poorer one. The streets were twisted and narrow and there were people everywhere.

"Here," the driver said. "Second floor, apartment on the right. Knock three times quick, once slow."

"Do you know anything about my wife? Where is she?"

"Your *wife*?"

"She freed me. She's in your group—she must be."

"You were freed by Nadja."

"Who is Nadja?"

"She was the nurse who attended you. She's one of ours. She's from New Jersey."

Flynn concealed his surprise.

"Get changed, and for God's sake, take a shower. They're not gonna let you on the plane smelling like that, let alone wearing that uniform."

The apartment door was answered by a young boy who looked up at Flynn with grave, scared eyes. There appeared to be nobody else in the house, so he went into the tiled bathroom, stripped off the uniform, and showered.

It hurt. A lot. His skin was rubbed raw, there were cuts, there was a nasty wound where the flaying knife had gone in, and the water made it all burn like hell. Still, though, it felt almost a little miraculous, and the mint-scented soap was soothing.

As he was drying himself, the boy said through the door, "Him say hurry now." Flynn wrapped the towel around himself and went to the bedroom, where a business suit was laid out on the bed. It was a good worsted, the cut British, the label inside the jacket Chinese.

Dressed, he went quickly through the apartment and back to the car.

"I almost had to give you up," the driver said. He pointed to a scanner embedded in the dash. "They're looking."

"The airport's gotta be closed."

"Soon. We need to hurry."

"I thought they were efficient."

"The moment they close Khomeini, every intelligence operation in Tehran will start trying to find out why. They'll be fending them off for weeks."

The car careened through the streets, the driver lying on his horn.

"How did you find me?"

"We looked."

"Who's we?"

Silence.

"Shouldn't I know?"

"Let's do a little trade. I'll tell you who's saving your ass and you tell me why in hell you offed that prof at the agricultural school."

In Flynn's weakened state, he couldn't be sure if he had revealed the shock that this question delivered.

Oh, they were clever. So very, very clever. This was just brilliant. He hadn't escaped at all. This was simply another interrogation technique. It had to be, because a Western intelligence agent would obviously know the answer to that question.

The Inquisition of the Middle Ages had used this technique—the false escape—to trick heretics into revealing themselves.

"I'm thinking I made a mistake," Flynn said carefully.

"But then why did you turn up here? What are you after in Iran?"

"Something is wrong."

"You nearly get yourself killed because of some vague suspicion? Why were you suspicious in the first place?"

"Who wants to know?"

"Mossad."

A lie, of course. He was still very much in the hands of the Revolutionary Guard. He played along. "What does Mossad know about Aeon?"

"Less than we'd like. We'd welcome a briefing."

"I'll try to make it happen."

"Really? How much do you know?"

"Less than I'd like."

They pulled into the jam-packed airport departure lane. "Good luck," he said.

Flynn stepped out into the surging crowd. Doubtless he was being tracked in a dozen different ways, but this transfer might also offer a chance to escape.

He now had clear questions—major questions—that led from Aeon to Iran and right back to the White House. The best answers were undoubtedly here but with Aeon giving the guard support, he was outgunned and he knew it. There was one, single objective now, which was to get out of Iran alive. He would take what he did know with him, and they would work from there. If there was time.

He leaned back into the car window. "What's my next move?"

"Everything normal. Pass through security, get on the plane, that's it."

Khomeini was large and, he hoped, complex enough to provide him with some sort of escape route. He couldn't bolt, because the instant he did it, they'd be on him. He had to play their game, pretending that he believed in the rescue. Just when he was stepping onto the plane, he knew, they would recapture him and drag him back. They would want him to taste freedom before they made their move. Their plan was to completely crush his morale, and with it his resistance.

Firmly, he choked off the hope that seeing Abby had given him. Damn them all, damn them to hell. Just for those few moments, he'd opened his heart again, and now all the grief of not knowing was back, waves of anguish exactly as powerful as they had been the day he'd acknowledged to himself the bizarre and horrific truth of her dissapearance.

Passport control moved him on with a perfunctory glance, and he was soon in the international departure zone. Quickly evaluating his fellow travelers, he located a man standing near a soft drink kiosk, looking away toward a distant mirror on a booth that sold scarfs.

He stepped out of the mirror's line of sight and the man turned slightly. So that was one. There would be more, and before he had reached the gate, he had spotted two of them.

They'd wait until he was seated on the plane, then move in.

Another man, this one dressed in women's clothing, was an obvious giveaway. Inept, that. Also carrying. He was wide open, believing that his flimsy disguise protected him. Flynn could get his pistol. Kill him.

But then what? He could escape in the pandemonium, but only for a short while. No planes would be taking off after a shooting.

Could he steal a jet? He was a good pilot, but he'd never flown an airliner, so it was too dangerous to try. In any case, Iran had an excellent air force. They'd blow him out of the sky.

There was an announcement in Farsi and Arabic, and people began lining up at the jetway. He joined the queue and began moving forward as the gate agent took tickets, the ringing of the scanner coming closer and closer.

If he got on that plane, he was trapped. Playtime was over.

Then he was at the front of the line. He handed the agent his boarding pass and got waved down the jetway.

The access door that led onto the tarmac below was open. He continued moving to ahead, watching the steward, who would greet each passenger, then turn, his eyes briefly following the passenger as he moved into the plane.

The couple in front of him entered. The steward greeted them. In that moment, Flynn stepped aside and through the door onto the small metal platform where cabin baggage and wheelchairs were stowed after landing, and which the captain would use after he'd made his ground inspection of his plane.

There were certain to be observers in the terminal watching the jetway, so he fulcrumed himself off the front of the platform and dropped to the tarmac, a distance of about twenty feet. He knew that he had at most a couple of minutes, probably less.

There was a baggage wagon nearby, empty and ready to be taken back to the storage area. But he couldn't drive it in a suit. Farther away, an old Jeep stood empty and unguarded. As he approached it, he saw an emblem on the door. It was some sort of security vehicle. He guessed that it was used for perimeter patrol.

As he approached it, a heavyset man appeared, armed, wearing a threadbare uniform. The man ambled toward the Jeep. Flynn crouched beside it, letting him get into the driver's seat. He slipped into the passenger's side and before the driver could react, he found himself looking into the barrel of his own gun.

"Understand English?"

The man looked perplexed.

"No? Then I have to kill you." He cocked the pistol.

"No! A little. What you want?"

"Do your job. I know your route, so if you try anything to attract attention, I'll kill you. Do you understand."

His eyes, fixed on the Webley in Flynn's hand, told Flynn that he understood very well.

As they started, the Jordanian jet began its takeoff run. For the split of a second, Flynn wished that he were on it and that all was well. Since it was rolling, however, his pursuers knew that he had slipped the noose.

The Jeep moved across the runways to the perimeter, and began going along the perimeter fence. It was electrified and about eleven feet high, with razor wire along the top. Beyond it, there was another fence, also electrified.

They'd been moving for maybe three minutes when police cars appeared on the tarmac, racing up and down with searchlights. A chopper swarmed overhead, then another. Huge lights glared down from above.

The car's radio came alive, the voice spitting with urgency.

"Tell him nothing's wrong." He drove the pistol into the man's ribs. "If they come this way, you die."

The man spoke into the radio, his voice calm.

Finally, Flynn saw what he was looking for: a slight wrinkle in the chain link. Animals—dogs, probably—had dug a hole under it. They obviously came and went here regularly, and then he saw why. There were rows of Dumpsters across the tarmac, stored in a dark area near the wall of the terminal. The dogs came to steal food, and in this impoverished country, people probably did, too.

"Now that you've lied to the Revolutionary Guard, you'll have to keep lying or you know what'll happen."

"I know."

Flynn opened the door and roll out. The Jeep moved off, and he slid on his stomach toward the little ditch, passing under the fence without touching it.

He followed a narrow path to another such hole, and went under that.

He was off the airport. Behind him, four helicopters were now policing the area. It was only a matter of time before they widened the search to include this barren stretch beyond the fence.

About a quarter mile ahead, there were a few lights—a poor neighborhood, probably, jammed up against the airport.

He was in light.

Dropping to the ground, he realized that it was an incoming plane, its landing lights glaring. It passed over him at an altitude of perhaps fifty feet, so close that he was choked by the thick, warm fumes of burning kerosene.

He got up and began loping toward the community, watching and listening as he ran.

If Aeon was on the ground in Iran, they could step in at any time. They could not let him escape. He might not know everything, but he knew enough to make a start at derailing whatever plan they were in the process of executing.

He'd escaped from them before, and more than once, and they would not have forgotten that. It also meant that they would act sooner rather than later, and he would be up against their disks, with all their speed and firepower, and technology so advanced that it could identify a man by his thought patterns from miles away.

As he moved closer, he heard tinny music, the occasional honk of a horn, then the voices of a crowd. Soon he could see that there was a night market running. When he entered the community, though, he discovered that it wasn't much of a market, just a few stalls, one with some withered beets, another selling rounds of bread, a third with boxes of cabbages.

The town itself was little more than a clutch of mud huts reinforced with cardboard and discarded lumber. People moved like ghosts, too tired and starved to give the bizarre appearance in their midst of a Westerner in a business suit more than a mildly curious glance. He was careful to keep the pistol concealed. It was an old, unbalanced weapon that had seen a good half century of use. Flynn hoped that he could fire it with useful accuracy, but he had his doubts. As to speed, forget it. Pull the trigger of this old mule too quickly, and you'd get a jam. There were at least some bullets;

he could tell by the weight. But it wasn't much firepower against what he was fairly sure would be the combined might of the Revolutionary Guard, Iranian intelligence, and the armed forces. Not to mention Aeon.

A fighter screamed past overhead at five hundred feet. For a moment, Flynn hoped that it was searching, but then it did a tight turn and came back on what he realized immediately was a strike run.

They had guessed that he was here. But then again, where else could he be in this flat, open area?

The people around him took no notice. They saw low-flying jets all the time.

A flash, then a loud, echoing *crack* and two missiles came streaking toward the village.

They were going to level the town.

Flynn threw himself into the deepest ditch he could find.

Dazzling light. Silence. Dust. Bodies, bits of furniture, fruits and vegetables speeding past. An almighty roar.

He raised his head to see a burning hell where the pitiful little village had been. The stink of cordite choked the air. Body parts lay everywhere. A woman, naked, her skin smoking, staggered down the middle of the street.

She may have been screaming, but Flynn couldn't tell—he had been deafened by the blast. Children appeared, digging themselves out of the rubble of one of the huts. One of them had lost the crown of his skull. His naked brain was covered with dirt. He was grinning wildly, one eye turned upward, the other down.

The jet lined up for another run, and Flynn could see a fat napalm canister tucked under its belly.

He did the only thing he could: He jumped out of the ditch, ran between two ruined buildings, and disappeared into the dark. Once again he threw himself down.

With a tornadic *whoosh,* a gigantic wall of fire rolled across the village. Flynn knew that he was plainly visible in its light. The intense heat of it made his clothing smoke, and the sweet-sick stench of burning napalm filled the air with choking fumes.

Keeping as low as he could, he ran out of the pool of flickering light, angling toward what he thought must be another village. Judging from the myriad dots of light, this one was more prosperous.

By his mere presence, Flynn had just gotten a lot of people killed, and he feared that exactly the same thing would happen if he made it to the other village.

He could not risk that. He would not. As he moved across the open desert, conserving his strength against whatever might be thrown at him next, a thunder of low-flying helicopters rose behind him. His infrared signature would make him an easy target, but he doubted that they would want to shoot him. Their purpose had been to flush him out of the village, not to kill him. They would want to do more questioning—a lot more.

If the day has been hot enough and it's still early enough in the evening for boulders to be warm, their heat signature can offer a man some concealment against infrared detection.

There weren't any boulders around here. In any case, the desert was already too cold. He ran on, feeling an increasing sense of hopelessness, knowing that if he was captured he would be ruthlessly drained by the Revolutionary Guard of every last bit of information he possessed, then handed over to their new allies to suffer whatever ungodly fate Aeon might have in store for him.

A chopper passed overhead and landed ahead of him. Another one, higher up, opened up its floodlight. Two others landed outside the pool of light in which he stood with his hands raised.

Figures came out of the churning dust and noise. They were armed with automatic weapons, hidden behind face masks, and dressed in hand-me-down Russian riot gear. Used gear or not, he could tell by the way these men moved that he was not going to be escaping from them, not on this night, and probably not ever.

Nothing was said. Nothing needed to be. A rifle barrel swung toward one of the helicopters. Flynn followed the direction, moving slowly, his hands still high. The men were extremely tense; he could see it in their rigid postures, in their fixed stares. They were scared of him and scared of losing him. Should he attempt to bolt into the dark, he would be caught, no question.

He got into the helicopter. Two of the guards entered with him, one on either side. They sat silently, each with a pistol in his ribs. He could feel their bodies against his. They were as hard as metal, these two kids.

The chopper's wing began to thutter, and then, with a great roar and dust pouring in both doors, it rose into the ink of the night.

Flynn sat in silence. He had retreated into himself. Next would come more torture, expertly managed and even more intricately ferocious. Like any man, in the end he would tell them everything.

The pilot turned on a radio. They flew on, to the tune of Persian pop music, four black-clad soldiers with their captive now in a hopeless situation and trying hard not to sink into despair.

CHAPTER ELEVEN

FLYNN LISTENED to the thunder of the engine, concentrating as best he could on what had to be next. His plan was to jump. If no opening presented itself, he would have to die with his secrets.

The chopper was floating in a dark sea of sky. There were no lights below and no way to determine altitude. But it had to be more than a couple hundred feet, which was easily enough to kill a man. He gauged his chances of taking over, seeing immediately that they were poor. He could take out one guard before the other fired, but not both. He looked over at the guard on his right, who smiled—and at once Flynn recognized him from the torture chamber. He'd hung back, watching like some sort of trainee.

Like a trainee, he kept his gun holstered.

Instantly, Flynn got the pistol and aimed it at the pilot's head. "Land or we're all dead."

The pilot flew on.

"I *will* shoot!"

No change.

"Does anybody in here understand English?"

"Fuck, we gotta blow it," the copilot said.

The pilot turned halfway back. "We're U.S. Special Forces. You're being extracted."

What the hell?

The guy was Iranian. So were the others. Had to be. Before they took off, they'd been speaking Farsi like natives.

"We're gonna declare an emergency and put you down. There'll be a vehicle to get you to the coast. There's a sub waiting."

Flynn considered. Could this actually be true?

The second guard spoke quickly in Farsi, his voice high with what was clearly fear. His partner responded, his voice harsh.

It sounded very much like a jailer speaking to a despised inmate.

The next thing Flynn knew, they were landing and the second guard was pulling his gun.

Whatever was going on here, it was not what it appeared.

The copilot turned around and shot the frightened guard in the face. His head exploded all over the cabin.

"Jesus!" Flynn yelled.

"Not on side," the copilot said.

The pilot shouted into the radio, then shot it.

The three who were claiming to be Special Forces operatives piled out of the chopper, pulling Flynn with them. They proceeded to shoot it up. Briefly, there was a stench of burning fuel, then one of them threw a match on it and the chopper burst into flames.

In the flickering light of the fire, Flynn could see a Corolla, its black surface now caked with dust. Could it be the same one that had been used in Tehran? Looked like it.

"Get the hell out of here," the pilot shouted. "And next time, will you please knock before you come bursting through our front door?"

"Sorry about that."

"Yeah, well. Now sit back and relax. You're about to see an Academy Award performance."

The pilot ran into the pool of burning gas, then came out rolling, his legs and back on fire. "Don't just stand there, move your asses, I'm burnin' up!"

Flynn and the others put him out. He lay there, his clothes smoking, laughing and grimacing in pain at the same time. "My story will be that I nearly got burned alive trying to save my helicopter. And you got away, and why? Because your friend the spy made sure of it."

"I don't understand."

"You will. We gotta go back to Tehran and keep playing like Rev Guards. Wish us luck."

Flynn saluted. He knew of no greater honor that one soldier could offer another. The pilot got to his feet. The three of them returned the salute, and Flynn headed for the Corolla.

He moved quickly, but not at a dead run; though it was dark, there could be eyes on him. The car was dark, too, seemingly abandoned. But as he approached, he could see a thickening of shadow on the driver's side.

He opened the passenger-side door. No interior light came on. When he slid in and sat down, the driver turned to him. It was Davood Ghorbani. "Let's roll, buddy," he said. "I'm coming out with you."

Flynn still had the pistol he'd taken from the guard. It felt very good to be armed again, especially in view of what he still feared was really happening here, which was that he was being played by the Revolutionary Guard in the same way an expert fisherman plays something big and powerful like a swordfish. Give it line, let it run, pull against it, tire it out.

Ghorbani started the engine and began driving fast down a dark, two-lane blacktop, lights out. "I hope I didn't fry your balls off, Flynn."

The comment was an invitation to engage, but Flynn didn't care to do that just yet. He was thinking this thing out, and it was complicated. The guard who'd been killed could have been a prisoner slated for execution. There were a few Iranian Americans who had returned after the revolution, so the other three could have actually been more Revolutionary Guards, and Davood Ghorbani could be a clever actor. All good interrogators had an element of the actor in their personalities.

He decided to let things continue to play out.

"I'm MI6," Ghorbani said.

"Special Forces, MI6? Who else is out here?"

"Tehran is spy heaven. The locals all hate the ayatollahs. People will practically pay for the right to help the West."

He decided to turn the conversation in a direction that might cause Ghorbani to reveal a little more of himself. "Do all those agencies know about Aeon?"

"We do."

"Obviously, given that you questioned me about it."

"I was asking prepared questions, remember that. Prepared by MISIRI."

"What do you think Aeon is, then? Personal thought."

"It's some sort of ultra-high-tech project. Biorobots, maybe. Stronger and faster than us. Maybe smarter, too. We want to know more."

He was a fine liar, very impressive.

"You told me during torture that Iran was allied with Aeon. How could it be allied with a biorobot project?"

"No, sir, that's what you told me, and I'm still wondering what you were getting at. I'd love to know."

Flynn caught his breath as he forced himself not to pull out the Webley and blow this brilliant bastard's head off. But Ghorbani had just slipped. Flynn had *not* brought up Aeon first, but Ghorbani was assuming that he wouldn't have clear recall. A mistake. Useful, too. Revealing.

Ghorbani was, in fact, so brilliant at his profession that it now came to mind that he might be like Louis Charlton Morris, a humanoid biorobot. Morris had been a criminal both here and on Aeon, but that was under the old regime. His side had won. If he had still been alive, he would probably be a member of their government.

Flynn had destroyed him, but he did not think that blowing another one to pieces would be the best move, not until he was certain about what he was dealing with.

He would play it out a bit more, see if he asked more of the wrong sort of questions. Human or not—that would decide the matter. He said, "What do you know about me?"

Ghorbani chuckled. "Enough to understand that you'll blow my brains out if I ask a question that makes you decide this is all another interrogators' trick."

The objective of this sort of interrogation is to go beyond the uncertainties of torture so that the responses are more likely to be truthful. You gain the subject's confidence. You become his friend—in this case, his rescuer. Then he opens up to you.

The firmament swept down to the horizon. Somewhere out there was

Aeon, hell in the glory. He kept an eye out, as always, for wandering stars.

They drove on for hours, crossing the ancient vastness of Persia, going higher and higher into the central massif that defined the country's geography. The villages were barely lit, the small cities were silent and looked very poor, and yet it was all touched by a mysterious beauty.

Finally, they were through the mountains and driving steadily across the coastal plain. Morning was coming soon, suggested by the rosy glow that hugged the eastern horizon. The morning star hanging in it was so vivid that it seemed as if it would be possible to touch it.

As a boy, he'd loved the sky. He'd spent time at the McDonald Observatory in Fort Davis with Abby and his old gang from Menard, looking up in wonder. When would it seem wonderful again? Ever?

Four A.M. came and went. Ramshackle trucks kept appearing on the road, and there were soon enough of them to slow progress. But there was no police presence, not a single official vehicle, checkpoint, anything like that. Also, not a further word had been said.

Ghorbani, as a consummate professional, knew that Flynn would be most off his guard if he started the conversation himself. "What's the plan?" Flynn finally asked.

"The plan is that we get to the sub, I get taken back to Qatar and reassigned. What happens to you, I don't know."

"No cops on this road."

"Once you leave the big cities, resistance to the regime fades. Thus no reason to police the area. This is ayatollah country, not like Tehran. They hate the regime with a passion up there."

"You're a good torturer."

"Learned my trade in Belfast, boyo. You're the toughest bloke I ever did, I'll tell you that. Damned eerie. Could've sold me on the idea you're a robot, tell the truth."

He thought about that, all that it might mean—all kinds of impossible, unbelievable things. He was human, had grown up human. There were no implants in his body. But he was no longer a normal man—that he could not deny. He turned in his seat, faced Ghorbani. "I sure as hell felt it."

Ghorbani was unbothered. "They have no rules in this country. No limits. And to think that they want the bomb."

"They gonna get it?"

"Not for me to say. I just follow orders and hope what I do matters."

Ghorbani abruptly turned onto a desert track. A moment later there was a burst of sound on the car radio, not quite static, but in that direction. "A signal from above. The good old U.S. of A. has eyes on us."

"What's our threat level?"

"Hard to say. None to total. Depends on how long it takes the Guard to figure this little escapade out."

"What was your position in the Guard?"

"Me? Sub-assistant flaymaster. Electrocutionist."

"You did that for them?"

"I did it for the West, my boy. For information. Knowledge. Guys in my line are respected in Iran. Trusted. Trusted with secrets. It'll probably take London a year to completely debrief me. I've been on station for four years. I know a lot."

Another major slip. A sophisticated Western intelligence operation would be debriefing an operative like him as often as it could.

"Aeon?" Flynn asked.

"They talk about it like it was a country. Russia. China. Aeon. What do you know?"

"That any country who makes an alliance with it is going to get damn well raped."

"Oh?"

"A deal with the devil. You can't win."

"Personal experience? The U.S. made an alliance with this entity? Is it another planet? What are you saying?"

He was so very good, it was too bad he worked for the other side. This man could think, and think well. He was playing his cards like a true master.

Flynn replied, "It's out for itself, Aeon. It's a taker, not a giver."

"Can you expand on that?"

"Just that it's very dangerous, whatever it is, and that we do not know."

"But a good ally, yes?"

A very revealing question. It meant that they were having trouble dealing with Aeon just like we'd had. They were looking for pointers; that was why he had been lured here. The alliance was established, though. He knew this because they had a Wire. It was where they had gotten their instructions about how to handle him.

The track petered out. A short time later, Ghorbani brought the car to a stop. "Far as she goes," he said. "There's coastal radars the other side of that ridge. They aren't gonna track on two guys, but they might see a car."

"Shore patrols?"

"Now and again. Down here, though, there's not a lot going on. They won't have detected the sub. FYI, we're about twelve klicks south of Bushehr. Qatar's a couple hundred klicks across the gulf."

They left the car and climbed the rise to see spreading before them, like a great shadow in the land, the Persian Gulf. It was still enveloped in the night. Here and there on its vast waters a fisherman's lamp shone, reflecting a fragment of gold on the glassy surface.

Flynn stopped.

"Hello?"

"We're under observation. Glint of light on a binocular a klick up the ridge." The gun appeared in his hand and Ghorbani blinked, then stared at it.

"How did you do that?"

"The binocular is still on us, moving slowly. Somebody on foot."

"I can't see a thing."

"You're lying," Flynn thought. "They're your people. They're here to pull me back." He said aloud, "It's two guys. One of them has a rifle ported."

"How can you think about a pistol shot at all? That thing won't be accurate past fifty feet, if that."

"Two hundred feet."

"Where in hell did you train, because I want on that program."

Flynn didn't even try to answer.

"Classified, eh? Not surprised."

"I'm human, that's for damn sure. You really beat me up and I really feel it. A lot." Flynn looked out across the water, which was gaining definition as dawn spread. The tide was out, leaving about a quarter-mile expanse of flats exposed.

"Do you clam?" Ghorbani asked.

"Clam?"

"Tide's out. We're going clamming. Throw the spotters a bit of a curve. If that's what they are."

They rolled up their pants, left their shoes on the shore, and went out onto the flats. "Got any idea how to do this?" Flynn asked.

"You don't know?"

"No clamming in West Texas."

Just then, another figure appeared on the flats, about a quarter mile to the north. It was a woman shrouded in black and carrying a basket. She began to clam.

It went on like that, with more women coming onto the flats.

The two shore patrols came along the ridge, still watching them with the binoculars.

"How long does the sub wait?" Flynn asked.

"Remember, the U.S. has eyes on us. The sub will wait until and if Langley is certain that we can't make it. So we hang out here until nightfall."

"Do we have that long? Shouldn't we swim for it?"

"*Swim?* It's a good two miles."

Flynn could handle that. "Do it slow. If you give out, I'll take you on my back."

"We'd never make it. Anyway, there are sharks. Lots of sharks."

Clearly, Ghorbani did not want him to enter that water. This meant only one thing: Escape in that direction—the real thing—was possible.

"I think we should swim."

"The shore patrol's gone. Let's find someplace to lie low."

"It's not gone. They're behind the ridge, popping up from time to time to have a looksee."

"Bollocks!"

"You're a native speaker—maybe you should approach them."

"And say we're down from the north clamming with the women? I doubt that'll work."

"They take bribes, I presume."

"Possibly, though down here they might be too loyal."

"Soon as they realize you're Revolutionary Guard and you've got an open wallet, they'll carry out your orders."

"You stay well hidden."

"You got that right."

"How could you ever come in here without even any Farsi?"

"Swiss arms dealers don't speak the local lingo."

The tide was coming in, so they headed back from the clamming flats to the beach. Flynn took the bag, sat down in the shadow of a dune, and began taking clams out, examining them, and returning them to the bag, pretending he knew what he was doing. Meanwhile, Ghorbani went across the dunes, then up along the ridge.

Flynn waited, listening to every sound he could detect over the hiss of the low surf. Each moment that passed, he was feeling less secure. There was something he wasn't seeing, he was certain of it. But what?

The crack of a shot echoed among the dunes, and Flynn instantly knew what the plan was. They would recapture him, and he'd end up in a cell with his so-called fellow Western agent Ghorbani. As they took their turns in the torture chamber, the real interrogation would be going on in the cell, as Flynn opened up to his fellow sufferer.

Even as these thoughts were passing through his mind, Flynn was running for the surf, keeping low, dodging from side to side. Shots followed him, smacking into the water like slaps. He strained for deeper water, but it took a while. The tidal flat continued out for a long distance.

A shot passed his head so close the slipstream of the bullet caused an involuntary jerk away. Finally he was wading. He threw himself into the water, swimming through the light surf as bullets whined past. Fire seared his left leg, causing him to cry out, his voice gargling as he swallowed water. As he choked up the salt water, still swimming, he tested the leg. Still working, meaning that it was a flesh wound.

Lethal in this water, though, as soon as the sharks got the scent. He swam on, seeing the lighter green below him give way to deep, infinite blue. He'd passed off the edge of the shelf. He dove. As far as the shooter was concerned, he had disappeared. If he was lucky, they'd see the blood and decide that they had accomplished their mission.

He swam fast, due south, getting out of the line of fire. When he had to surface, he turned on his back, bent his neck, and lifted only his face into the air. He inhaled a series of deep, oxygenating breaths, then let himself sink again, being sure not to create the least ripple on the surface.

When he was back under the water, he heard the deep thrumming of a big diesel, then another, and farther away a third.

Three patrol boats were on their way. From the sound of the engines, about two miles out.

He dove again and swam harder. He had no means of navigation and no idea of the coordinates he was looking for, as if he could even estimate coordinates.

The intensity of the sunlight could blind him if he wasn't careful. This close to the water's surface, the effect was the same as the glare of arctic snow. He swam on for half an hour, stroking now more easily and smoothly, conserving energy, always making sure that the coast was behind him.

So far, no sharks. The bleeding slowed and he was hopeful that the wound was only torn muscle that would soon swell closed in the salt water. Blood in the water didn't inevitably trigger a shark to attack: It depended on how hungry it was. But if there were several in the area, more than one or two, any attack would undoubtedly become a feeding frenzy, and he would be done.

As he swam, he continued listening to the engine notes, which faded, then grew more distinct, then faded again. They were operating a grid search a few kilometers north of his position, working their way in this direction. He was a small target in big water.

The shark appeared without warning, racing up at him in full attack mode. Instantly, he ceased all movement. The shark's mouth was closed, so it was still scouting him. Opening his eyes in the warm salt water stung, but when he did, he could see more of the sleek, speeding shapes below him.

It came in again, sweeping past him quickly. As it turned and came back, he delivered a quick jab with his closed fingers to its eye. The soft, cool tissue gave a bit. He pulled at it and the shark reacted by swimming away fast.

This interested others, which began rising. But he'd stopped bleeding, so he had a chance, although a slim one. He'd been lucky to get an eye, the shark's most sensitive point. If the others came in, one of them was going to take a piece out of him. Then the feeding frenzy.

He hung in the water in absolute stillness. The sound of the patrol's engines was loud now. The southernmost limit of their grid was probably no more than five hundred meters away. If they saw shark fins, they would locate him at once. So which would he prefer, getting flayed alive by torturers or eaten by sharks?

Duty answered the question clearly. Torture would lead to him revealing vital secrets. He would have to choose the sharks.

Above all this, though, was an overriding and overwhelmingly urgent need to get back, or at least get his message to Diana: Aeon had changed sides and was in the process of forming an alliance with Iran.

One of the patrol boats came roaring straight toward him. Still, he remained motionless. It bore down on him, its engines thundering like some kind of wild enormous heart. The wake shoved him like a remorseless great hand, tumbling him over and over. He bounced hard against the screw cage and counted himself fortunate that the hull had one. Otherwise, he would have been cut, probably dismembered, and the sharks would have eaten the scraps.

The force of the screw's thrust propelled him a long distance, taking him far from where he'd been leaving blood in the water. So at least he was free of the sharks for a few minutes.

The searching patrol boats moved south, and did not return. He remained absolutely still. No sharks appeared.

Warm though the water was, it was still well below body temperature, and he assumed the "Help" posture, crossing his arms over his chest to retain as much heat as he could. As the sun crossed the sky and began to drop in the west, he considered the idea of returning to shore for the night.

The surface water would cool down in the dark, and he could already feel the thick weight of the fatigue that came from exposure.

He was trying to estimate how far out he might be by now, and whether or not he could manage the swim back, when he felt himself being lifted by deep pressure. He thrust his face under and saw perhaps thirty meters below him a vast, gray shape moving at a slow, searching pace.

No question: It was a submarine. But how to attract its attention? He couldn't catch up with it and he couldn't swim down ninety feet to rap on the hull.

Then it was gone. He fought down the disappointment that came from knowing that he had lost his main chance.

As the sun set, he found himself alone in a vast circle of water. Maybe he was three miles out by now. He could not survive for long, but he also couldn't swim back into the hands of Ghorbani and his kind. His choices were to die here or to die in Tehran.

But he'd already made the decision. He stopped swimming, stopped treading water. He floated, his eyes lifted toward the evening sky, the gulls shining white in the last light, above them the first stars.

Here, now—this would be his grave.

CHAPTER TWELVE

UNSEEN CREATURES broached and sighed in the dark—whales, he assumed, maybe dolphins. The stars danced in the water. For hours, he'd been floating, raising his head to breathe, then floating again, staying in the "Help" posture, conserving all the energy he could.

It was well after midnight when a searchlight swept the water about three hundred yards out. Was it the sub? An Iranian patrol vessel? He waited, then saw the light point downward into the water.

It was a fishing boat. They were trying to attract a catch.

He swam toward it. As he drew near, he could hear voices and smell raw fish and cigarette smoke. Diesel fuel. It wasn't much of a vessel, an ancient dhow fitted with an outboard motor to move it when there wasn't any wind.

When he reached the side, he found himself looking up into a great, painted eye, an ancient symbol in these waters. Egyptian sailors would paint them on their ships to guide them through night and storm. The water around him was now a hazy green, the light a white column that played out in the dark below. The bright shaft of it was rapidly filling with speeding, darting squid.

Feeling his way along, he came to some netting and lifted himself just far enough to see four men. They sat around a gasoline lantern, its hissing a counterpoint to their low voices. What were they speaking, Farsi or Arabic? He was unsure.

Then he saw, lying against the mast, the dark but unmistakable form of an AK-47. Were they pirates, then? No, not in these waters. Pirates needed a wider and more anonymous expanse, like the Indian Ocean. The weapon revealed nothing. Anybody out here at night, no matter their purpose, would be carrying some kind of a gun, and you could buy an AK in any bazaar in the Middle East.

One of them, his face invisible in the deep shadows that surrounded the dhow, stood up and came peering over the side. He leaned far out, looking down at the squid.

Flynn moved around to the far side of the boat and waited. After another few minutes, they ran their net out and dropped it. As it sank into the mass of squid, one of them did what Flynn had been waiting for and began pulling the starter cord on the old engine to bring the net back up.

They were all on the opposite side now, and the clatter of the engine nicely masked whatever small sounds Flynn made as he lifted himself into the boat. At once he went to the mast and secured the AK. He thumbed the safety back. He could kill these men in an instant, take their boat, and sail it southwest until he reached Qatar. He could, but he wouldn't. His killer instinct did not extend to the innocent.

The ancient engine clattered and spit oil as they drew their net in. It was a fine catch, the net packed with frantic, squirming squid. The fishermen's voices rose with excitement as they guided the net across the deck and dumped the squid into the hold.

It was then, while they were opening the net, that the first of them saw him. He was standing by the mast waiting quietly, prepared for anything, especially for any hand movements on the part of the one carrying the pistol under his soiled old dishdasha.

One by one, they turned toward him. The squid continued sloshing down into the hold, where they kept up a frenetic splashing. Flynn took a step forward, reached down, and cut off the little engine. The net swung free, but the fishermen ducked rather than move to stop it. Slowly, then more quickly, it came back and then hung still.

He could see the confusion in their faces. He was wearing a tattered shirt and a pair of underwear; that was it. The gash along his left leg was puckered and white from the salt water. He assumed that his face was corpselike. From the fear that was replacing their confused surprise, he knew that they were finally understanding the situation, that a dead man had come up out of the ocean and was pointing their own gun at them.

"Anybody speak English?"

Slow looks, one to the other. "I," one of them said. "You fall from plane?"

"Boat."

"Ah." He gestured toward the gun. "You rob?"

"No. I pay. How much to take me to Qatar?"

The one who could speak English conferred with the others in what Flynn was now sure was Arabic. He turned back. "Where you money?"

"In Doha."

"You fall off boat? What boat?"

"Pirates stole my boat."

He spoke again in Arabic, relief clearly audible in his voice. "You thirsty? Hungry?"

"Yes."

Judging from the stars, they were sailing south-southwest, which probably was the correct direction. Flynn had no idea how the Qatari port officials would react to him, but if he could get them to call U.S. Central Command at Al Udeid Air Base, he was fairly sure that he would be all right.

When they heated lamb stew over a camp stove, Flynn's body reacted, and he didn't think he could remember ever before feeling so hungry or so thirsty. They had orange sodas and bottled water to wash the food down. He could have consumed everything, all the drink and all the food, but he was careful to take only modest portions.

He stationed himself in the prow of the boat and fought sleep as they plowed along in what was becoming a heavy swell. They muttered among themselves and watched the ring that had appeared around the moon. It was October, but maybe there was still the risk of a simoon. The boat began falling into the troughs of waves. The right sort of wind could quickly turn the narrow Persian Gulf into a surging maelstrom, which a boat like this would not weather well, if at all.

They knew it, too; they had trimmed their sail as close as they dared, and the little boat was racing. The sail of the dhow is designed to survive sudden, intense winds, but a lengthy storm would be too much.

"How long?" Flynn asked, looking at the moon, which was now flying in tattered cloud.

"One hour."

"Until the storm strikes, or until we reach Doha?" Flynn asked, but got a blank stare. The English was too complicated.

The storm came on them with the suddenness characteristic of the region, a roaring surge of white-hot wind stinking of the desert, bringing with it sand-thick spray. The boat leaped and then heeled, cords whipping, the sail as tight as a wineskin, and the crew began shouting the cry of despair universal to the Moslem world, "*Allah o'Akbar*," again and again, as much an incantation against the storm as a prayer of resignation.

The sky had turned to ink swirling with spray. Close to the boat, pale, roiling surf thundered. The rest was darkness absolute. If they were still on course, God had indeed enacted a miracle. Still, the Persian Gulf isn't like one of the great oceans. You can get lost in it for a while, but it's no trackless waste. Sail east or west, and you will come upon land in a few hours. You can't get out into the Indian Ocean without passing through the Strait of Hormuz, and a storm is certain to run you aground or drown you first.

The calling on God changed to cries of terror when, in a lightning flash, there appeared an onrushing wave so huge it looked like a great wing of water tipped with delicate pale feathers of foam.

The crew were cowering in the prow, so Flynn went to the stern and took the tiller. It would bite, then run free as the stern was lifted high out of the water, then bite again when she smacked back with a timber-shuddering crack. He got her prow into the wind, but she kept falling off, and he knew that it would not be long before she foundered.

He watched the crew in the prow. Their dark, resigned faces looked back at him, blank with despair. The boat shot into the trough of a wave and into a sudden silence. Gulls scudded, seeking fish in the wall of the oncoming roller. Then the boat began to rise, then faster, then so fast their ears popped, and suddenly they were in the roaring surge of the storm again. The boat crested the wave and went speeding down into the next trough like a surfboard.

Finally realizing that they weren't going to die immediately, the crew broke out hand pumps and began working against the water building up in the hold. Still, the prow fell off dangerously as they climbed every wave. To really raise this boat in the water, they would have to dump their catch. Without Arabic and needing to stay back on the tiller, Flynn had to just hope they figured it out.

When they crested another wave, he glimpsed, just for an instant, a shimmer of light that shouldn't have been there. It wasn't lightning—too steady. So there was something out there, dead ahead.

They went deep into a trough, the boat wallowing, the men pumping furiously, then rose again to the next crest. The lights were there again. A distant city? Doha, maybe? Or could it be something far stranger than that? His worst fear, the one that could wake him up screaming, was of being kidnapped and taken to Aeon.

The next time he saw the lights, he also saw a dark outline, and understood after a moment that they were the running lights of a huge ship. Not only that, but it was less than a mile off. He was face-to-face with a true giant of the seas, an aircraft carrier. It was so large that it could only be American. No other country floated anything like this.

Salvation, then—or death? If they stayed on this course, they would slide along its side and be spit out through its props in the form of kindling and bloody pulp.

Flynn shoved the tiller hard astarboard. The fishermen began shouting and waving. The boat was now racing toward the carrier, drawn by a deadly suction.

The tiller helped, but not nearly enough. Either they attracted the attention of the ship's company or they were dead. He had to leave the tiller and risk everything to find flares, if there were any. When he took his hand off it, the boat swung wildly and the crew lost their footing. Finally, they realized what he was doing, and the youngest of them, a boy of probably about twelve, threw himself at the supply chest. He pulled at it, dragging it open, and came up with a canvas bag. In it were three flares, wet but still possibly serviceable. He pulled one out and the four of them huddled around it, trying to get it lit with a cigarette lighter.

Finally, and much to Flynn's surprise, a white flame erupted from it. With it, they lit the other two, and soon they were dancing on the deck for all they were worth, screaming and waving flares.

The stern of the carrier came up and went past, and once again the full force of the storm hit them hard. The dhow twirled like a top, its sail swept away into the dark.

The carrier sailed on, her lights almost immediately swallowed. The dhow was now little more than a canoe with a hold full of squirming squid and a deck awash in terrified fishermen.

Flynn stayed with the tiller, fighting to keep some kind of trim by using the sodden sail like a sea anchor. He did this because of what he had heard, which was the carrier dialing back its engines. The reason they were still alive was that the captain had reduced the prop suction, sparing the dhow.

It was then that he heard a new sound rising above the roar of the storm, an ominous thunder of rushing water. A moment later he saw it, an immense line of foam pale and churning in the darkness, so high that it might as well have been a mountain racing across the crazy seascape.

The next thing he knew, he was in the water in a swarming school of squid. Then the squid were gone and he saw two heads, members of the crew, also in the water.

He struck out toward them, but by the time he'd completed ten strokes, they were gone. He was alone in the ocean, treading water now, keeping his head up, letting himself be carried by the waves.

This continued for long minutes. In all of his life, he had never felt this absolutely alone. He would be carried down into the trough of a wave, into the silence, then up again into the screaming storm, and so it went, again and again.

A streak of light appeared, flickered, and was gone. Was it a searchlight? Had the carrier released a tender? Flynn waved, shouted, then swam toward where he'd seen the light, but carefully, conserving his strength against the greater likelihood that he would end up still in the water.

The light appeared again, sweeping through the trough of the wave Flynn was riding, passing so close to him that he impulsively threw himself toward it—and went splashing and tumbling, sucked under by ferocious wave action.

He was dragged deeper and deeper yet, into the silence of the wave's undertow. He sensed rather than saw some enormous presence near him, a whale of some kind, and then saw, far above, a light flickering on the surface of the water like the shimmering wing of an angel.

His head burst to the surface and as he gulped salty air he was flooded in that wonderful light. It was a tender, pitching in the waves, being handled expertly. This was no Iranian patrol boat. This boat belonged to the carrier, had to.

He cried out from the depths of him, from the hidden core that is within us all, that seeks for survival from the deeps of blood and soul.

A bright orange life ring splashed into the water a couple of yards away. He grabbed it and at once found himself being drawn through the water toward the pitching tender. Four sailors pulled him aboard. He tried to stand—actually, to salute—but his body said no, and he sank down on the deck and the lights went out.

CHAPTER THIRTEEN

THEY TOOK him into the tender's tight, neat cabin and wrapped him in a blanket. Nobody spoke to him, not sailors working a boat in a fearsome sea.

Waves crashed against it again and again, causing it to shudder and its engines to scream, but Flynn felt safe from the storm. This was the U.S. Navy. They weren't going to sink.

As the boat heaved and tossed and plowed, his stomach gave a few slight turns, but no more than that. He'd been close to death this time, too close, especially given the information he had obtained.

In perhaps half an hour they were in sight of the carrier, and in another twenty minutes Flynn was aboard. He was taken to the sick bay and lay down on a bed so astonishingly comfortable that he had to fight not to sleep. A medical ensign came into the bay and peered at him.

"I'm an American," he said. It was a barely understandable croak.

"Yeah?"

"I need a secure line right now."

"Can you identify yourself?"

He did not reply.

"You need us to look you over before you do anything else."

"Secure line. Now."

"You're injured, sir. Suffering from exposure. You need treatment."

"I need to continue my mission, Ensign. Urgently. I need a secure line in your code room."

"Do you want to confer with the intelligence officer?"

"He's not gonna be need to know on my mission. I'm way behind and I'm in a hurry."

The ensign picked up a wall phone. "The vic's a citizen. He's saying he wants a secure line. On a mission." There was a pause. "Yessir." He turned to Flynn. "We can give you that line." He reached down and Flynn gripped his arm and let him lift him to his feet. He was too exhausted to move, but that didn't matter. He had to move; he had to overcome his fatigue. Above all, he had to make that call.

As they navigated the carrier's labyrinthine corridors, Flynn stumbled more than once on a doorjamb or a pipe, or slipped on narrow steps. The ship was big but so is the ocean, and the footing was precarious as the enormous vessel heaved and wallowed.

The communications center was at the base of the command island, a large space crammed with digital systems. Flynn looked for the telltale black-mirrored face of a quantum communicator. This was a supercarrier, and if the navy had this system, you would find it on subs and on ships like this.

The technology, developed from the Wire that had been given us by Aeon, was the only communications system believed secure enough to transmit messages that Aeon shouldn't see. They could decode literally anything in an instant and they monitored not only all electronic communications systems, but also the minds of everybody they had implanted.

"I need to see the signals intelligence chief, the intelligence commander, and the captain. Right now, and I need them here, and I want this room cleared of all other personnel."

The ensign picked up another of the internal phones. Flynn took it from him and hung it up. "No. Go personally. No more use of electronic equipment. Never mention me on a phone, an intercom, anything. Don't e-mail or text about me, don't write any digital notes. Just go get these men."

"Sir, they're busy, especially the captain. We're in a storm."

"I noticed that. Tell them I need them now. It's a national emergency. Immediate dire threat to the nation."

The ensign went pale and hurried off. Flynn sank down into the nearest chair. He leaned back and closed his eyes.

"Sir?"

He opened them. He'd fallen instantly asleep. Not like him, and a mistake he must not repeat.

"I'm Captain Petersen. But let's be informal. You can call me 'Captain' and I'll call you what?"

" 'The guy in the underpants.' Look, I can tell by your layout in the intelligence center that you have a certain system so highly classified that only two of you have ever laid eyes on it. Am I right?"

His silence affirmed Flynn's suspicion.

"I need to use it."

The captain shook his head. "No can do, not without orders."

Flynn had expected this. They had no idea who this man they'd pulled out of the ocean really was. "I'm an intelligence officer with urgent information to send to Washington, and there is no means of doing it secure enough except the QX."

"Do you know how to use it?"

"I do, and I have a personal identifier that it will recognize."

"I'll need to signal the admiral for the OK."

"Not in the clear, and everything except the QX is considered in the clear by our unit."

"Which is?"

"Classified."

"Clear the room, please, gentlemen, we're going to pull out the egg."

He waited until the room was emptied, then he twirled knobs on a safe embedded in a pillar. Captain Petersen opened the safe and drew out the QX, which was a gleaming black orb, looking something like a black crystal ball. When he applied power, the same endless darkness that made the Wire so eerie covered it, seeming to suck at your soul. There was something evil about these things, as if they were somehow a perversion of the order of reality.

The captain sat down at the keyboard. The letters he was typing floated onto the screen, then slowly faded. "IO pulled from sea requests permission QX use. No creds."

On the flagship, which was over a thousand miles away in the Indian Ocean, response would take some time. Their QX would signal an incoming message and their intelligence station would then need to be cleared, the message decoded and considered.

Flynn pulled up a chair. He didn't want to reveal to these men how weak he actually was, but standing here like this, he wasn't going to last much longer.

They waited. The intel officer—his name tag read ANDREWS—said, "Rough night out there."

"I'm lucky I made it. The four fishermen I was with didn't."

"It's a treacherous body of water."

Flynn laughed mirthlessly.

The signal came back: "If he can code-activate it, allow use. If not, brig him."

Smart admiral.

Flynn took a seat at the console. He completed his code sequence and it completed its facial recognition scan. The dark screen lit up, then opened into that black infinity that nobody liked to see. He typed, "Flynn here. Come back."

The system was very smart. It would deliver the message directly to the detail's office in the basement of CIA HQ. Diana would be there, he knew, waiting. She would have been there from the moment she had realized that he'd gone to Iran.

Words drifted up out of the darkness of the screen. "I thought you drowned."

He had to admit that it felt good to be back in touch. Damn, damn good. He typed, "Aboard the *Abraham Lincoln*. Sub rendezvous failed."

"I'm aware."

"I have information as follows: Aeon hasn't just abandoned us, it is in the process of forming an alliance with Iran. Possible also that Doxy was a MISIRI asset. Could mean deep penetration of White House staff. Confirm receipt of message."

For some time, the screen remained black. Then, "Get back here. I'll have a plane ready."

The closest Aeon had ever come to destroying him had been when he was in a plane.

"Get me to Dubai. I'll disappear into the crowd, go commercial."

"You have creds in your underpants?"

"You get them to me."

"How?"

He typed, "You figure it out," and terminated the connection.

When he turned back to the captain, there was the eerie sensation of reentering the world from some dark and distant place. The QX and the Wire both did that. They left you with a lingering uneasiness that could go way south on you if you let it. More than one of the Wire clerks in the old days had ended up blowing his brains out.

"You guys use this thing much?"

The captain shook his head. "Except for the orientation session, this is the only time it's been in use."

"Be careful with it. Gets under your skin." He was glad to see it pushed back into its safe and the door closed. "At this point, gentlemen, I need civilian clothes, food, and sleep. But the instant a package arrives for me, you're to wake me up."

The captain raised his eyebrows. "Excuse me. Do you understand that you're aboard a ship at sea?"

"As soon as it arrives, wake me up. How far are you from Dubai?"

"Two hundred nauticals."

"Get her within striking distance of your fastest tender. Soon as the weather clears and the creds are in my hands, I need transport to the Port of Dubai."

"A chopper?"

He shook his head. Aeon might look at a helicopter, but far less likely a tender apparently taking seamen on shore leave. "I want the tender to be populated with a shore party and for them to look like guys going on leave. I'll join them. I'll need to be in uniform for that portion of the trip."

"Somebody's watching you? Eye in the sky?"

Flynn nodded.

He showered in the captain's expansive stateroom, taking delight in the billowing steam, the feel of the fresh water on his salt-raw skin, even the scent of the soap that he lathered on again and again, paying special attention to his gash and to his matted hair. Afterward he found that the captain's orderly had laid out a razor for him. Soon his face had reappeared, its hardness framing the eyes that Diana told him made people look away. They stared back at him out of the cave of secrets that was their home.

The uniform had been laid out for him, the suit packed in a duffel. It was a conservative gray, the sort of thing a naval intelligence officer might wear on a confidential shore mission. You might as well have hung a sign on it that said, YEP, I'M A COP. But he wasn't going to be getting any choices. The Florsheims that came with it were weathered but serviceable. Were these the intel officer's civvy togs, stuff he wore to funerals, maybe?

In the tender, he'd be Chief Petty Officer Evans. There were upward of five thousand personnel aboard, so nobody would be surprised that they didn't recognize him. Wherever they were stationed, they'd assumed he was stationed somewhere else.

In the small dining room that was part of the captain's suite, he was served a meal of steak, corn on the cob, mashed potatoes, and ice cream cake, all of it chased by iced tea. He ate every scrap of it. He thought he could feel his starved body putting it to use, racing the protein to his wounds and his depleted blood, the carbs to sagging muscles.

Given that there was now nothing to do except wait, he wrapped himself in what he assumed was the captain's robe, lay back on his bed, and let the stately rolling of the enormous vessel lull him into an uneasy sleep.

Sometime later, he began to dream a familiar and terrible dream. In it, he saw a face, sleek, almost featureless, human but too slick, a face that was at once plastic and alive. For a moment, he didn't recognize it. But then he did, which was the point where the dream became a nightmare.

He was in a coffin, wanting to claw, wanting to scream, sucking the bad air, his body twisting in anguish and agony. From outside came the sound of dirt hitting the lid.

He'd once been buried alive by Louis Charlton Morris. To him, humankind was ripe fruit, there for the taking. He stole people, DNA, sperm, and eggs, whatever he could sell on the black market. He had stolen Abby.

As he struggled, he heard Morris laughing. It was the softest, most chilling laughter Flynn had ever heard, the sound of a machine pretending to be something it was not, and smart enough to hate that.

Then he was running. Morris had set dogs on him, lean and black and quick, with eyes that should have been in the faces of men, eyes of despair and the rage that is born of great suffering.

The dogs were fast and he was falling, going deep into silent water.

The dogs were flying like bullets, leaping in after him, their paws churning.

Morris laughing. The dogs closing in. The silent depths of the lake.

He woke up and found himself looking into the eyes of the cabin steward. "I have your package, sir."

Morris was dead. The hybrid dogs were dead. The trauma of that fight, though, would never die.

He said nothing; he couldn't talk—his mouth was too dry. He'd lived that dream, lived it and somehow survived. But that's what life was for him—a series of impossible escapes against horrible odds, odds that had to run out sometime, that had nearly run out that time, and again this time.

"Sir?"

"Sorry. Heavy sleeper." He took the package, but waited until the steward quietly left before opening it.

Another Swiss passport, this time for Hermann Rung. A ticket on Emirates, Dubai to D.C., first class. Fifteen thousand dollars in cash.

He looked out the porthole at a morning sea full of glaring chop, illuminated by the brutal sun that scoured this part of the world.

The Emirates flight was scheduled to take off in six hours. He called the bridge.

"The sleeper awakes," Petersen said "We have a guest stateroom, by the way."

"Sorry about that."

"No problem, I used it. Nicer than my setup, to tell you the truth. It's where admirals park."

"I need to get moving."

"Good."

He sounded cheerful, for which Flynn did not blame him. It must be worrisome having him aboard, a guy with significant pull and no identity. He put on the uniform and heaved the duffel onto his back.

Once again, an ensign led him through the bowels of the ship. This time he was more stable, but still far from fully recovered. At the embarkation port, he found a bouncing tender full of sailors. As he climbed in and took the last seat, the engines started and they were under way. Nobody so much as glanced at him. Been ordered to keep their mouths shut, no doubt.

The journey in took forty minutes in this fast little boat, and when they arrived at port customs he looked back at the gulf, but the carrier, outside the twelve-mile limit because this wasn't an official stop, was invisible below the horizon.

He went through customs with the sailors, having his passport stamped with a day stamp. From there it was an easy matter to get a cab to the airport. He arrived with two hours to spare, entered a men's room and changed, leaving the uniform, stripped of any identifying marks, in the duffel. He stuffed it all into a waste bin.

The businessman who tacked out into the wide lobby drew not a glance. He spent the next hour eating another meal, but in a different restaurant from the one he'd used on the way in. He passed effortlessly through first-class embarkation and set up in the lounge, looking at *Der Spiegel*, as befitted a German-speaking Swiss. Not that he'd need it, but he spent the time working on his German, sight-translating an article about U.S. national security surveillance capabilities. The tone of outrage fit the subject. A man's individuality is bordered by his privacy. When that's invaded, he becomes less.

The moment his flight was called, he boarded. One of the first-class hostesses met him, greeting him by name. She even spoke a little German. Fortunately, he spoke a little more. She showed him to his compact stateroom. As he closed the door, she reminded him that she would open it for takeoff. "I don't want to be disturbed," he said. "No food, no drink." He smiled. "I've a lot of work to do, and I'm desperate to sleep." He'd used halting, thickly accented English.

"Of course, sir."

He slid the door shut, sat back, and closed his eyes. It was absolutely magnificent to be alive, and incredibly satisfying to know that he had communicated that crucial information to Diana. Even if he didn't make it back, he had at least given her some sort of a chance to fix what was wrong. Whatever in hell it was.

One thing was clear: It threatened the president. But how? Not assassination—Aeon wouldn't care about that. Something else, but what?

The President of the United States was a powerful man, but only in certain ways. The system of checks and balances prevented him from carrying out much of an agenda, and Bill Greene was turning out to be no exception to that rule. He was too conservative for the Republican center, but too liberal for its right wing. So he had no real constituency in his own party. Powerless. And yet, they were targeting him. Somehow, they could use him, and that was very, very worrisome.

The plane taxied and took off, and Flynn's long hours of uneasy, isolated worry began. Aeon could easily make an entire plane disappear. They'd done things like that before, never with an A380, but he had no doubt that they had the capability. Still, he had covered his tracks, he thought, with the greatest possible care. He had no electronics on his person. He'd been in a storm at sea, for God's sake, in the dead of night and swimming for his life. Surely even they would have lost him then. He knew that he wasn't implanted. So maybe this was actually a safe moment in his life, one of the few.

He adjusted the seat to a deep recline. He slept, but uneasily, and when there was movement in his cabin, he came to full wakefulness immediately.

"Hello, Flynn."

No. Impossible.

Louis Charlton Morris was sitting across from him in the small conference seat, and it was no dream.

Flynn did the only thing he could. He responded, "Hello."

Morris raised his hands. "Unarmed." He smiled that liquid smile of his, the lips lifting mirthlessly away from the ugly little pearls of teeth. "You'd like to kill me, yes? Again."

Flynn said nothing.

"I've been sitting here for two hours. I could have done you, Flynn. Would've looked like a heart attack, yes? Clean job, nothing to it. But you are here and I am here and we really must talk."

Flynn thought of the pen in his pocket. One quick, smooth move and it would be jutting out from between Morris's eyes.

Morris touched his lapel. Flynn's hand slipped down to the buckle of his seat belt, ready to loosen it so he could leap at the creature's throat.

Morris raised his hands defensively, palms up. "Now, just relax." Carefully, he slipped two fingers into his suit pocket. "Your pen, my dear. I could see by the way you were looking at my forehead that you were missing it."

Flynn took it from him.

"We're relatives, you know," Morris said. "I am, as it were, fashioned from your rib." His teeth appeared again, a crushed, brief, and extremely sinister smile. "When you were a boy, you and Abby were out on the prairie. You were twelve. You were lying side by side. Do you remember?"

"The meteor night?"

He continued. "I wasn't born of a mother. I'm not really alive. You have a soul; you continue into higher realms. But I do possess one thing of yours, which is your marvelous DNA—or rather, a deeper element of the life force. There's no word in English for it yet, as you haven't discovered it. The closest would be the Chinese chi, but that's not the half of it. Still, let's just say that you and I share your exceptional chi." He spread his pink, fat hands. "But this is as far as I go." The smile became a leering jack-o'-lantern grin. "Nature's largesse doesn't extend to us toys."

"I don't understand."

"No, and it's not even important, is it? My fate? Less important than the fate of a dog. About as important as the fate of your Ferrari, I would think. Destined to be junked and forgotten, though not until after a good run."

He leaned forward. Flynn prepared to fight. "No, no, we need each other now."

"How did you do it?"

"Survive?" He shrugged. "Machines don't die, they break. 'Broken' can be fixed."

"By whom?"

Morris chuckled. "You never stop, do you? Calculating, questioning."

"Trying to understand."

"As you know, there was a revolution on Aeon."

"Which you won."

"Me? Hardly. Creatures like me are less than slaves there. As I said, I'm a toy. I was raised in a factory, schooled with implants, then sold to an elderly woman who used me sexually. I escaped, got myself out onto the wild frontier of Earth, and started my little business."

"Stealing people."

"Part of it, yes, as you know. Which I may not be able to continue."

"Why not?"

"That would be why I'm sitting here now."

"I don't believe we could ever have mutual interests."

"You want to preserve humanity. I trade in humanity. Mutual interests."

Flynn looked into the strange, dead eyes. "What are you getting at?"

"How much do you understand of the revolution? Its motives? Policy toward Earth?"

"The new regime is setting up an alliance with Iran."

"But do you know why?"

Flynn said nothing.

"So you don't. But I do. For me, mankind is a resource—a gold mine, as it were. Rich DNA pool, strong chi. You're the richest pool we have ever found. Oh, Flynn, we can do wonders with human material. Create genius animals, biological robots with the minds of gods and the skills of warriors or whores. Anything you can imagine, you can do with that magic clay. Right now, human beings are the most valuable commodity in this galaxy, and I want to continue to reap that harvest."

"But you can't?"

"The new regime considers mankind dangerous. Human slaves on Aeon are nearly impossible to control. Fortunately, I can still sell elements." He gazed into the middle distance, and Flynn could see that he regretted no longer being able to sell slaves. How he had enjoyed killing him. How he would enjoy doing it again, only this time he'd put the remains in the burn at Wright-Pat. This *thing* would never be reconstructed again, not if he could help it.

"What about Abby?"

"You know she was dispersed."

"I don't know."

"Sold in elements, Flynn."

He had only a vague idea of what that meant. He had encountered dogs with human eyes. He knew a tiger that was as smart as a man and was, in some way, human. Probably they were creatures fabricated by these evil beings.

"She's not conscious, not in any form?"

Morris shook his head. "Her intelligence is probably in use, but in some mechanical context. There would be no memory."

"So they consider us dangerous. Seems like that'd encourage them to stay away."

"From a planet like this? Earth is a jewel, Flynn. They plan to colonize it, very frankly. To do that, they have to get rid of humanity. Kill you off."

"Thus destroying the planet. That doesn't make a lot of sense."

"No, the animals and plants stay. You do not."

"Where do we go?"

"You die."

"When?"

"It's imminent. That's why they've been trying to neutralize you, Flynn. You're probably the only opposition worth worrying about."

"I take that as a compliment."

"You're a small worry, believe me. An irritant, nothing more."

"How can they kill us without killing anything else? Hard to see how that would work."

"For me, too. That's another reason we need to pool our resources. Unless we can understand this, we can't stop it."

Flynn was torn. Morris could be telling the truth. On the other hand, when it came to misdirection, Aeon was masterly.

"You're still wary of me."

"Of course."

"Then let me give you something of real value. We biological robots have a vulnerability you don't know about."

"I'm listening."

He leaned forward. "Feel my forehead."

It was cool.

"My running temperature is eighty-eight degrees Fahrenheit. Otherwise, there will be overheating at various biomechanical junctures." He smiled.

If this was true, they would be able to detect biorobots much more easily.

"You will find that I've given you two very valuable pieces of information. It won't stop you from at some point assaulting me, and I don't expect it to. But if you're as bright as you seem, you will join an alliance of convenience with me, at least for now."

Flynn did not respond.

"You will; I can see it in your eyes." As he stood up, he added, "There are two plainclothes officers in the bar, compliments of Diana. They're both heavily armed. If you don't want to ally with me, all you have to do is identify me to them."

Morris left, sliding the door closed behind him. But then he opened it again. "One thing: You're right not to trust Diana's house."

"I don't."

"When you meet with her, do it outdoors. An open space, but with cover from above."

He could think of a few such places, parks with forested paths. "Do you have any specifics in mind?"

"Better that we don't talk specifics."

When he left, Flynn sat back. His mind raced. Was Morris a trustworthy ally, or was he actually working with them? As always, battle with Aeon unfolded in a dark labyrinth.

He sat watching the afternoon, the ocean sparkling far below, a cruise ship tiny in the great waters.

The airframe shuddered as the airspeed dropped. Descent had started. They would be on the ground at Dulles in an hour and a half.

There remained way too many questions, given the urgency. He could still lose this, there was no question about that, and now it appeared that the stakes were more appalling than he had dreamed and the danger more immediate that he had feared.

The enormous plane landed so gently, it was as if it had settled onto a cloud. He and Morris filed out together, not speaking. They were expedited through customs with the other first-class passengers, and in a moment Morris had slipped away, disappearing like a wisp of smoke.

A moment later somebody was running out of the crowd of waiting families and chauffeurs, and then Diana leaped at him and was in his arms, and he was twenty years old again and, Abby or no Abby, he was just so damn glad.

CHAPTER FOURTEEN

"FLYNN, WHY do you put me through crap like this?"

"I did what I had to do."

He and Diana were walking together in Dumbarton Oaks Park, Flynn having taken Morris's advice and brought her here so they could talk outside of earshot of any listening devices. He wouldn't tell her about him, though, not yet, not until he had a clearer idea of what to say.

"That's all you've got for me?"

"It's what happened."

"You walk out of the house and just keep going. The next thing I hear, Mossad's signaling that an American has been captured by the Revolutionary Guard and it's damn well *you*. Can't you ever get it into your thick skull, there's a chain of command?" She stopped suddenly. He could hear her gobbling back sobs. "You make me so damn mad."

He felt her pain, and his own regret. But he couldn't express feelings like that; it just wasn't in him. He wanted to be tender, but it did not work. He said, "The information I obtained is crucial."

"I need to know what to do with it, Flynn."

"That's our next step."

"Tell me what happened out there. I want details."

"I was captured immediately. I was tortured. I was helped to escape by what might have been a Special Forces operation. Or I got away from the Revolutionary Guard while they were being too clever for their own good.

I'm not sure which. In any case, I escaped and by some miracle survived sharks and a storm at sea. Those are the details."

"You were tortured by an American agent who wished to hell he didn't have to hurt you and admired your iron resolve, as he should. You were allowed to escape thanks to an operation mounted by Mossad that appeared to be U.S. Special Forces, and our guy saw you to the coast. The Arabs on that fishing boat were Saudi agents sent out to find you after you missed the sub."

"They were killed. They drowned."

"They were taken aboard the carrier fifteen minutes after you arrived in the sick bay. You were an actor in a play, Flynn, from the moment I caught up with you." Still gobbling sobs, she gripped his hand as if it were the last ledge on the tallest building in the world. "That agent—the one called Davood Ghorbani—he risked his operation, his life, everything to get into that torture chamber with you. They would have tortured you to death, Flynn, if we hadn't had him there. You owe him your life."

"I'll have to thank him."

"When he comes out, you sure as hell will. If he does. He's at risk now."

"Because of me."

Her silence accused him, and that made him angry. "We can't lose sight of the bigger picture. If we can't find a direction to go in, this is all going to happen before we have a chance to stop it."

"What do you suggest?"

"We figure out two things. How they intend to get rid of us without destroying the planet, and why they need the president, not to mention the Iranians."

"You left him terribly exposed. Not to mention Cissy and Lorna."

"What could I do? Talk about it in your house? In the office?"

"What about bringing me here? Ever think of that?"

"There wasn't any time."

"You just wanted to go charging off on your own, as usual." She hunched, the speed of her walking increased, and she thrust out her chin.

He caught up with her and spun her around to face him. "There's no time for this, either!"

"You left Greene exposed while you wandered off in a spectacularly unprofessional manner. Who knows what might have been done to him by now? Although I fail to see how he could play a part in the end of the world. Not even a president has that kind of power."

"But he does. He must."

"Nuclear war?"

"The planet becomes a radioactive hell for thousands of years to come. So no."

"Why not? Sounds like a plan to me. For them."

"They want the lions and tigers and the butterflies. The amber waves of grain. Just not us." He gestured toward a flaming maple. "They want that." He pointed to some kids playing soccer. "Not those."

"And we know nothing, essentially, about what they're going to do?"

"I got us one leg up, not two."

"You're always so calm, Flynn. It never ceases to amaze me."

"Battlefield behavior. Put one foot in front of the other, keep your head down."

"The president has to be told, then. With all the problems that this is going to bring down the road."

"If there is a road."

She dropped down on a bench. "The question is, what the hell do we say? He's gonna be on quite a learning curve."

"Plus, Lorna's going to be all over it, and her response will be to look for angles. How she can play it to advantage."

"Sounds like a real patriot."

"She is. To the Lorna Nation, population one. Bill's just a means to an end."

"Then we need to keep her as far away from it as we can."

"But we have to let Cissy in."

"Why?"

"She can help us with her dad. His initial reaction is going to be total, complete, and absolute disbelief. We'll get tossed out on our asses if Cissy's not there to back us up."

"Right now, I'd like to get hammered," Diana said.

"Right now, we have to go to the White House."

"We need an appointment."

"You figure it out. That's what you do. And thanks for the ticket home."

"Please call it what it was, a rescue, so please don't do anything like that again."

As she was speaking, he'd seen a telltale gleam on a roof, just a flicker of light. But it was immediately clear to him what it was. As he threw his arm across her back and began pulling her down, the first bullet passed her head with a quick whisper. He rolled with her behind a bench.

"What the hell!"

"Shooter. Roof of the Danish Embassy. There's a team."

"How did they find us?"

He thought back to the plane, and to Morris. "They never lost us." Now it seemed that the meeting had been just another turning in the labyrinth of war with Aeon. Morris's mission, at least in part, had been to lure Flynn into an exposed place. He'd baited the trap with information, though, some of which Flynn thought could be true. Or maybe it was all true. In this war, you never knew.

Another shot passed so close to his head that he felt the heat of the bullet's wake.

Behind them was a dense urban wilderness. Ahead were the spreading greens, beyond them Dumbarton Gardens, though few flowers this time of year.

Death probably waited in those woods, but crossing the greens would be suicide. Staying where they were, inevitably they would be picked off.

"He's missing because he's using a silencer. Plays hell with aim."

He sensed rather than heard the faint crackle of footsteps in dry leaves. Very careful, very stealthy. "Somebody's back in the woods, coming this way." He slid his pistol into his hand.

"Thank God you have that."

It was the little Glock he kept in his Audi, which she'd used to pick him up.

From perhaps thirty yards behind them, there came the distinct but muffled sound of a bullet being chambered in an automatic pistol.

In other words, a mistake. Flynn turned and fired three shots in a tight pattern. The shadow that had been there flew back into the trees as the explosions echoed, crashing back and forth between the buildings that surrounded the park. In the distance, Flynn saw a couple of cops begin trotting this way, their hands on their weapons.

"We need to go," Diana said, taking his wrist and drawing him toward the woods.

"We're alive because they want us to break cover."

"You're gonna end up on a murder charge, Flynn!"

"It's a permitted weapon and we were attacked."

There was more movement back in the woods.

"They're cleaning up the mess right now," he said mildly. He stepped out into the broad lawn, in the long gold of the sunset. The cops broke into a run. As they came within earshot, Flynn said, "Back there." He pointed toward the woods.

"Sir, a weapon was discharged."

He pointed. "It was back there. There's people. Something's going on."

The movement in the woods faded quickly, but not so quickly that the cops didn't see the shadows and give chase.

Flynn forced Diana to walk casually with him, not hurrying, two lovers in deep conversation.

"I'm with you an hour and I'm getting shot at again."

"And not getting killed."

"How did you even know that we were being attacked? I didn't hear or see a thing."

He didn't bother to answer. The Iranian kill team had been well placed but poorly prepared.

"We need to move on this, Diana. Ignore these distractions."

"I think the way to go is to call the private number and tell them who you are and you need to see him immediately. And could we get out of the line of fire? Do you mind?"

"The operation failed and they're gone. Smoke in the wind."

"Until the next time."

"I guess."

She handed him her cell phone.

He raised his eyebrows in question.

"The president's on the line."

"That is very impressive." He took the phone. "Mr. President."

"Flynn? What the hell do you want?"

"I need a meeting."

"Everybody needs a meeting. Let me guess. That crook buddy of yours who corrupted my daughter is up shit creek again."

"Bill, I wouldn't call if it wasn't critical."

"Is he gettin' under her tail feathers again? Damn crook needs to stay away from the First Daughter."

"This has nothing to do with him."

"Or with you hiding out over here the other night? What in hell was that about, old buddy ole pal? You bangin' her now?"

"Bill, this is national security stuff, and it's urgent."

"There's a committee for that."

"Your ears only."

"I don't want to hear any spy bullshit, Flynn, it mixes me up."

It was easy to see why they'd gone after Greene. Whatever it was they were doing, he was not going to be hard to handle.

How had Bill gotten into office? Lots of money, fabulous smile.

"Bill, this is about you. You know Bob Doxy's boy, who—"

"—committed suicide?"

"It's about why he was murdered."

Silence. Beat. More silence. Flynn could hear the brain creaking. "How in hell do you know that?"

"Here's another surprise. He carried a paper file into the White House before he was offed. That file contained classified information about the most sensitive organization in the government. He was killed for it and for what he knew."

"And how in the world does a cop from grungy little Menard, Texas, know this?"

"It's my unit, Bill. I'm not working in Menard anymore."

"Get the hell over here." He hung up.

"He's on the hook," Flynn said.

"Now what do we do?"

"Bury him in bad news."

"He's not going to like that."

"Presidents spend their lives buried in bad news. It's what the job is about."

They reached the sidewalk, and Diana hailed a cab.

At the White House, they were directed by the guard at the gate to scram. "Closed until tomorrow nine A.M.," the officer said, his voice bored.

"We're here to see the president."

"Oh? And you have an appointment?" Mirth in the voice now.

"We do," Diana said.

His eyebrows went up and a crooked smile broke out on his face. He was a study in amused skepticism. "May I send your names in?" he asked with exaggerated politeness.

"Flynn Carroll and Diana Glass."

He picked up his phone. Flynn noticed that two other officers were coming down the drive. They weren't hurrying. Their holsters were snapped shut. Kooks arrived claiming appointments with the president on a regular basis.

The officer hung up the phone. The smile was gone. He input a code into the gate's security system. As the cab rolled forward, two plainclothes Secret Service agents appeared in the portico. They stood, legs spread.

Flynn wondered if these two would recognize him. He wondered, but he didn't care.

"Sir," one of them said, "we'll need the pistol."

"Of course." He took the Glock out of his side pocket and handed it over.

He could see by the agent's face that he had noticed that it had been fired recently. As his partner opened the door, four more agents met them in the front hall. This was an unplanned and unexpected meeting, meaning they were operating at a high security level.

They were led to the family elevator, and two of the hulking agents crammed themselves in with them.

Bill Greene was in the West Sitting Hall, lounging on a couch in front of the big arched window that had long ago held Tiffany glass. A sheer curtain was drawn across it, so no paparazzo could get a snap of the President of the United States in Jockey shorts and big, fluffy slippers smoking a cigar.

He gestured toward a silver humidor on the gleaming coffee table in front of him. "Cigar? They're H. Upmanns."

Flynn started to take one, but Diana pulled his hand back. "Nope."

Bill's eyes twinkled. He was married to a female powerhouse; he knew the signs.

The West Sitting Hall is a large space, and the Greenes hadn't managed to lay it out for intimate conversation. The result was that the president sat on a crushed velvet couch at one end of the room, and Diana and Flynn on its twin thirty feet away. Lorna's interests did not extend to interior decoration.

At that moment, as if cued by Flynn's passing thoughts, she came striding in, her heels clicking with the clipped precision of a hyperactive metronome. She hadn't yet said a word, but her snapping gait might as well have been a curse.

She stood in front of them, all five feet of her. She was wearing silk that flowed around her nakedness like a cloud. Flynn wondered if her girlfriend was waiting back in their lair, longing for her return.

"You better not bring that criminal friend of yours into the White House is all I can say, Flynn."

"Excuse me?"

She sat down beside him, enveloping him in, of all things, crème de menthe breath. "That creep MacAdoo Terrell who knocked Cissy up when she was seventeen."

"I did not know that."

" 'Course you did. You two are thick as thieves. You'd be a crook, too, if you had any guts."

"I knew they had a relationship. I didn't know about any pregnancy."

"A-damn-bortion. Could've cost us the White House." She looked past him to Diana, obviously wondering who she was. She put a hand on Flynn's knee. "Why are you here, Errol, dear?"

"I let them in," Bill called from his distant couch.

Flynn turned to Lorna. "I thought you guys were dead set against abortion."

"That crap's for the zombies, Flynn, wake up. God's been dead for years."

Flynn kept his thoughts about that to himself. He believed that there was good out there somewhere; he had to.

Lorna went over to the other couch and sat down beside Bill. The socializing, hard-edged as it was, was over. From her position of power and safety beside the President of the United States, she looked across at Flynn and Diana. "So, why are you here? You don't barge into the White House at this hour for fun."

The president walked over to the fireplace. Standing in front of it with his elbow on the mantelpiece, he seemed so completely presidential that even God might have become convinced that he could do the job.

"We're a specialized unit that works in the area of terror suppression," Diana said, "and we believe that you are under threat. The murder worries us. It's why we're here."

"The kid killed himself. As I believe I've already said. So that fish don't swim."

Flynn said, "He was beheaded by an Iranian agent because he'd discovered a secret that doesn't want to be revealed. I know what that secret is and you don't, but you need to."

"Go on."

"Have you ever heard of Aeon?"

"No."

"There are aliens here."

"There are. And I've criminalized illegal immigration."

"Not that kind."

There was a brief silence. Lorna choked out a scornful laugh.

"From another world, then?"

Neither Flynn nor Diana responded. He needed to come to this on his own.

"What are you two tripping on?" Lorna asked.

"This planet—or place; we're not sure exactly what it is—is in possession of powerful technology. They can control minds, among other things. And they do not like us."

"The United States?"

"Mankind. They want us gone."

Greene sunk into himself. Then his eyes bulged with belligerent anger. "A god-for-damned alien invasion, and it happens on my watch. Shit!"

Lorna's smile faded. A confused frown replaced it. "How long has this been going on?"

"More than one alien species has come here," Diana said. "But right now Aeon is the only situation we have to deal with."

"These are the things with big eyes? From the movies?"

"That was another species. Very mysterious. As far as we know, they left when Aeon came."

"Except that their faces are on every kid's lunchbox in the country."

"Communicating with them was a challenge we couldn't meet. In any case, what Aeon mostly fields are biological robots, complex mixtures of living tissue, electronics, and machinery." She glanced toward Flynn. "He's an expert at destroying them."

"We should catch one and learn how it works," Lorna said.

"That hasn't been possible," Flynn responded, remembering the disastrous early attempts at it.

"So where do we come in?" the president asked. "What do you want me to do?"

"They're in the process of concluding an alliance with Iran, and we assess the situation as being extremely dangerous. Once this alliance is in place, Iran will be the most powerful nation on the planet."

Flynn then saw something that made every muscle in his body grow tense, as if some sort of physical assault were about to take place. Greene had pulled a large black briefcase made of soft leather out from behind the couch. The football should have been in the care of a military officer. And in the White House, where there was communications equipment both in the Situation Room and in the President's Emergency Operations Center beneath the East Wing, it shouldn't have been in use at all.

"Know what this is?" Greene asked.

"Yes."

He opened the football and laid it on his lap. "I punch in a code and a flight of Minuteman missiles turns somebody into a nuclear cinder. Russia. China. Iran. You name it, they've all got codes."

"There's no code for Aeon."

"Then I need one."

"Aeon is in outer space," Lorna said.

"So? We have astronauts, don't we?" He opened the football.

"Bill—" Flynn heard the worry in Lorna's voice.

"Take a look at this thing, Flynn."

"Bill, close it. Everything in there is classified."

"Flynn's a big genius, he wants to see it."

"Put it away!" Lorna was now shaking, but not with fear. She was furious. She'd have liked to tear his heart out; you could see it. She'd hated him for years. Despised him, this faithless husband who swung all sorts of ways, but never with her. At the same time, though, here she was in the White House, honored as First Lady. Flynn didn't envy her that conflict, eating her heart as certainly as cancer eats the gut or the brain.

Greene snapped the football closed. "You're talking to the most powerful man in the world about hostile alien entities, Flynn." He put it back down beside the couch and advanced on Flynn. "Next time, you bring crap like this to a shrink, not to the White House. 'Aeon.'" He shook his head. "Sweet Jesus."

"Don't be a damn fool," Lorna blurted.

"I'm going to need proof. Serious proof. An alien invasion!" He shook his head again in disgust and disbelief. "And how much money do you people spend? Who's paying you?"

"Sir, our budget is not large," Diana said.

"It better not be." He lifted his thumb toward the door. "*Vamanos!* I'm sleepy."

Flynn and Diana left, not speaking, not in this captured place.

If the White House didn't already belong to Aeon, they sure as hell would have no trouble gaining control over it.

The last thing Flynn wanted to do was assassinate the poor dumb guy.

But if the fate of nation and species was in the balance, he would not hesitate. At least the vice president, Harlon Durward, the former senator from Kentucky, was no fool. Mean as a snake and somewhere to the right of Hitler, but no fool.

CHAPTER FIFTEEN

THE SENSE of urgency that had settled in when Flynn saw Bill Greene with the football, then heard his nonsensical reaction to the news of Aeon, now rendered him silent as he and Diana returned to the Georgetown house. Diana also said nothing, certainly not in a taxicab. They'd been careful to cross the street and hail it well away from the White House.

But when he saw her house, its elegant façade glowing in the streetlights, a surge of exhaustion swept through him. It was a black wave, the storm returning in all its crushing rage, sucking him downward.

"Flynn?"

"Sorry!" Incredibly, even as they were getting out of the cab, he had fallen asleep. He'd slept a little on the carrier, and he'd even less on the plane, not after he'd woken up and found Morris in his face. All of it was imperiled sleep, where the body lies still but the mind remains on watch.

But the house wasn't safe, either, obviously.

"Shit . . ."

"Come on, you're passing out."

The interior smelled like his lovely old home in Menard, the family homeplace for four generations—of beeswax coming off the furniture, of the indefinable perfume of a place where a woman lives, of the flowers that stood on the mahogany side table in the sitting room. As had his mother, Diana lived elegantly. Her taste was discreet. Nothing too flashy;

no statements. He loved the way she kept this house: the beauty of the rooms, the sense of permanence and peace.

"I need to shake this."

"In the past four days you've been tortured, gone through a storm at sea without so much as an inner tube, flown ten thousand miles, been shot at, and discovered not only that the end of the world is at hand, but that the President of the United States is even more of an idiot than you thought. So you're tired. Bone-tired. And you're not going to shake it."

"I have to! We just got stiffed by the president. He wants proof. We've got to get it to him."

She took his elbow and directed him toward the stairs.

"We can't stay here, it's too dangerous."

"Flynn, it's dangerous everywhere, and here at least we have one of the most sophisticated security systems on the planet."

"A toy."

"You have to sleep. You have no choice. You can't afford not to. You're losing your edge."

"We have to get over to the office, we have to pull the whole team in, and we have to do a massive search of every single bit of UFO lore and alien lore that has been recorded anywhere in the past year."

"And?"

"We're looking to prepare for some pattern, some clue, that might tell us what the hell they're doing."

"Flynn, you're asking us to sift through a gigantic dumpster for a single gold button that might not even look like a gold button. Mission impossible."

"Then I have to kill Greene. I have to go back there tonight and kill him."

"Kill the president in the White House? That's an ambitious plan, I'll say that for it. But what does it get us? Next stop, the vice president. Then after that, who? The president pro-tem of the Senate? Then on down the line how far, Flynn?"

"The veep's not a fool."

"Flynn, tell you what. I'll get the work going if you get some sleep. I'll also provide the president the proof he needs."

"How will you do that?"

"That's my business, but I have the resources we need."

"What? Not a body. You know those damn things come back to life." He thought of Morris. "They're machines, so they can be fixed."

"I don't have anything physical like that, and I don't need it."

"Greene." He shook his head. "Di, the man has to go."

"I don't like the way you're thinking. Some good stuff, but mixed in with some really bad, dumb stuff. Toxic combination."

He remembered something Morris had said. "Another thing. Get in a supply of infrared thermometers."

"What for?"

"The humanoid bios might have a lower-than-normal temperature."

"You're kidding. How did you find that out?"

"Morris. I remembered how cold he was." He did not tell her about meeting him on the plane. Probably should have, but he was compulsive about not sharing information unless absolutely necessary. You give what you have to give, no more.

"I'll do it. Now you get to bed."

"I'm going back to the White House."

"The hell you are!"

"We could be talking about the end of the human race, and all because the asshole in the Oval is a pitiful, vulnerable little jerk."

"You will not assassinate him! It's not like you to be so damn dumb. Stubborn, yes, but not dumb."

"Assassination is far from dumb. It's smart. It's essential."

"Sleep is what's essential here."

He knew she was right, and the moment he admitted that to himself, reality took over. Offing Greene would only create chaos at the top, and God knew what Aeon would be able to do with that.

It was all he could do to get himself up the stairs to the luxurious master suite. The huge marble bath, which he hadn't really wanted, now looked like a corner of heaven.

Once the taps were gushing, Diana bustled around, laying out a thick terry cloth robe, mixing a combination of Dead Sea Salt and lavender oil into the steaming water, clucking with wifely concern when she saw the huge bruises, cuts, and burns that covered his body.

"That bastard Davood was damned enthusiastic," she said as he slid into the steaming, scented bath, "for one of ours."

"If he is. I have my doubts."

"He got you out."

"Unless I escaped."

The water was wonderful. Lovely. His eyes slid closed, his habitual wariness fading. For just a few minutes, he tried to put aside his watchfulness.

"I thought I was gonna buy it, Di."

"You're a soldier, Flynn, not a spy."

"Too dumb, I guess."

"You're the smartest human being I've ever known. Smartest hunk, anyway." She sat down on the side of the tub and laid a gentle hand on his forehead. "God, you're beautiful. My great, shining warrior." She stroked his forehead, then her fingers drifted down his cheek. "I'm glad Davood stayed away from your face." She leaned over and kissed him. "How does that feel?"

"Um, good. But—actually . . ." How could he tell her a man recovering from electroshock torture does not want to become sexually excited.

She laughed a little. "Maybe you deserve a little pain with your pleasure."

"You're still mad at me."

"No, that wouldn't be accurate. I'm absolutely furious at you."

He took her hand and kissed its smoothness. "Forgive?"

"Damnit, of course I do."

The next thing he knew she was naked and in the oversize tub with him. It turned out that not even the intimate injuries that had been inflicted on him were enough to stop him.

They churned up a storm in the foaming, scented water, but this one was dancing with joyous waves, far from any savage ocean torrent. In fact, given his size and his power, it was fortunate that the bathroom floor was well sealed, or a lot of water would have ended up downstairs.

Finally they lay in the remains of the bath together, floating in grateful silence.

"There's no more time," he said as he pulled himself to his feet on the gleaming brass handrail that ran along the wall beside the tub. "We gotta get to work on this right now."

"Flynn, you're done in. You can't work."

He stepped out of the tub and grabbed the robe. "I have to work. I have to get some kind of traction on this thing; there's too much at stake." He went into the bedroom to get his clothes on. He'd been here an hour. Way too long. There weren't going to be any second chances.

He sat down on the bed. He and Abby had shared a queen, but that wasn't Diana's style. The senator's daughter lived large, and this bed was vast. He lay back. It was also damn comfortable. Too comfortable.

He didn't know exactly when he drifted into sleep, or when Abby replaced her in his dreams. Abby in the sea long ago, swimming in the blue waters at Port Aransas, then going back to their condo and making love, then driving down Padre to the Padre Isles Country Club for a dinner of redfish and chardonnay, then having sex again, this time on the broad deck of the condo in the moonlight.

When it came time to wake him up, she had to throw ice water on his face. He felt it like a memory of the storm and it brought him up in bed shouting.

"What time is it? How long have I been out?"

"It's midnight."

"Damnit!"

"The team's working right now. Anything that looks promising, we'll see it right here. You have no need to go to Langley. Probably dangerous to be on the streets, anyway."

"I have to go to the White House."

"Hell no!"

"Not to kill him. To stand guard." He got out of bed—and then sat back down. "Damn."

"It's called exhaustion. Something that happens to other people fairly often. To you, not so often." She drew him back down to a prone position.

"There's no time!"

But there was time. There had to be. He could not rouse himself; it simply was not possible. In fact, all he could do was let his eyes drop closed. He wanted to stay awake, he wanted to get the hell out of here and get moving, but his body would not respond.

In his uneasy sleep, he called Diana Abby, breathing the word like a sigh from his soul, and she took him in her arms and silently wept. She so wanted Abby to leave him—the memory, the ghost, all of her. Listening to his slow breathing, her arm across his broad chest, she gradually fell asleep, too.

Flynn was right about the urgency, even more so than he realized. Had they understood the fearsome truth of what was about to happen, they would not have slept for an instant. She certainly would not have. She would have guarded him with a gun, and shot any shadow, no matter how fleeting, that passed into the room.

She slept on, and the night deepened and the danger grew.

CHAPTER SIXTEEN

IN THE places in Washington where night guards patrol, they made their rounds. They walked the halls of the great monuments, the echoing Capitol, the Pentagon and the State Department, the White House, and all the offices that formed the sinew and muscle of government.

In the White House, Lorna Greene read poetry to Ginny Bowers. Bill Greene, loaded with lorazepam, slept like a dead man, not dreaming, hardly breathing. Cissy, by contrast, lay with a pistol beside her. Her eyes were wide open, as they had been, for the most part, since Al Doxy's murder. She was watching for movement, and would shoot if she saw it. Where was Flynn? Why hadn't he stayed? Had Daddy thrown him out or had he left in disgust? What was going to happen next, what terrible thing, in this haunted, awful house?

Flynn was drawn to full consciousness only slowly, by the pressure of the hand that had been lying on his forehead for some little while. He knew by its weight that it wasn't Diana's hand, and then he became aware of its distinct coldness.

"You wake up very carefully," Morris said. "I admire that, brother."

For the split of an instant, Flynn thought he must be dreaming. But no, that familiar face was actually there, floating in the darkness beside the bed. It was Morris, no question. He had gotten into this house and come right up to this bed without being detected. He was way too good at this sort of thing, clearly.

"I'm not your brother."

"You are. Remember the meteor night."

"I come from a long line of Texans going back to pioneer days, and before that to old England. I repeat, I am not like you and I am not your brother."

The hand went away. "If we stay here, Diana's sedative is going to wear off. That would be inconvenient, brother."

"Get out."

"I'd love to, you shit."

Flynn rolled out of bed. Diana lay as if dead. He was familiar with the way this particular kind of sedation worked. It was accomplished with sound, not drugs. When she woke up, it would seem to her that the time she'd spent in this condition simply didn't exist. Do this to somebody while they're awake, and it can be very disturbing. Do it while they're sleeping and they never suspect a thing.

They went down to the library of the old house. As they descended the elegant central staircase, Flynn noted that the alarms were still armed. The house had deep protection: approach sensitivity, heat and motion detection, facial and voice recognition, and, of course, acoustic monitors to pick up sounds of breakage. Magnetic switches that were installed on every door and window. Even the attic was alarmed.

They entered the library, filled with Diana's history collection and his art books. His friend Mac was becoming a serious collector, and Flynn was beginning to consider it.

"How did you get in here?"

He wiggled the fingers of his left hand. "Fingerprint reader. You need to face the fact that I'm formed out of you. Flynn's rib."

There was a reader on the service door in the alley, used by Flynn and Diana and the office messenger. It allowed entrance only into the pantry. "We don't share the same fingerprints."

Morris smiled. "Sometimes we do, sometimes we don't."

Flynn was powerfully reminded of how advanced Aeon was. Still, beyond the pantry, facial recognition would be necessary, and Morris did not look like him. "I repeat, how did you get in here?"

"We have at most three days, Flynn." He went over to the small liquor cabinet that was set into one of the bookshelves, and poured himself a generous bourbon. He sipped it neat. "It's not a lot of time."

"Why three days?"

"They'll implant the president tonight, if they haven't already. They'll do it from a distance. But the signal will need to be amplified if you're going to override the target's core instincts, the strongest of which is survival. So there will be an amplifier installed in the White House, and somebody will need to put it there."

"He had the football out while I was there. He was obsessing on it."

"I did not know that he was a sportsman."

"Do you know what the football is?"

"Leather-clad sports ball. Pigskin, to be perfectly accurate."

"This is a different sort of football. It's used to order the release of the country's nuclear missiles."

"That wouldn't be it, then. Nuclear Armageddon would ruin the planet. They want the planet intact."

"So what are we looking for?"

"You tell me. That's why I'm here."

"I don't believe you. You've already tried to have me assassinated. And Di."

"No."

Flynn sighed. It was remotely possible that the Dumbarton ambush had been set up by the Iranians. "Maybe not, but I don't trust you."

"I don't trust you."

Flynn imagined what it would be like to slam into him, seize his head, and snap his neck.

"I'd like to kill you, too," Morris said. He sipped his drink. "What a pleasure that would be." Morris's eyes lit for a moment with a surprising inner fire—surprising for somebody who claimed, essentially, to be a program.

"You can feel anger, I see."

"I can feel any damn thing I please."

They sensed the approaching presence at the same time and went to their feet at the same moment. They both found themselves looking down the barrel of a Casull Raging Bull at the same second. Diana was handling Flynn's big pistol expertly. He was silently impressed, and he knew that Morris was, too, because he could feel the fear pouring off him. If she pulled the trigger, his head would be blown apart, an injury too extreme to fix.

"You've been practicing," Flynn said. He'd find out later how she had defeated Morris's sonic incapacitation, which was one very powerful tool. He looked over at Morris. "She won't miss."

"Help me," Morris said, his voice dead and hopeless. Flynn could hardly imagine how it would feel to know for certain that death was the end for you. Not good, especially if you also suspected that others survived the death of the body—or, as in Morris's case, knew it.

"What the hell is going on here, Flynn? Do you realize who this is?"

"I do."

"Then—what?"

He stepped over to Diana, but when he reached to take the pistol, she swung away from him. In that instant, Morris darted between them.

"Shit!" She whirled, but it was too late—he was already out the front door and gone. Following him would be futile.

She came into the library and slammed the pistol down on the desk. *"What in hell?"*

"I was going to tell you."

"Just not right now. What are you two up to?"

"He claims that he wants to work together against Aeon."

"That I do not believe."

"We flew here together from Dubai."

"That is the first thing you should have told me."

"I didn't and it was a mistake. I'm sorry."

"Flynn, we can't afford mistakes. If I hadn't come down here when I did, God knows what would have happened."

"You should have been knocked out until morning."

"I was never knocked out."

"His device didn't work?"

"There's a counter-acoustic barrier covering the entire house. Nobody in here can be knocked out with a sonic pulse device."

"So you heard everything."

"And I am now more certain than ever that you have a fatal flaw. Your fatal flaw is, you're a compulsive loner."

"I could've told you that."

She picked up Flynn's Raging Bull. "I sure have been practicing," she said. "Do you know we have your entire body mapped, inside and out? Those functional MRIs you did have enabled me to learn just how you make your moves, and train my own body to do the same. And train others." In a split second, the Bull was raised pointed at him. "It's a learning curve, Flynn, nothing more. It can be taught."

"But not tonight. We need to get out to Langley."

"We can patch in from here via the QX."

"We need to leave. If he can penetrate, they all can. This place is a death trap."

He went upstairs and threw on some clothes, and she followed and did the same. They went across to the garage. Instead of taking one of their own cars, Flynn chose one that was well crusted with dust, an elderly Oldsmobile, entered it, and wired it.

There was half a tank of gas. The engine clattered like a sewing machine.

They pulled out into the street and drove slowly off toward the Key Bridge and, beyond it, the GW Parkway.

Morris had said three days, but what truth was there in it? Flynn's sense was that they might have less time than that, maybe a lot less. And still, even at this late moment, they still had no real idea what they were up against.

The U.S. president. The football. Mind control. The extinction of mankind, but without destroying the planet in the process. "So how," Flynn said into the darkness across the bridge.

"How what?"

He didn't reply. There was no reply. He drove on, deep into the night.

CHAPTER SEVENTEEN

THE LANGLEY Central Intelligence Agency complex never really sleeps, but as the night wears on, the shifts grow thin and the long corridors grow quiet. In the main building there are many different types of restricted areas, ranging from the secret to the highly classified. There are a few areas that are so secret that finding them would require detailed knowledge of the structure and of the misleading names on the doors that conceal them.

Diana and Flynn walked across an empty open-plan office belonging to a group of economic statisticians and went through a door marked simply with the word STAIRS. In silence they went down one flight, then another. There was a discreet number keypad on another door. Diana punched in the code and they entered another corridor. With a whir and a final clunk, the door they'd just come through closed and locked itself.

Concealed from them around a corner of the hall they had entered, a guard drew his weapon. He did not show himself, but if either of them failed the body identification and recognition scan that they were now undergoing, he would step out of his post and kill them both.

The identification system was invisible, embedded in the walls. If they had failed, their first awareness of this would have been death itself. You don't hear the bullet that kills you.

As they passed, the guard pulled the door that concealed him closed. He waited until he saw them entering the facility itself to open it again. He did not know who they were. He knew only his duty, and he fulfilled it with absolute dedication. His orders were never to allow himself to be observed. Diana had given him those orders when she had appointed him.

By contrast with the empty, silent corridor that seemingly led only to a storage room, the detail's bullpen was brightly lit and humming with intensity. As always, Flynn tried to minimize contact. It was compulsive with him: Of course everybody in here knew what he looked like; everybody knew what he did. He strode quickly between desks, heading for the refuge of Diana's office.

"Flynn?"

He went through the door and closed it. In Diana's outer office there were four desks. Now only one was manned. "Mr. Carroll! Hello!"

"Who are you?"

The woman behind the desk jumped to her feet. "Sly Crawford."

"You're a spy and your name is Sly? Fix that." He headed for the inner office and Diana's overnight suite behind it, the most secure area in the facility.

"Flynn!" Diana had come storming in behind him.

"No."

"Get out of here! We've got work to do that doesn't involve your various neuroses."

"Security isn't a neurosis."

"It is when you're in one of the most secure facilities on the planet."

"There are no secure facilities on the planet."

"Oh, fine. OK. That makes it simple. We've lost and we all need to go home. Why did we even bother to come over here?"

"Look, Di, I'm here because I'm willing to try. In fact, I'm willing to die trying."

"No need for melodrama. We're all desperate and we're all terrified."

He didn't say it, but when it came time to be on the front line, it was going to be him, not her and not the rest of the staff. Still, she was right about what he had to do, and right about the fact that there was no reason to hide back here. It was instinct, though, and far from illogical. In a war like this, without boundaries and with an enemy that could penetrate the deepest recesses of your secure areas with undetectable surveillance, there was every reason to be more than normally careful—to say the least. Unless, of course, it just didn't matter.

He went out into the bullpen. "OK, folks, listen up. We want patterns. Anything that suggests some kind of plan behind it. Right now, though, I need reports. As much as you have. Map it all and throw it up on the screen in Di's office. Do it now."

He returned to her office and sat down in her chair.

"Thank you," she said, sitting in one of her office chairs. "What are we looking for?"

"I don't know."

An image appeared of a world map. On it were dozens of circles and triangles, green, yellow, and red, each representing an unknown object present in the sky. Gene Fox, director of data services and former Wire technician, came in.

"Green are identified, yellow are possible, red are definite unknowns. Let's roll through it over the past seventy-two hours."

The map began to animate, with circles and triangles appearing and disappearing.

"Can you drop out the civilian reports?" Flynn said. "There's too much static; you can't see a pattern."

"There are no civilian reports here."

"Military only?"

"Military and airline flight crew. These are all from classified channels."

"My dear God," Diana muttered.

It was, in fact, a huge worldwide incursion. Normally, there would be ten or twelve of these on a given day, if that many.

"We're looking at something like three hundred an hour, and those are just reports of things that were observed and tracked. And it's escalating."

"Zoom in on CONUS," Flynn said.

The map of the United States grew until it filled the screen.

"Now roll back until the level was normal, then roll forward to the present. Slo-mo."

He watched as the number of objects declined to almost none, then rose day by day. The image stopped at the present. As they watched, two more triangles appeared on the screen, reports from control towers at Hobby Airport in Houston and a radar facility in North Dakota.

"Thanks, Gene," Flynn said. "Keep us posted."

Gene took that as a cue to leave.

"Why did you do that?"

"What?"

"Ditch him like that. Not exactly a morale builder."

"Need to know. By the way, are those thermometers here?"

"Yes, in the outer office."

He returned to the map, looking at the sea of dots. "Do you see a pattern?"

"Not so far."

Taking one of the thermometers with him, he went back out onto the floor. Gene was huddling with members of his staff. Silently, he ran the device over the group. It threw an infrared beam, which measured temperature from a distance. No cold spots in the group. He drew Gene aside. "What I need are all the individual courses you have, each one you can verify as being a single object. I know it's complex. A lot of calculation. Your expert judgment."

"Can do. Take some time."

"Gene, we don't have time. I need it within ten minutes."

"It's a day's work at least!"

"Not in wartime, it isn't." He left Gene gaping at his back. As he returned to Diana's office, he heard the man start barking orders.

Soon, tracks began appearing on the map, showing where objects had been first and last sighted, with dotted lines for probable courses.

"See that?" Flynn said, pointing to two courses that both ended in the same place.

"I do not."

"You know what's in Minot, North Dakota."

"Malmstrom. Now I see it. My dear God."

He went back out onto the floor. It was silent. People were working furiously, deeply concentrated. "Gene, I need you to do the same thing for Russia."

"Our data isn't as robust, obviously."

"Concentrate on their ICBM launch facilities."

"There are hundreds of them, plus a lot of mobiles. They're not as centralized as we are."

"Do what you can as fast as you can."

The U.S. watched Russia's ICBM launch facilities from eyes in the sky, in addition to listening in on any and all communications.

The map changed, showing the vastness of Siberia. Over the intercom came Gene's voice: "This is without courses yet. But you need to see it." The map went to a point where there were few circles and triangles, but by that time, Flynn was already at Gene's side.

He reached over to the intercom button on his console and switched it off. "Next time, knock."

"Excuse me?"

"No intercom. Could be a surveil on it."

"In *here*?"

"In here."

Flynn returned to the inner office. Once again, he watched as the number of objects blossomed. He returned to Gene. "I want you to overlay a map of all Russian ICBM launch facilities."

Yet again, he went back to the inner office. In a moment, the known locations of all of Russia's fixed ICBM bases appeared, then the locations of all parked mobile launchers.

"Where are we going with this, Flynn?" Diana asked.

"Look closely."

Slowly, Diana got to her feet. She walked over to the map, then stood back from it. "What's their point? Why are they doing this?"

"That I don't know. But they're sure as hell overflying ICBM sites in both countries. Doing it again and again."

"They are, I agree. But I can't see why our missile defense would matter to them. We target against each other, not them."

"It matters, though."

Silence fell. Could they be retargeting the missiles? That had happened before, back years ago, to both countries.

She said, "Are they developing an ability to fire them?"

"If they do that, then they don't get the planet."

"What it if they don't actually care about the planet? After all, planets are plentiful. We know that much."

"I need you to put together a team for me. First, I want nuclear experts. At least two leading nuclear scientists, people who know everything there is to know about nuclear weapons. No air force personnel."

"What's the plan?"

"We're going on a tour of Minuteman bases. Inspection. And I'll need an identity that's far enough up the chain of command to smooth my way."

"You want to impersonate a general? Could backfire if you run into somebody you're supposed to know."

"I need to be Department of Defense. Civilian. Undersecretary level. Somewhere down in the cracks."

"I'll make certain all verification requests come my way."

They set about preparing the team, which turned out to take many phone calls and more explanations than Flynn liked. While Diana and her assistants worked the phones, he discreetly moved through the big room with the temperature sensor. He didn't pick up anything unusual, not from this shift, anyway.

He returned to Diana's office as she put down her phone. "You getting on OK?"

"Did you know that most of the scientists involved in nuclear weapons research are dead?"

That was disturbing. Maybe also a clue. "Meaning?"

"Nothing sinister I don't think. They got old and died. Cold War's over. Nuclear weapons design is a backwater. Pencil-pusher country."

"So get me the best pencil pushers you can find."

"What do I tell them they're looking for?"

"I don't know."

"Flynn, you are so damn difficult." She went back to her phone. A few moments later, she said, "Madame Secretary." She and the secretary of the air force spoke together for a few minutes. "That was Secretary Culpepper. She's got me a name. Guy at MIT. He's got major cojones when it comes to nukes. Plus he knows the facilities. He's an expert in weapons miniaturization, which is about the only active field of research at present."

Flynn thought about that. "That would be the cutting edge right now, for sure."

She shrugged. "He's the best nuclear engineer she knows and he's got a heavy-duty clearance, so we don't have to worry about getting him to sign his life away; he's already done that. I know you're not gonna want to fly from here, so I'm assembling your crew at Wright-Pat."

"OK, good."

"It's four now. If you drive all night, you'll be there by dawn. Your group will be assembled on the flight line. You can pick a plane at random and you'll be taken to Malmstrom."

"As long as it's not like the last time. That general was ready to have me shot." He'd commandeered an air force general's plane during a previous emergency.

"You took the man's plane while he was actually going aboard. You threw him off his own assigned aircraft. So yes, he was a little annoyed. This time, you outrank the generals."

"So when I'm on the flight line, I can get in a plane at random?"

"Of course not, Flynn. You'll have a plane and crew assigned. A flight plan filed."

"Scratch that. I'll tell them where they're going once we're rolling."

"But not a random plane. That I cannot do."

As was his established procedure, he left without saying anything to anybody—not a goodbye, not a word. He never, ever forgot that his life depended on his skill at deception, and Aeon was very damn good at seeing past most of his tricks.

This time, he would use a new procedure. Instead of going to the parking garage and pulling out the car that was kept there for him, he'd take a company car to Dulles, signing in under one of his working aliases, Richard Kelvin. Kelvin had retired two years ago, but his identity had not retired, and could still be used for chores like acquiring a car and driver.

He waited in the vast, sterile lobby until the car pulled up in front. Head down, he walked quickly to the vehicle. He instructed the driver to take him to the Silver Spring Metro station, then sat back with his eyes closed and, as far as was possible, blanked his mind. But of course, the mind keeps on, and that's what Aeon's surveillance experts counted on. Once they had a DNA signature—and they had Flynn's—they could find a person by the electromagnetic pattern generated by his brain, the same pattern that we measure with an electroencephalogram. Worse, they could do this from an unknown distance, probably from Aeon itself. A unit in the National Reconnaissance Office, as secret as their own, was supposed to be searching for some sort of base in our solar system, but so far nothing had been found.

As he hurried down into the Metro station, a cold, wet autumn wind blew reefs of leaves down the street. People huddled past in coats and jackets. The station was crowded, which was good. He boarded a train bound for Union Station. There, in the echoing hall, he bought a Greyhound ticket to Pittsburgh, using cash. The bus would leave at 7:55 and get in at 2:15 in the morning. He then went to a newsstand, where he found throwaway cell phones for sale. He bought four, again with cash. He used one of them to call Cassey Air Charter at the Allegheny County Airport, chosen at random. The GSMK phones were possibly secure, but only when calling other phones that were similarly equipped. He had taken one of them with him, but he wouldn't use it unless he had no choice.

"I'm looking for a flight to Dayton. I need it at three fifteen."

"Not a problem. Name, please?"

"I mean this morning. Not tomorrow afternoon."

"Oh. Hm."

"Does that create a problem?"

"No, it's just . . . What are you carrying?"

"Just myself. My dad is dying."

"Oh, jeez, I'm sorry. We can get you a plane, sure. Cost triple-time money, though, for the pilots."

"I gotta be at my dad's bedside." Flynn gave him credit card information from one of the aliases he carried. He waited as the card was run.

"Your plane will be waiting. You know how to get here?"

"I do." Flynn closed the phone. He then went into a men's room and opened it. He fished out the SIM card and flushed it, then threw the rest of the remains in a trash bin. There was still half an hour before the bus left, so he entered a stall and waited there. Unless necessary, he would not expose himself for more than a few minutes in any public place, not given that there was an active assassination effort under way.

He told himself that he wouldn't worry about Di, which started him worrying about Di. Now that she was in the facility, surely she would stay there until they got some kind of a handle on this thing. But was the facility secure enough? Could everybody be trusted? There were no biorobots in that shift, but what if some of them were implanted? The whole staff was checked weekly, but maybe somebody had been hit in the past few days. And what about the other two shifts?

He left the john. It was too confining. It felt like a trap. His mind swam with worry and indecision. Maybe he should return to the White House. He'd faced the fact that killing Greene would gain nothing and cause all hell to break loose, so he needed to both protect him and prevent him from carrying out some kind of nuclear strike, but he also needed to figure out why Aeon even wanted to induce a nuclear war.

Watch the president. Check out the missiles. Which one mattered most?

He decided that the missiles were the best move. Greene was being such a jerk, he needed to come back to him with rock-solid evidence.

Of course, the deeper question had to be asked: Was Greene under mind control, or was he still free? And there was no way to get him into an MRI scanner, given his attitude.

The time crawled. Crept. People came and went, trains were called, buses were called. Finally, he was able to get aboard.

He took a seat in the back row and leaned up against the window so his face couldn't be seen from the outside. As the other passengers came aboard, he watched them. Elderly couple, black. Young woman, cheap coat, gum, furious eyes. Couple of guys, looked like college kids. Why were they on a bus to nowhere? A mother with a baby in a carrier. The baby was asleep. For now. Over ten minutes, the bus filled. That was good; it made it easier to be overlooked. The only better alternative would have been if he was alone. Alone, just him and the driver, what could go wrong?

He abandoned that train of thought. Any damn thing could go wrong. Anything could go wrong now.

Taking a bus was an ordeal, but he felt that it was absolutely necessary. In fact, of all the modes of transportation he'd used in the past, buses had been the safest. There had been only one incident, and it hadn't been major. By contrast, purchasing a car for cash had been extremely danger-ous. They'd found him fast and come damn close. Using a small private plane had been even more nearly lethal. He hoped that this unlikely mode of travel and the fact that he was clean of implants would set them back. But he sat, tense, his shoulders hunched, compulsively feeling his weapon, the modified Raging Bull that hung under his arm, a heavy and reassuring hunk of pure power.

The bus wheezed along. The minutes crept into hours. The bus seemed to stop at every other gas station. People came and went, with the number of passengers dropping steadily.

When the driver called out "Pittsburgh," he awoke, his eyes flying open and his right hand going for the pistol. He'd been asleep. Dead asleep. And all that time, he'd been horribly vulnerable.

The bus entered the station on 11th Street and emptied quickly. To his surprise, Flynn found a cab easily enough, meaning that he didn't have to waste another of the throwaway phones. He gave the driver the address out at the airport. The driver didn't ask questions and Flynn was glad. When he traveled, the talkative troubled him. He always told them that he was an accountant. Their eyes would glaze and silence would fall, blessed silence.

He got out of the cab. Cassey Air Charter was in a trim aluminum struc-ture. Nothing fancy, but it didn't look like a sty, either.

As the cab drove away, he went to the door, which was locked. He knocked, then rang the buzzer. For a horrible moment, he thought that he'd been ditched, but at length he saw a shadow coming toward the door. A man in a gray coverall appeared and looked out at him suspiciously.

"I have a charter waiting," he said.

The man opened the door. "You that plane out there? Come on in, sorry, we don't get many riders this time of night."

"My dad's dying. I've got to get to Philly."

"Oh, my, I'm sorry. Well, your plane's ready to go."

He went through the empty facility, past a softly rumbling Coke machine and a row of plastic chairs, then through a double door and onto the tarmac, where an elderly Lear 23 stood with its windows glowing. A generator roared under the nose, and as Flynn climbed aboard he saw the lone ground crewman unplug it. The lights flickered as the plane went on batteries. He entered the cabin.

"I'm Gene Curtis," the pilot said. "Sorry about your dad."

"It was very sudden. We were golfing two days ago."

"That's rough. Look, we're gonna just go straight across. There's some weather north and west, but it's not moving fast enough to catch us, doesn't look like. We'll be landing in an hour and fifteen minutes."

As the man spoke, Flynn watched him. Too bad he couldn't use the temperature sensor he had with him, but he just could not see how to explain that. He couldn't afford to raise suspicions. He needed this flight to happen.

He gave the sad sort of smile a grieving son might offer. "Thank you."

The pilot went into the cockpit. Before he closed the door, Flynn glimpsed the copilot, a woman. A recent hire or not?

He stood and knocked on the door.

The pilot opened it.

"I'm just wondering—I'm sorry to ask—but I'm an uneasy flier, and—"

"I've been pushing iron through the sky for thirty years," Curtis said.

"So have I," the woman added. "I'm Cassey. The wife and the company's namesake."

Flynn took a seat and belted himself in. Maybe they were OK.

The plane started moving at once, and was soon bouncing along the runway. The 23 had not been produced since the 1960s, so this aircraft had to be pushing fifty. Maybe Aeon wouldn't need to come after him. Maybe the plan would simply fall apart.

Once they were airborne, he sat listening to the shriek of the engines and feeling the uneasy trembling when they encountered pockets of rough air. But that ended quickly. Since 23s cruise at forty-five thousand feet, the air was soon as still as glass, the plane seemingly motionless.

They had been flying for under half an hour when the pilot came back. His face was pale and his eyes full of worry. "There are numerous aircraft out there declaring general emergencies," he said. "ATC is saying they're losing instruments." He fixed steady eyes on Flynn, who looked back with what he hoped was the blank stare of the ignorant passenger.

"Are you saying to turn back?"

"I'm telling you what's happening. Turn back, keep on, I have no idea. Just want you to know, we could get real busy up front."

Flynn rarely felt fear, but he felt it now. This was Aeon, had to be, doing this. They knew he was out here somewhere, but not where. In hope of getting him, they were going to strip the sky of planes. "Let's land right now."

"Dayton's our closest field."

"Will we make it?"

"I've never seen anything like this in all my years of flying, so I don't know. So far we're OK, but I might have to put this baby on the ground wherever we happen to be. I just want you to know that."

Flynn said nothing. He'd been a damn fool to even try flying, but how could he avoid it, and what about the longer flight ahead from Wright-Pat to Minot?

The pilot returned. "Four affected aircraft have landed, two have lost contact."

"Are they down?"

"Out of contact may mean down. ATC isn't saying."

"How many are still in the air?"

"Six. Four affected, two unaffected—us and a Cinci flight out of Louisville. A Citation."

"Do you know anything else about the affected planes?"

"A couple of UPS haulers, an air force whatever—we don't get told—some other charters. No sardine cans this time of night."

A stall horn went off in the cockpit. Curtis turned and hurried back. A moment later, the horn stopped.

The lights went out. From the front, Flynn heard, "Shit!" They flew on. The darkness was absolute, like being in a cave. Only the windows revealed anything—a few stars and, far off, lightning.

The intercom crackled. "We're having avionics issues, sir. Please remain in your seat. Do you know how the brace position works—" The intercom crackled again and then was silent.

Would he die now? It seemed likely. If so, would the world die with him? That thought made him break out into a sweat. It made him feel both helpless and essential. Maddening.

He felt the plane shudder, then slow. For all he could tell, a normal descent had commenced. A moment later, though, they wallowed to the right, the right engine screamed, and they straightened out. Then the same thing happened as they wallowed left.

Curtis was guiding the plane with engine thrust. He didn't have his vertical rudder. What else didn't he have, then?

Flynn could see lights below. Dayton? No way to tell, no way to ask. The plane pitched, the engines dropped back, the nose fell, and the stall horn sounded. Again, the engines screamed. The stall horn stopped. The engines cut back and in a moment the horn was blaring again.

It went on like this as they dropped lower and lower. Flynn now understood that they had no hydraulics and no backup electrics. Wherever they were, this was going to be a very dangerous landing.

Lower they went, and lower still, the engines alternately screaming and cutting back as the plane pitched and yawed and wallowed across the sky like a leaping sea creature.

Immediately below them, Flynn could now see a runway, a wide one. Fire equipment pulled in beside them and dropped back as the plane failed to lose speed. They were coming in much too fast.

Flynn leaped out of his seat and went to the rear of the plane, where he took the seat closest to the bulkhead. He fastened the belt and braced himself wrapping his arms around his knees and bending as far forward as he could.

A roar, the tube of the fuselage twisting, a haze of smoke and fire, then a ferocious pull to the right and a long, screeching slide that never seemed to end.

His head took a blow, he saw flashes of light, then another blow, then he was thrown to one side with such force that he blacked out.

Orange light. Pain in his face. Heat. More heat.

Screams, long and awful with despair. A specter wreathed in fire, dancing across the runway. Then it fell. It kicked, it shook, its fists hammered the air.

Flynn understood that he was still in his seat. Then he further understood that it was lying on its side on the concrete. The burning figure over there was Gene. Gene was burning.

Flynn tried to get out. The man was dying, screaming and writhing and dying.

He couldn't get the belt off, couldn't reach the pocketknife he carried for such emergencies. Using all his strength, he forced himself to a kneeling position. He dragged himself forward, the seat still attached to him. He had to put that fire out; he had to save that man.

Then it started raining. A storm? No, snow. It was snowing, but not enough to help the poor damn pilot. He had to hurry—people don't last long in fire. He went to his feet and staggered ahead, bent forward under the weight of the seat.

"What in hell is that? Look at that seat!"

"That's a guy, asshole, help him!"

The seat suddenly took on a life of its own, then Flynn was on his back looking into the face of a fireman. Then he was free. They hauled him out.

"Careful, get the gurney, get him stabilized."

"We've got fire under the starboard wing tank—move, move, move!"

Flynn pushed them aside. "I'm Ok," he shouted. "Get the hell out of here."

"You don't know if you're Ok. We're getting a gurney."

Flynn ran, trying not to stagger, forcing himself to ignore the pain in his back and leg.

As they followed him, a great light came, casting their shadows far ahead of them, along with the knotted, bulky shadow of Flynn Carroll. Then came heat, searing, like boiling water poured down your back. Flynn kept running, then flung himself down in the grass divider and rolled.

The fire set up a crazy quilt of flickering shadows. The firemen went about their work, their pumps thundering, their foam hissing. A winter wonderland, except it was still autumn and the snow stank of ammonia and jet fuel. Everything stank of jet fuel. A little farther away, the body of Gene looked like a mound of snow somebody had plowed up and left behind.

Gene. Dead because of him. Another notch on his gun, was that it? And the copilot, a woman just glimpsed.

"Sir, you need to get on the gurney."

"Yeah, later. Where's the other crew?"

The fireman shook his head sharply.

So it was two more down, poor innocent people out trying to make a little money, trying to help him out. Were there kids at home? If so, Flynn would do what he could.

In the distance, he could see flashing light bars. He walked off toward them, going faster as he regained his orientation and his strength. There was back pain, considerable. Right knee. Also considerable. His head didn't hurt and there was no blood. Internal injuries? None of the burning sensation such things usually entailed.

Forcing himself not to stagger, not to stumble—in fact, not to just lie down and surrender—he went on.

The light bars resolved into a flood of official vehicles. Flynn shuffled into the lights.

CHAPTER EIGHTEEN

HE FELT for his throwaway phones, and found that one was still in his pocket. As he walked, he ripped it open. He'd have to hope that Aeon's surveillance experts weren't monitoring Diana's father.

It rang once, twice, three times. A female voice answered, thick with sleep. What time was it? Flynn didn't care.

"Grace, put the senator on."

"Who is this?"

"Flynn."

"Is Di okay?"

"Absolutely fine. She's safe in the tomb. I need to talk to Walt right now."

A moment. Silence. Shuffling. Then the senator. "Flynn, what the hell?"

"I want you to go to Langley. Di's in the tomb. You go down there and tell her to put a spin on the crash story that'll be developing."

"What crash story, Flynn? Where? Are you OK?"

"I'm good. There've been a number of crashes across the Midwest. We need Homeland Insecurity to spin them as terrorism."

"My God, what happened?"

"You get to Di, you do it personally."

"I can't enter the tomb."

"I'm going to text you a number sequence. Send it to Di from your phone and she'll make sure you can get in. Now, listen, you tell her to make certain that I'm listed among the dead. Certain! And no matter who asks,

Flynn is dead. That's all she's to say. Dead in the crash of a chartered jet at Dayton International."

"OK, I'm in motion."

"Thanks, buddy, I owe you."

"Hell, Flynn, that tab's always paid in full. God go with you, wherever you are."

He closed the primitive little phone, crushed it, then picked up the SIM card and threw it off into the dark.

Now he was among the light bars, meatwagons, local fire, local cops, state cops, uniforms everywhere, radios crackling, general tightness and silence as people waited to hear what the hell was happening. He saw some braid and brass and walked up to it.

"I need transport to Wright-Pat," he said. "It's a national emergency."

"Sir, you need to leave this area." The officer looked Flynn up and down. "Sir, were you on one of the planes?"

"Lieutenant, you listen up. I need immediate transport to Wright-Pat. Do you hear me?"

"If you were on one of those planes—hey, Mike, get over here—you need to talk to CID."

"If you want to keep your brass on your shoulders, you need to do as I say. You need to designate a squad car and have that officer drive me to Wright-Pat immediately."

"I have a survivor here!" the cop shouted over his shoulder.

Flynn would have no more of it. He took the man by his lapels and lifted him off his feet. "This is a national emergency. I'm a federal officer. That's the end of your need to know." Shock finally delivered compliance; Flynn could see it in the surprised eyes. He put him down. "Now, I repeat, you *will* transport me to Wright-Pat, and you will do it forthwith. Personally."

"Yessir!"

The lieutenant led him to his vehicle. Flynn sat in the back. He didn't want conversation, and he didn't want to be observed any more than he already had been. The shadows, the night, were his home. He was not comfortable interacting with outsiders of any kind.

He'd survived again—somehow. But there had been collaterals, a lot of them, and he hated that as deeply as a man can hate. He hated Aeon too, with every cell of him, with his blood and his soul.

He took slow breaths. No emotions, only thought. Analysis. His feelings needed to stay in the vault of his heart.

"Take back streets," he said to the lieutenant.

"Sir?"

"No highways. Too exposed."

The cop pulled the car over and turned around in his seat. "I need to know what I'm dealing with."

"No you don't."

"You sit there and tell me you're in danger and I have to ask, what the hell is this about?"

"No you don't."

"For chrissakes, I'm a cop. Protect and serve!"

"You can't protect me unless you follow my instructions."

He squared his shoulders and drove on.

As they arrived at the main gate and the guard came out, Flynn realized that he had forgotten the identity he was using. Then he remembered, it was "Richard Kelvin." It was just an infrequently used pickup, enough to establish identity for the charter operator.

He opened his wallet. The Grauerholtz cover was still there, but it didn't have any clearances.

"May I see your identification, sir?"

"You need to wake the commandant."

"Sir?"

"It's a national emergency."

The guard looked toward the trooper lieutenant. "Sir, can you help me here?"

This was it. Either this fell apart right now or it didn't.

Once again, the trooper turned to Flynn. "Who are you? I think I do have a need to know."

"I'm the reason all those planes fell out of the sky, and my mission is absolutely urgent, and I can't tell you another thing. You just get me into this facility. I have a team waiting for me on the flight line and I need your help right now." He added to the guard, "You have to let us through."

"Sir?"

"Or call your commandant. Do something!"

"This watch isn't waking up the commandant. We don't have the authority."

Flynn leaned forward. "Somebody does. Call them."

"I'm sorry, but I can't let you onto this base without some kind of authority, not at this hour."

Flynn said to the trooper, "Drive through while the bar's up."

"I don't think—"

"Do it if you're a patriot. It'll all sort out in a few minutes, I promise you."

The car didn't move. The barrier began to drop.

"Do it!"

The trooper gunned the engine and the police cruiser leaped forward. They went through and onto the base.

"Curve around on Skeel Avenue," Flynn said. "There'll be a small cluster of buildings on your left, then a larger structure and a second one. Stop there. Second structure."

Sirens rose in the background. The trooper slowed down.

"Hit your siren, put on your light bar—do it!"

The trooper complied, and none too soon, because the first security vehicle passed them going in the opposite direction and did not stop.

"Hurry, they're gonna figure it out in thirty seconds."

"What happens to me?"

"Stop! Right here!"

The trooper jammed on the brakes and Flynn leaped out and sprinted into Flight Operations.

"I'm Flynn Carroll," he said to the reception orderly. "Where's my crew?"

"Yes, sir. Just a moment."

Sirens rose outside.

"Your group is in the assembly area."

The rush of relief that surged through him was like air to a drowning man. "There's been a mistake outside. My transport—will you take care of it?"

"Your transport?"

"The state police brought me and they didn't have the right permit. Take care of it—do it now!"

"Yessir!"

Flynn strode past him, turned to his left, and entered the assembly area.

Tim Fletcher was there, and Will T. Berman. They were both scientists from the old exobiology team that had been trying to study Aeon. They'd made the mistake of believing that more advanced societies would be more ethical, not stopping to think that the Nazis were the least ethical society in human history, and had grown like a cancer in one of the most civilized countries in the world. Time does not eradicate the madness of men, and apparently that goes for aliens, too.

There were three others he didn't recognize.

Fletcher came to his feet. "Good to see you again."

"Yeah. I want to be briefed on the plane, but only if you've got something sensible to say." Fletcher had many times tried to get Flynn relieved of duty on the theory that he was upsetting to Aeon. He was upsetting all right—damned upsetting.

Fletcher smiled, and in it Flynn saw the sadness of defeat. Good. He'd faced his mistakes. Fletcher said, "This is Al Quint from MIT."

"You're in bomb design, am I right?"

"Well, I'd hardly—"

"Don't give me any bullshit shyness, please. Are you capable of analyzing nuclear weapons and determining their degree of readiness?"

Quint drew himself up. "I am capable of that."

"You have all your equipment? Everything you need?"

"Stowed."

"Let's go." Flynn hoped that this flight would be uneventful. His best guess, based on past escapes, was that he had until about eleven this morning before Aeon discovered that he was still alive.

There was a typical USAF-issue general officers' plane waiting for them.

It was nicely equipped, but more utilitarian than the private-charter Lear, which had been luxurious . . . until it had turned into a death trap.

They took off immediately. The crew already had their marching orders, so Flynn didn't have to explain anything to anybody. Unless Aeon blew them out of the sky, the next stop was North Dakota.

"OK, ladies and gentlemen," Flynn said, "what we're going to be doing is analyzing every aspect of the Minuteman operation at Malmstrom. We will want to check control systems, missile guidance programming, and the condition of the warheads, the fuel, and the rocket engines. Everything."

Quint said, "Can we know why?"

Flynn answered carefully. "Something in these systems is wrong. We're not sure what it is."

Robert Hardy, a man with wild white hair and an air of unease, said, "They have their own technicians out there."

"We need an outside inspection."

The only woman on the team, Linda Bartlett, said, "So somebody's not loyal. Is this terrorism? Because if it is, I'm not going and the hell with the fee."

"You're already going," Flynn thought, but did not say. They were well west of Dayton, probably climbing through ten thousand feet.

"Yeah," Hardy said. "I'm not going into some nest of terrorists, either."

Flynn smiled. He said mildly, "You're all agency assets and you're going where you've been ordered to go."

"'Ordered'? Where the hell do you get off, mister?"

"Let me be clear. You will be doing the most important single thing that you have ever done, all of you. What hangs in the balance I cannot tell you, but it's a lot."

Flynn had imagined that his feelings were hidden, until Linda Bartlett sat beside him and said, "I believe you're very afraid."

Flynn looked away from her. He said nothing.

"Why? What's out there?"

"Your job is weapons design, am I right?"

"I lecture on nuclear weapons design, yes, but I don't build bombs."

"You know bombs: how they work, how they're constructed, what sort of fissile materials they require."

"Yes."

"Then you do your job, which is to evaluate the warheads at Malmstrom."

"Are we in danger? Because we have a right to know that."

He realized that he had to tell them something. He stood up in the aisle. "OK, listen up. We're going to be attempting to see if terrorists who infiltrated the 230th Missile Wing at Malmstrom succeeded in sabotage of the missiles, retargeting of the warheads, or any sort of systems revision designed to make the units malfunction in any way whatsoever. Now, with regard to danger. I cannot say that there won't be any danger. What has happened is that an infiltration unit has penetrated into the 230th command structure. We know that they deployed missile technicians, among others. They are no longer an actionable unit."

"What does that mean?" Quint said.

"To be blunt, it means that they're all dead," Flynn lied. "The 230th no longer has a terrorist component infiltrated into it."

"Then why not use the USAF techs? They know their systems. I haven't been on a missile site in ten years. More."

This was followed by a murmur of agreement.

Flynn said, As I've said, "we need people from outside. Out of an excess of caution, let's say." He didn't want to go anywhere near the truth, which was that the airmen involved could be implanted, that there could be biological robots involved, and that therefore nobody at Malmstrom or any other missile site anywhere in the world was to be trusted.

There was silence, then. He could see the questions still in their faces, the uneasy anger there. He knew that they'd all been coerced in one way or another to leave their lives at a moment's notice to do this. None of them wanted to be here. None of them believed his lies.

He went back to his seat. Somewhere down there, the airwaves and the Internet were filling with the story of the mysterious crashes. Soon Diana would bleed his name into the list of victims.

The hours oozed past like dark lava, slow, deadly hours.

He remembered being naked on the moonlit beach at Port Aransas, the surf flinging its mystery up the uneasy strand, their bodies chill in the wind and the flying spray. Her hand in his, a dove at rest.

A partner dies, but the conversation continues on in the mind of the survivor. Slow words in the midnight . . . her whispered desires, his whispered desires.

Diana gleaming in the bath, her body oozing invitation.

How alone could a man be?

The plane slipped through the sky. Somewhere other minds, cruel, cold, full of the lust of greed, sifted through the sparking electronic threads of life on Earth, looking for a certain strand, the echo of a fragment that would lead them to him.

At the appointed time, they touched down. This once, he'd made it across the bridge of the sky without being attacked. He thought long, though, of the men and women dead in the fields of Ohio and Illinois, whose planes had mysteriously failed them.

On their first operation together, Diana had gotten her whole crew killed except him. He'd thrown it in her face a couple of times, but now that he knew how it felt, he would never do that again, not to her or to anybody else.

The cabin steward, who had hidden in the back when he realized that his plane was carrying civilians, now emerged and cracked the door. With a loud whir, the steps dropped. They had landed not at Malmstrom, but at Great Falls Airport in Montana. The Malmstrom runway had been closed for years, and the only air operations facility there was a heliport.

Flynn waited until the others were filing out, then crossed the windswept tarmac among them. As always, he kept his head down. He hunched to keep his height from being too noticeable from above.

At this hour, with dawn just a red glow on the bare edge of the eastern horizon, the airport was almost abandoned. They walked quickly through its silence.

Before they left the lobby, Flynn gathered them around him. He would not brief them in an air force facility. There was no way to tell who might be watching and listening in such a place. He always tried to brief in unexpected places, at unplanned moments.

"Quint and Bartlett, you're to proceed to Echo 1. Your mission is to choose one of the missiles at random and analyze it. Bartlett, I want the state of the warhead to be evaluated. What is it emitting? Does its condition suggest anything unusual about it? Quint, you determine if the control and navigation systems have been changed or even addressed recently. Is the missile correctly targeted? What is the condition of the system? Could it have been altered or redesigned to give somebody outside of the system access?"

"Hardy, you inspect the missile bodies on Oscar 1. At no time should the three of you be out of each other's sight. The team now present there has orders to stand down when you arrive. If you see anybody else nearby when you are working, all three of you leave the area and radio me at once. Is that understood?"

There was general agreement. "Are we expecting violence?"

"That's an unknown."

"Shouldn't we be guarded?"

"We go in and out as quickly as possible. You'll be choppered to your sites. Fletcher and Berman, you're to visit each Launch Control Center and evaluate personnel. You've been briefed."

"These things?" Berman held out one of the temperature sensors they'd been given by Diana before they left.

"Check their body temperature. Then you're to go onto the base itself and do the same with all missile staff there." He did not add that anyone with an impossibly low body temperature would be dead before sunset.

The silence that fell after he was finished was absolute.

"I'll be with the commandant and available at once by radio. Everybody: If anything—anything at all—falls outside of protocols and standards, I'm going to want an immediate report. Do you all have radios?"

They all did. There was no question in his mind but that Aeon would notice these radio calls, and that was what he wanted. If they took action, he would be able to observe and see what they chose to do.

They proceeded to the Malmstrom flight line in a convoy of SUVs. The abandoned runway was a vast expanse of concrete gleaming in the morning sun, which had just come up over the horizon.

As he watched them go, he wondered which ones might be coming back. His best guess: none.

CHAPTER NINETEEN

COLONEL WILLIAM Finscher had been commander of the 230th Missile Wing for four years. He sat across his desk regarding Flynn with a carefully neutral expression.

"I'm sorry to descend on you like this, Colonel. But I'm going to need to ask you a few questions."

"May I know why you're here? I got notice from the Pentagon an hour ago."

"It's unusual, I know, and I'm sorry about that. I need this conversation to remain in this room. The first thing I require is a list of all personnel changes on the wing in the past month. I need it in hard copy, handwritten. It must never pass through any electronic device. I need it as soon as possible."

"Where are you from? Because if there's something amiss in my command, I have need to know on that."

"Did the secretary brief you?"

"Yep, and never mind the chain of command, I guess."

"This has to stay as small as possible. I can't tell you where I'm from, and if there is anything wrong here, it has nothing to do with you as a commanding officer and you do not have need to know, I'm sorry. Now, let's refer back to 1967. I assume that you're familiar with what I'm talking about."

"I am."

There had been a penetration of Malmstrom's missile systems by glowing objects that had hovered overhead and caused the missiles to drop off-line by shutting down their guidance systems. "So my question is, has anything like that happened while you were in command?"

"No."

"Recently, has anybody reported any glowing objects, disks, unusual events, anything like that near any of the Launch Control Centers or launch facilities?"

"I'm not aware of any reports like that."

"Would such reports have been made?"

"Standing orders require security personnel to note any unusual event whatsoever."

"What would happen to a report of a UFO hovering over an LF?"

"The report would be filed."

"But not transmitted up the chain of command?"

"A flying saucer? No."

"Then I want any and all security reports that have been filed in the past ten days. Again, hard copy. Nothing electronic."

"Will you tell me what is going on here?"

"No."

The colonel went to his feet. "I get an order from the secretary of the air force to give you every courtesy. You have a universal clearance and your people are cleared for all assigned tasks. And I have to say, I'm impressed. But now you sit in my office jabbering at me about flying saucers. Jesus Christ! So let me be frank. The little green men all left yesterday." He threw himself back down into his seat. "You'll have the paperwork you need in ten minutes. I'd prefer you wait outside."

Flynn had half-expected something like this, but the intensity of the reaction concerned him, as did its similarity to Bill Greene's reaction. Were both men implanted, and being controlled by the same mind control script?

He got up. "Thanks for your cooperation, Colonel. I'll be glad to wait in the anteroom. I'm sorry to be such a bother."

"Pain in the ass, to be specific. You got me out of the sack at dawn.

I didn't even get a chance at a damn cup of coffee before you're in here grilling me about flying saucers." He shook his head. "Please step outside, now."

The phone on the colonel's desk buzzed. He turned quickly to it and grabbed the receiver. For a moment, he listened. Then he said, "Are emergency measures in operation right now?" He hung up. "A chopper is down between here and Echo 1."

That would be Quint and Bartlett, by far Flynn's most critical team.

"Any more information?" he asked.

"It's down! We'll know more in a minute."

Flynn's first impulse was to reach out to his people and abort the mission, but he knew that he had to stay at the center of things.

"Are there any fighters in the area? That could get here immediately?"

"What the hell are you talking about?"

"Fighters to escort the other choppers! Here, damnit!"

"No fixed-wing aircraft on the base," the colonel said coldly. "The runway's been closed for years."

Flynn knew that fighters probably wouldn't matter in this situation, but Aeon's ships were sometimes careful of them.

"Then I want the other choppers to land right now."

"Where?"

"Wherever they are, Colonel!"

Finscher picked up the phone and gave the order. Immediately, another line rang. "Yes!" He listened, then slammed it down.

"My pilot and copilot are DOA. One of your guys is DOA. The other is shaken up, but unhurt. They're choppering him in to the base hospital as I speak."

"Stop them! Do not move any more helicopters without my say-so. Which man is it?"

Finscher returned to the phone. "Keep the helicopter on the ground. Please give me the name of the survivor." He turned to Flynn. "It's a she. And she's demanding an immediate return to base."

"Continue her on her mission. Put her in a vehicle. Send vehicles for the others and continue them, also."

"A man dies and you continue the mission? Without even evaluating your situation?"

"This is war, Colonel. In war you don't stop until you can't go."

"War with whom?"

Flynn was silent. A moment later, his radio chirped. He listened. It was Will Berman. "We have—"

"Report to the commandant's office immediately. No chopper. Vehicle." He turned off his unit. No more radio use. Aeon was right on top of this operation and as efficient as always. A moment later, his secure phone vibrated in his pocket. He took it out. "Colonel, leave the office, please."

He smiled, incredulous, then laughed.

"Get out of here! Now!"

He pushed back from his desk. Regarding Flynn as he might a cobra, he withdrew.

"Go ahead," Flynn said into the phone.

"I need you back here pronto. Something's wrong with Greene. Cissy just called. He's holed up in the Yellow Oval with the football. He's, like, guarding it."

"Look, I can't move—we're under attack here."

"Flynn, don't say that! I need you NOW!"

"I can't fly. They've got the air."

"OK, look, there is a plane that might make it."

"Not a TR?" This was a close-in surveillance aircraft that was responsible for half the UFO reports in the world. In fact, it had been developed to mimic some of the functionalities displayed by actual unknown objects.

"I'm pulling it out from Grady right now."

Grady was an underground airfield that flew TRs up and down the West Coast. The TR was capable of perhaps two hundred miles per hour. "It'll be six hours before it even gets here, and twelve hours to Washington."

"No."

"Come on, I know the specs on the aircraft."

"Not on this one. Get your socks packed, it'll be there in an hour." She hung up.

He would obey her orders if it made sense to do so. He was in battle here, and maybe he'd be able to disengage and maybe not.

The situation was not only out of control, it was deteriorating fast. He was trapped between two urgent necessities, and that was not how you lost battles, that was how you lost wars.

Fletcher burst into the office, followed by Berman. "We've got a positive," Fletcher said. "Public relations director, Major George Gleason."

"How can you be sure?"

"Mobile infrared temp clocks him at eighty-eight Fahrenheit. Humans don't roll that low."

"Check the colonel."

Berman stepped out. A moment later, he was back. "Colonel's gone, but the desk clerk checks in at eighty-eight."

The wing was completely infiltrated. He went back to the secure phone. Diana answered immediately. "You need the secretary to send out an order that all missile operations are to stand down."

"How is that going to work?"

"Just do it!"

"Only the president has that authority, Flynn."

"Claim it's a presidential order."

"Flynn, that would be treason."

"Do it!" He closed the phone. He knew that she'd try her best, but that it was hopeless. No doubt every missile wing in the United States was infiltrated just like this one, and in Russia, and in the rest of the world, too.

He now had an idea what might be happening, but he wasn't sure of the physics, if it was even possible.

He thought back to Al Doxy, to the file he had been carrying and the implant that had been removed from him. The Iranians had taken it because they were hungry for mind control technology. They'd used a weapon from Aeon, but it was an unimportant one, given to them, no doubt, to gain their trust, the same way European colonists bought off Indians with steel knives.

Iran had some sort of a role, obviously, but it wasn't central. Or was it?

He would have to deal with that later, because he did have a job left to do here.

His radio crackled. He drew the thumb-sized transceiver out of his pocket. "I have some information." It was Linda.

"Where are you?"

"Echo 1 LF, and the first warhead I did an emission analysis on came up as not a hydrogen weapon."

"Means?"

"Whatever they've got on that missile, it's not a normal warhead. It looks like one, but it doesn't have the emission signature—"

There was a roar, then the radio went dead. "Linda?"

Nothing. No signal at all, no carrier, nothing. Her radio was history.

"Missile rising," an intercom voice announced from the outer office. "Unauthorized firing. Repeat, an unauthorized firing."

Flynn rushed out. "Call the LCC, get them to blow it! NOW NOW NOW!"

The clerk just stared at him. "Sir, I don't know who you are!"

Flynn went to the desk.

Over the squawk box there came a laconic voice. "Missile destroyed. We will need a cleanup team to the site of impact at once."

The launch control officers had acted on their own initiative. So this place was infiltrated, yes, but it didn't belong to Aeon completely, not yet.

"How can I talk to those guys?"

"Sir—"

Flynn pulled out the Raging Bull. "I repeat, put me through to those officers. Now!"

"I can't!"

"Do it!"

"The communicator is in the colonel's office."

He went back and looked over the ancient intercom system he'd seen on the desk. Old, predigital systems were still in use on missiles because they couldn't be hacked. Everything was analog and at least forty years old. Among the many keys were four labeled with Launch Control Center identifiers. Flynn opened all of them.

"This is an emergency. The colonel isn't available and a missile has just—"

He was hit from behind so hard that it almost knocked him unconscious. He flew into the intercom console and over it, landing on his back on the floor of the office.

The colonel stood over him, his face impassive. The Bull had flown out of its shoulder holster and was across the room, but the smaller pistol was still in Flynn's ankle holster. Flynn drew it and did a head shot. The colonel flew backward into the wall and sank down. From outside there came a cry of "Jesus God," and then nearly incoherent screaming into a phone. The air police were being called, and Flynn had to get out of here. There would be no way to explain to these people what was happening. As far as they were concerned, a completely unknown civilian had barged in and blown their commanding officer to kingdom come.

A glance at his watch told Flynn that the specialized aircraft that Diana was sending would be here in forty minutes, but he did not have forty minutes. He probably didn't have forty seconds. He grabbed his big pistol off the floor and stepped quickly into the outer office, brandishing both guns.

"OK, stay calm," he said. "This is official business. This base is under attack from within."

The clerk had his hands up. "Don't hurt me," he said. "Everything's fine, we believe you." He plastered on a smile that looked like it had been bought in a costume shop, and not a very good one. "We believe you!"

Flynn headed into the corridor, then out into the parking lot. Three AP vehicles came screaming up to the building as he flipped the locks on an elderly Ford, slipped into the driver's seat, and wired it. As the APs rushed into the building, guns drawn, Flynn drove slowly out of the lot and headed for the main gate.

He got on the secure phone. "Di, you need to get eyes on a gray Ford Fusion now exiting the base. This place is crawling with bios and I had to off the commanding officer."

"Oh, great. I'm so happy."

"I've got the thing figured out. The warheads have somehow been altered, and my guess is that this applies to every warhead on every missile on the planet."

AP vehicles appeared behind him.

"Shit, I'm blown. I'm gonna have to take extreme measures in a second."

"What measures?"

"No idea. But you need to get that transport to wherever I am when it arrives."

"What's with the missiles? I see here that there was a launch and remote destruction."

"Only way they could kill Linda Bartlett. She was in the silo reporting to me on the warhead. There can be only one logical solution. The warheads will now emit intense radiation fields with low-level blast effect, and the radiation will be short-lived."

"They're going to sterilize the human population but leave the wilderness intact."

"You got it, and it's going to happen right away." The AP cars were coming up his tailpipe. Ahead, he could see the flashing light bars of a state police vehicle. "I'm going to run this thing into a field. Where's the aircraft?"

"Twenty minutes out."

He swung the wheel and the car leaped off into the stubble-covered field. Then he smashed the gas pedal to the floor and the car lunged forward.

"Why in hell did you do that?"

"You'll see."

Behind him, the state police vehicle slowed down, then the three AP trucks fanned out, centering on the trooper car. The group of them came forward, keeping pace with him but no longer attempting to close.

"They don't realize that I'm going to have transport. The troopers will have vehicles ahead of me in a few minutes. They think I'm trapped."

"Flynn, it's going to be a near thing."

"Then you better be prepared to get me out of jail."

"How?"

"Not my problem."

A shuddering *crack* startled Flynn. "They're damn well shooting at me, and somebody's good." The state police vehicle swerved and stopped in a cloud of dust. "The APs just shot out the state cop's tires. They want me dead and they don't want civilian authority in the way. They're coming in for the kill."

"Turn due west. At sixty miles an hour, you'll intersect with your transport in four minutes."

The car bucked as bullet after bullet struck it. Flynn began twisting the wheel, but his pursuers were very good shots. Machine-like in their skill . . . just like him.

He realized that he had to take them down or they were going to win this. In a situation like this, four minutes might as well be four years. Even with his Bull, a shot at this distance, which he estimated at about 2,450 feet, was going to be difficult on a moving vehicle.

He had to stop. He had to aim. He had to do this, now.

He pulled the car around so that its length was between him and the oncoming AP vehicles, fronted by the bulk of the engine.

"What are you doing?" Diana screamed into the phone.

"Getting screwed to the wall. Where's that plane?"

"Three minutes out."

The AP vehicles opened fire. "I'm looking at eight weapons—six pistols, a machine gun, and a sniper rifle," he said. "Can't that thing go any faster?"

"It's maxing out!"

He braced the Bull and fired into the radiator of the lead vehicle, then repeated the action on the other two.

Nothing happened.

He fired again, this time trying the windshields.

One of the vehicles stopped, the other two sped up.

He waited. Their guns blazed away. The car shook and clattered as bullets poured into it. He began to smell gasoline.

He fired again, and a second vehicle stopped. But all three of them continued to fire at him. He stopped the third vehicle, which was just five hundred feet away. Two APs rolled off into the dirt. They began working their way around Flynn's flanks.

A shadow flickered past. He looked up into the base of the blackest thing he had ever seen. Its darkness was so deep that it looked like a triangular hole in the blue sky. Then he could make out the black-on-black image of an American flag on the fuselage. One of ours.

The two air policemen engaging in the flanking maneuver broke cover and came running toward him. He hated to do it, but they were probably under Aeon's control one way or another. He neutralized them both with shots to the legs. If they were just innocent kids doing as ordered, they would survive. If they were biorobots, they would be destroyed by their infuriated masters.

He ran toward the black fuselage, in the sweet of morning, in the bird-song and the whipping autumn breeze, and heard geese far above.

The plane, if it was a plane, offered no way to enter, no ladder or stair. He found a curved metal lip, and drew himself up into a dark interior crowded with cabling, which at first he could not even begin to understand.

Then a cylinder wrapped in wire that dominated the center of the cabin began to rotate, and he saw the land below dropping rapidly away.

"Hello, passenger." A female voice, young, a kid.

He could see no sign of a cockpit. "Where are you?"

"At base."

"This is a drone?"

"It is. And stay where you are. You're in the service bay. You don't want to get near that cylinder above you. It's gonna fry you."

"What the hell is this thing?"

"A dirigible, basically, but a lot smaller, obviously. The helium lift is supported by electrostatic propulsion. It's capable of six hundred klicks an hour and it can reach near space. But not with you aboard. It's not pressurized. Close the port, please. It's setting up drag that I don't need."

The world was racing past below him. "There's a handle?"

"Feel forward, you'll find one. Pull it toward you."

When he slid the door closed, all sound ceased. There was no wind noise whatsoever. Around the whirling cylinder just above his head there was a blue glowing cloud, some sort of ionizing energy, he thought.

"Aren't people seeing this?"

"Sure, it'll show up on YouTube. UFO, whoa! AFOSI types will slay it with negative comments. Prove it's a computer graphic."

"Nice of them."

"I dated one. They're not nice. Hey, we've got observers. You are a popular boy."

"What observers?"

"Dunno. Up there, though. Way high. Incoming. We're gonna evade."

A thick electricity filled the air, the blue glow extending out from the engine until the entire interior danced with St. Elmo's Fire. It got hot, then hotter. The airframe shuddered a little, then more, then a lot more.

"What's going on?"

"Who are those guys, mister? They do not like you."

"Lady, I can't see, I don't know where I am, and at least tell me what the hell they look like. Are they planes?"

"You know they aren't. Right now, we're invisible to them. Radar is being absorbed and light's being bent around our fuselage. We're at an altitude of three meters."

"That's nine feet!"

"Very close."

"You can't fly at nine feet! How fast are you going?"

"Classified. I'll have you home in twenty minutes."

This thing went a hell of a lot faster than any three hundred miles an hour. In fact, it must have been going thousands of miles an hour, and practically at ground level.

He found himself feeling proud of it. What an incredible engineering achievement. The relationship with Aeon might not have worked out, but we had gained some technology, at least.

What else might there be, and how might it help him? He had so much trouble with travel, but he could fly anywhere in a thing like this. So why had it been withheld from him? He was fighting a war alone, and he needed all the help the government could put in his hands.

He thought of the birds singing out in that bloody field. He thought of how nice it would be back in the bath with Di, splashing in their big tub. He imagined himself floating, the stars flowing past . . . and then—what the hell? What in *hell* was he thinking?

The ship around him seemed vague, as if it was becoming insubstantial, disappearing. . . .

His ears popped, then his head seemed to crack. It was getting cold, very cold.

"We have a problem," he said.

"I know it. I don't know what's happening."

"I'm losing consciousness."

"It's ascending at a thousand klicks a minute; you're passing through twelve grand."

They were hijacking it. They'd take him up till he died. "Get the engine shut down."

"It might not restart."

"Do it now!"

The whirring that had filled the air abruptly stopped.

"It's descending," she said.

He could feel his head clearing. "Can you still maneuver?"

"Somewhat."

"Keep it pitching, rolling, turning, whatever you can do."

"Leaving twelve. You're crashing, you know that."

"Do as I say!"

It pitched sickeningly, then the nose went up, and it rolled, tossing Flynn round and round in the repair bay. The skin of the thing clattered like a tin roof in a hailstorm.

"Descent slowing."

"Can you reduce the helium lift?"

"It runs critical."

"Good, drop it."

Once again, the wind rose as the descent resumed. What was happening was that a disk somewhere overhead was drawing the TR upward. But every time its weight was changed, they had to adjust their tractor beam.

He threw open the access hatch. A patchwork of farmland spread below. "Where am I?"

"Maryland. That's Maryland."

"Get it on the ground."

"I can't put this down in some field!"

"Do it; we'll send a protective unit."

"Descent slowing."

"Drop lift! Get me down, goddamnit!"

"I'm trying. I'm going to reverse the motor—hold on!"

Overhead, the wire-covered cylinder shrieked, then spread a pink glow through the confined space. The ground began getting closer, then rushing up.

He would not survive this. "Slow it down!"

"I'm trying! It's not designed for this."

A stink of hot wiring spread through the fuselage. "We have a fire onboard," he said.

"I know it."

"There's flames appearing around the motor. Get me on the ground!"

"Descent arrested."

"Blow the helium."

"It'll crash—you'll be killed!"

"Blow it!"

There was a screaming hiss and the ground rushed up.

Blackness. So peaceful. He was floating, a man in a pool of dark water.

"Sir?"

He knew he needed to wake up.

"Sir!"

Fire was dancing along a dangerous road.

"Sir!"

What was he seeing? Hearing?

"Sir, it's moving; you need to jump!"

He saw a silver object slide into view. At first he was confused, then he understood that it was a roof—and not only that, but in another two seconds it would be too far down to jump to with any hope of survival.

He rolled out of the access hatch and felt himself dropping like a stone. Wind shrieked, then he hit the roof, which sagged, breaking his fall. Overhead, there was a bright white flash, then a rain of burned plastic ash began sliding down around him like gray snow.

She'd run a destruct program. Hadn't mentioned its existence, of course. Need to know. He moved to slide off the roof—which proceeded to give way. The next thing he knew, he was covered from head to foot in frantic chickens.

"What in hell, holy Christ, stop the line, stop the line!"

As he struggled to get out from under the clucking, scratching, flapping mass, he could hear machinery grinding down.

"Get outta there!" he heard a voice scream.

He saw why—just ahead was the black maw of an automated chicken slaughterer. He could hear its knives slashing, could smell the reek of chicken blood and hear the frenetic clucking as the massive, breast-heavy hens were drawn into its works.

It was slowing down, but the process was far from immediate. It became quickly clear that if he didn't get out of this thing, he was going to end up in a grocery store. The sides were high enough that the chickens couldn't flutter out, but not so high that he couldn't jump to his feet, balance himself on the uneasy rubber conveyor belt, and leap to the floor.

"Where in holy hell did you come from?"

Flynn thought fast. How could he explain himself in a way that would sound reasonable? "Skydiver," he said. "Sorry."

"Skydiver," the operator said scornfully. "You must be some kind of an idiot skydiving in country like this."

"Winds aloft. Not predicted. Blown off course. We were diving in Virginia."

"Yeah, yeah, whatever. Look, I gotta get the boys in here, get this operation running again."

"Could you call me a cab?"

"Call yourself a cab; there's a pay phone over by the dorm." He gestured toward a narrow door at the far end of the huge room. As Flynn walked, he inventoried himself. Nothing broken, no question there. He hadn't taken much of a hit, so no internal injuries. His pistols were still on his person. So he was intact, if you didn't mind a few feathers. Or rather, quite a few.

He brushed himself off as best he could and called the number of a taxi company scribbled onto a rain-weathered yellow pad that was hanging beside the ancient phone. There came an uneasy moment as he dug in his pocket, but he had just enough change, a dollar fifteen.

Behind him, the plant started up again, filling the air with its huge roar. He wondered what Aeon thought of what had just happened. They were in hot pursuit, and nothing seemed to throw them off. Would this have done it?

"Red Ranger."

"I need a cab."

"Where to?"

"Langley."

"Got it. You're where?"

"Big poultry plant. I just dropped in, I'm not sure of the address."

"No problem," the dispatcher said. "That'll be Peerless Chickens. Only poultry factory around here. We'll be out front in five."

The plant manager came running up. "Wait a second, here, I want some ID. I got a hell of a mess in there. Somebody's gotta pay."

"Of course." He gave him the Grauerholtz ID. It was tight, and he still had some of the credit cards in his wallet. And why not? From the moment they had gotten word of the Doxy murder to now, just six days had passed. He'd been in the White House for an overnight, then in Iran for two days, then traveling for a day, in the White House another night, and then last night this part of the program had commenced.

As he walked out through the office structure, the manager followed him. "You understand it's gonna be ten, twenty grand to pay for the damage you did."

"I'm sure."

"You don't seem to care."

"I don't."

"You must be pretty damn rich."

Flynn stopped. "I am. But I also have excellent accountants and lawyers. Overcharge me one red cent and I'll be down on you bastards like bird flu."

"Hey, I saved your life!"

"You did, and I thank you for it."

The cab was at the end of the walkway, sitting beside the enormous, weathered PEERLESS CHICKENS sign. Flynn walked up and got in.

"Wait!"

"No."

"Where's your chute? 'Cause if it's on the roof I don't want it blowin' in; it's gonna cause a major megillah, it gets sucked in."

"I left my chute in the plane."

The plant manager gaped.

Flynn closed the window and leaned forward. "CIA headquarters." As they pulled away, he watched the manager staring after him. Grauerholtz would get a nice, fat bill from the guy, probably double- or triple-padded. Fine. He had indeed saved Flynn's life. And what a way it would have been to go, the alien hunter himself, sliced into nuggets in a chicken factory.

CHAPTER TWENTY

DETAIL 242'S bullpen was humming with activity, but what they were all doing was a mystery to Flynn as he headed for Diana's office. By the time he reached her door, total silence had descended.

He went through into her outer office, then into the inner sanctum, where she was sitting with her father, Senator Glass; CIA director Boxleitner, and a thin, very pale man with powder-gray hair and, on his narrow lips, the gentlest of smiles. Flynn didn't know this man.

"Flynn!" Diana said. "At last."

The newcomer came to his feet. He extended his hand. "Flynn Carroll. I'm deeply grateful for all you do."

"Yeah, well, who are you, a tourist?" He turned to Diana, eyebrows raised. "Who is this?"

"We've been back to the White House. Their attitude has been revised."

"I need a bath," he said. "I'm covered in chicken shit." He strode into her private suite and started pulling off his clothes. She came in behind him. "That man is our supervisor. He and Boxy and my dad got with the president."

Originally, the detail had been attached to the FBI as a specialized policing unit. Last year, very quietly and without Flynn's being told a thing, that had changed. The fact that he wasn't need to know on the meaning of the change had been a constant irritant.

"So we're in the CIA chain of command now?"

"Not exactly. We rent this space from them."

"Then who does our supervisor report to?"

"He and I direct the operation."

"May I know his name?"

"You know that would compromise security. Flynn, may I ask why you smell like that? And the feathers?"

"Because Aeon caught up with that drone and I ended up in a chicken coop." He peeled off his undershirt. "They're running after me, all out. They're doing this because this thing is going down fast, and I'm an irritant."

He showered quickly, threw on some jeans and a pullover that he kept here, and returned to the outer office.

"Sorry about that," he said. He looked from face to face. "We're out of time, folks."

"We still haven't put it together completely," the nameless supervisor said in his quiet voice.

Flynn dropped into a chair. "Can you give me a name? What do I call you?"

He smiled. "What about I take over the Grauerholtz identity? It's about blown anyway. Call me Stephan."

"That ID is mine, and what if I need it? I'll name you if you won't."

"It's George. Now, you tell us what you've discovered. Brief us."

"OK, here it is. The missiles we tested did not contain hydrogen bombs. What they have done to those weapons I don't know, but they are not going to destroy infrastructure, they're going to destroy population."

"Like a neutron bomb?"

"So it would appear."

"How could they do that to hydrogen weapons?"

"Fascinating question. But whatever it is, they're doing it now. This is what all the flyovers of missile bases have been about. And when they're finished converting them all—at that second—they are going to trigger a nuclear paroxysm. Every converted warhead will be launched toward its target."

George leaned forward. "The result?"

"Obviously a huge number of people killed outright. Followed by social breakdown, infrastructure collapse, more dead. My guess is that they've got it figured out to the man. Once we're gone, they're going to show up in droves, turn the lights back on, and settle in."

"There will be people left," the senator said.

"A hundred million? Two hundred? They'll be hunted down. Aeon is very good at that, you have my word."

Diana jumped up and tore out of the room. Standing in the doorway to the bullpen, she said, "I want eyes worldwide on every known missile silo or launcher of any kind outside of the ones we've already looked at. Give me India, Pakistan, Iran, China, Israel—I want it all. I want a report on my screen detailing *all* bogey activity picked up around those sites for the past week, and I want it at once."

She came back and dashed through to her suite. A moment later, he heard gagging. She was tossing her cookies.

"I didn't understand the scope," she said hoarsely as she came out. "I thought—"

"Look at the world stock of nuclear warheads as a single gigantic neutron bomb. The only question left is, what's the fuse? And I think we have our answer. Bill Greene is the fuse."

Senator Glass said, "How do we fix this?"

"I hate to say it," George said, "but we need to neutralize Bill."

"That was my initial thought," Flynn replied. "But think about it. Aeon will go to Plan B and we'll once again be in the dark about what's happening. As things stand now, we know their plan. They're going to cause Bill to launch Minuteman, probably our undersea nuclear force as well. This will result in an all-out Russian response. They'll hit Britain, too, so the British will launch. I assume the rest of the nuclear powers will get pulled in, too."

A map came up on Diana's monitor, covering the east from Pakistan to China, with all of its 480 known missile sites showing as pulsating red dots. There were white dots near three quarters of them.

"That's a live feed?"

"Those white dots are reported unidentified objects. This means that they're finishing up the last few warheads. When those bogeys pull out, they're going to make their move."

"We need to figure out what to do about Bill," Boxleitner said.

"I think they're pulling out right now," Flynn replied. "Fewer every minute."

"Oh, Christ."

George stood up. "I'm too old for this." He looked toward Flynn. "I trust you'll get it sorted out."

With that, he left. "That man has confidence in you, Flynn," Senator Glass said.

"I hope he's not a damn fool," Flynn replied.

Diana said, "We need to move."

"I have another challenge for you, love. Getting me to the White House alive. That's what we need to concentrate on right now."

She reached toward him, touched his hand. "'Love,'" she said, "don't say that to me unless you mean it."

In that instant, he realized that Abby was now, finally and absolutely, part of the past. Diana, all five foot nine of her, the dark hair, the bright, hopeful eyes, the loveliness of her and the sense of loss that clung to her—she was here, now. She was real.

He said again, "Love."

For a moment, she was silent, but only for a moment. "We've got to do this now." She strode out into the bullpen, Flynn behind her.

Boxleitner and Glass followed. "What's going on?"

Flynn turned to them. "We're heading for the White House. We need to make certain that Greene is unable to do anything rash."

"By what means?"

"By whatever means, Senator. Of course, we want to avoid assassination. That's a last resort, but it's going to stay on the table."

Boxleitner said, "I don't see why you'd be safe going to Washington. Or anywhere."

"We can't do this on the phone, obviously."

"No." But the DCIA was right. How would they get to the White House alive? But then he thought, how had he gotten here safely, and why hadn't they just blown hell out of the place and been done with him?

At some point, after the destruction of the TR, they had changed their approach. They had backed off hunting him down—but why?

When it hit him—when he truly understood—his guts gave an enormous, sickening heave. He said, "Car's fine; we'll make it. Let's go."

"*Car?* Are you nuts?"

"We'll make it."

"*Flynn!*"

He was halfway down the hall before he heard her running behind him. "Oh, God, Flynn, please let's do the bus-and-train thing. We can take the Cheverly Line, I know how to do it, we'll be at the White House before six."

"We'll take my car. You'll need the Highway Patrol to clear us in."

"What? What are you saying? Your car's gonna be loaded with tracking. Talk about a death trap."

"They want us in Washington."

"*Why?*"

"So they can be certain we're spinning our wheels while they do this thing."

"I'm lost."

"Trust me."

They went along empty corridors to the underground garage where specialized vehicles and those requiring high security were kept.

When they arrived at the guard post, it became necessary to check the car out. They weren't on the guard's list, so he was very careful and very slow. Flynn was tempted to just hit the gas and breach the barrier, but he didn't need the hassle.

"Get us rolling," he said to Diana.

She got out, leaned into the guardhouse, then returned to the car.

The barrier went up.

"What did you do?"

"Scared him to death."

As they pulled out toward the parkway, she got on the phone and ordered up a Highway Patrol escort.

This had to look to Aeon's agents exactly as they expected it to look or they'd kill Flynn in an instant. They were conservative; they would always err on the side of safety. They possessed spectacular predictive algorithms, though, and had probably gamed his every move, right down to the moment he would fail.

She twisted in her seat, tried to look up, then opened the moon roof.

"No."

"We need to watch for disks!"

"They're going to let us through."

"You keep saying that, but why?"

"They've misled themselves."

A trooper car pulled past them and switched on its light bar and siren. The traffic ahead melted as they accelerated through a hundred miles an hour. As they headed into the city, Diana worked the phone.

They were pulling up to the private gate when she said, "It's a no."

"Shit."

"Lorna."

"Give me the phone."

"Flynn, Lorna's not gonna even talk to you." She handed him her iPhone. There was no reason to use a secure instrument, not when the other end was substandard, and Lorna wasn't going to be making any effort to secure the call.

He called Cissy. "Where are you?"

"Flynn, where are *you*? We need you!"

"At the gate. Lorna won't let us in."

"She's a fool! Boxy and that weird guy were here with Senator Glass. Daddy's not doubting you now."

"Can you get us in?"

"I don't know, I can try."

He returned the phone to Diana.

"What did she say?"

"She's gonna try."

"So we wait."

"Yep."

"What do we do if we get in? What do we say?"

"Tell Lorna that she needs to believe Boxleitner and your dad."

"Why doesn't she already? That's what's so strange."

Diana's cell phone vibrated. "Yes?" She listened. "OK, got it." She said to Flynn, "Cissy's waiting for us at the West Wing Entrance. The marine on guard at the moment is a friend of hers."

The gate began to open. Whatever Cissy had done, it had obviously involved getting the perimeter guard to stand down as they drove in. He swung around to the West Wing Entrance. Cissy was there, standing with the marine guard, sharing a smoke.

Flynn and Diana got out of the Audi.

"Hey," Cissy said to Flynn. Then, with just a shade of curtness, "Hello, Diana."

They followed her into the empty lobby, then through to the outdoor colonnade and into the Residence. They were stopped by a Secret Service officer stationed at the entrance. Flynn had not seen him before. He wore the usual dark suit. He was trim and muscular. He said nothing, but he scrutinized Flynn and Diana with a professional eye. He hadn't been on duty when Flynn was here previously, so there was no sign of recognition.

"They're friends of mine, Henry," Cissy said. "We're gonna play some bridge."

"Three-handed?"

"Ginny will join us."

He stood silently regarding them. He wasn't going to let them pass, not just yet. "I'm sorry," he said, "but I need ID."

"On my friends? Since when?"

"Since these are friends I'm not recognizing."

Was Flynn looking at a biorobot here? Was this trim and polished thirty-something actually Aeon? He had lost his temperature sensor in his fall.

Flynn went for the Grauerholtz ID. Thankfully, it hadn't been taken from him.

"These are my friends, Henry. We don't do this with my friends."

"They're not in the book. There's no prep."

"They are my damn *friends,* Henry, come on!"

"No, it doesn't matter, Cissy," Flynn said as he held out the passport.

That was enough for Henry, and he let the three of them pass.

Once they were in Cissy's room and the door was closed and locked, Cissy faced Flynn with shattered eyes. "Where the hell have you been?"

"Busy. Problems that couldn't wait."

"The only problem that can't wait is right here in this building. Daddy's in the Lincoln going slowly crazy and Mom's full of pills."

"What were they told?"

"That you and Di should never have been thrown out."

"Any details beyond that? Were you there?"

"I was there. They were told that Aeon is real and it's dangerous. Then we got the switchboard to look for you, Flynn. You're unfindable! Not even Boxy could find you." She turned to Diana. "Did you know where he was?"

"I knew why he was out of communication. But he's here now."

"What's the lay of the land, Cissy? Your mom's on pills and your dad's haunting the Lincoln because?"

"They know something's wrong. Horribly, horribly wrong! And they don't understand and it's driving them crazy."

"I can understand that."

"Can you? To be the most powerful man in the world and know something horrific is going down but not know what? Can you even begin to imagine what that would be like? Billions of lives might be in your hands and you have no idea what to do. That's stress, Flynn, and you belong right here because you might be able to help. You actually might."

"Look, I've known Bill for a while, at least from a distance. I have to ask: Is he drunk?"

"Not yet."

"Does he have the football?"

She nodded.

He got up and left the room. She came right after him. "Where do you think you're going?"

"Bill's got the football. That's where I'm going."

"Wait a second. Am I understanding you that you're concerned because he has it? You don't think he'd do anything with it?"

"I don't know."

She blocked his way. "I said he was going crazy with worry. He's not insane, Flynn."

"He's alone with it and apparently very scared, so I need to get in there."

Shaking her head, she stood aside. "I don't know what came over me. Of course you do."

"What came over you was the fact that you're no longer just the daughter of Wild Bill Greene. You're the daughter of the President of the United States."

The three of them went down to the Lincoln Bedroom.

A Secret Service agent stood at the door. "I'm sorry," he said, raising an arm to block their passage.

"Dave, don't do this."

"Miss Greene—"

"Stand aside."

"I can't do that."

"Look, these are friends from Texas. They've known him since college."

"Our orders come directly from him."

Flynn didn't want to incapacitate this man, but time was not on their side. "We'll have to go in," he said.

The man was now stone, staring fixedly. It was a rough situation for him, and he obviously wanted to be just about anywhere else. Something like this could easily break a Secret Service career.

Flynn said gently, "You didn't get an order, you got a request, am I right?"

"The president doesn't give orders. He doesn't have to."

"Right now, he needs help, and it's your duty to help him. We're help."

The agent raised a finger to his earpiece. He was going to take this up the ladder.

"No," Flynn said. "We need to be in there right now."

The finger hesitated.

"We've been friends for years. That's why Cissy here called us. When Bill gets into a state like this, he needs support. He's got a really rough decision to make and he's having trouble. That's why he's closed himself off in there. If we don't intervene, he'll start hitting the bottle. You don't want to get your ass blamed for letting that happen."

The tightly constructed young face had gone pale.

"You can't prevent his daughter from seeing him."

Slowly, the hand came away from the earpiece. He stood aside.

The room was dark, even the faint light from outside shut away by heavy curtains. The familiar Lincoln Bed that Lincoln hadn't actually slept in appeared to be empty.

There came a voice from across the room. "Flynn?"

"Bill?"

"Close the door."

Cissy shut it and locked it.

"Where in hell have you been?"

"At Malmstrom."

"Kill anybody?"

"I think you know what I did. I think you've gotten a briefing and you're getting some things figured out."

"You're very damn good at killing. It's what you do, I mean. Professionally. Back at UT, I always saw you as a wimp. You and that pretty girl you were running after with your tongue on the ground. Whatever happened to her?"

"We got married."

"All the best, Mr. Murderer. Is that why you're here? Boxy sent you because I'm unstable? Incompetent? I got elected by the American people, fella. Boxy and Glass and that odd creep came over this afternoon. Told me I needed to listen to you."

Flynn said carefully, "I don't kill people."

Bill got up from the chair where he'd been sitting. Flynn saw the football beside it.

"I've been doing some snooping," he said as he came toward Flynn. "The kind of thing I can do only when Lorna's not peering over my shoulder." He laughed, a sinister sound. "She's not right in the head, you know. What we used to call them—inverts? She's like Eleanor Roosevelt, with a girl in there warming her bed at night. I guess it's a tradition in the White House, am I right? Call it the sexual intensity of the place. Power makes the juices run." He glanced back at the football. "They're after me, Flynn. The tiger is in the tall grass. My own people don't think I can do this." He went over and picked up the football. "They think I can't captain this ship, but they're wrong. Did you know that the Soviets have a sub in the English Channel right now? Why is that there? You know that the bastard Chinks have two more off the West Coast? Again, I ask why? You could fire a missile off one of those things and in three minutes, L.A. is done. Three minutes, Flynn!"

Diana's secure phone buzzed. She held it to her ear.

"Dad," Cissy said, "there are no Soviets. It's the Russian Federation."

"Same damn difference. So what do the saucer people think, Flynn?"

"Aeon is extremely dangerous, Bill. I'm glad you've been made aware of that." Greene had to be gotten out of here right now, and secretly, and taken to a surgical facility to be scanned. If brain surgery was called for, then that had to be done, too. Tonight. Right now.

Diana said, "Just got word in that the incursions have ceased. Not a one in the past fifteen minutes, anywhere in the world."

"Di, how do we move the President of the United States without the Secret Service interfering?"

"Move me? Goddamnit, I'm not a piece of furniture!"

Flynn decided to try the straightforward approach. "We need an MRI. We need surgeons standing by. But not in a place where you'd be expected."

"Am I supposed to understand this?"

"Trust us, Bill," Diana said.

"Come on, Bill, we need to get this done."

He drew back. "Come on? Come where?" He held the football to his chest, both arms clutching it tightly.

"You need medical attention."

He put the football down. The desperation in his eyes was terrible to see—raw, stricken, roiling with panic. "They come in my dreams," he said. "It's Moscow; the bastards have done something to me, the Commie shits!"

"Dad, there is no Soviet Union!"

Slowly, his lips peeling back away from his teeth like an uneasy dog's, he went to his daughter and put his arm around her shoulder. "You let me live and I'll go quietly. I ain't no president, Flynn." He shook his head. "I have absolutely no damn idea about anything."

"We need to go, Mr. President."

"Don't call me that!"

Diana said, "The Chrysler's at the private entrance."

"Secret Service?"

"They've been told you're headed for a drunk farm in Virginia."

"You have a MRI facility ready?"

Diana nodded.

Would they ever be able to accomplish this under all the watching eyes—the Secret Service; foreign powers with various agendas; Iranian intelligence, which still had murderous agents running free in Washington; and, above all, Aeon? His conflicts with the aliens had always been a chess match, but never one this difficult. Then again, in the end, it had always come down to a physical confrontation, and he had always won that part of the battle. But so far this time he had not once had the opportunity to resolve anything important with weapons. And it was too bad, because Bill was right: He was a killer. It's what he did well.

Bill was also right about another thing. When he'd said, "I don't want to hear any spy bullshit, it mixes me up," he had been dead-on.

They headed down the Grand Staircase, toward the main entrance where the car waited.

"I still don't understand this. Why are we in motion?"

"Bill, we're going to resolve this," Diana said.

"Is this it? Am I going to be taken to some garage and shot like a gangster?"

Cissy took his hand.

Flynn said, "I will not hurt you, and I will immediately kill anybody who tries."

They reached the bottom of the stair. Flynn could see the car waiting outside, its black surface gleaming.

"How dare you!"

Lorna's voice echoed through the silence, stopping everybody. She stood on the staircase. Her heels clicked on the steps like gunshots as she came down. She wasn't steady, and Flynn saw that her pupils were dilated. Lorna was indeed stoned, which was a real surprise, and a mystery.

She went up to Bill. "Just where do you think you're going, out to scratch for a whore?"

"Mother!"

"And you, you whore." She shot an ugly look at Flynn. "This dog's beneath your station, Cissy. Is that why you want him to fuck you?"

Cissy walked up to her, positioned herself carefully, and slapped her mother so hard it sounded like a firework exploding. Lorna gasped, then choked out a cry. Her hands clawed at her reddening cheek. Then her face collapsed and she went to her knees before her daughter and threw her arms around her waist.

"Ciss, baby, forgive me. Forgive your mother." Her eyes shifted to Flynn, and he was shocked to see the sorrow in them, and the devastated emptiness of a defeated human being. "You. You're a good man," she moaned. While Cissy held her mother's head against her waist, Lorna reached toward Diana. "You stay with this man, and you two will drink of the water and the wine."

Flynn knew that it was time to take charge. Above all, he had to keep them on mission. He lifted Lorna to her feet. "I'll need you to come with us."

She nodded, her head bowed, her face hidden behind her fallen hair.

Secret Service agents opened the doors of the car as they approached. Ahead and behind, there were black SUVs.

Flynn went around to the driver's side of the Chrysler and said to the agent behind the wheel, "Out."

When the agent looked up at him, he recognized Flynn at once. "You're that weird guy, the alphabet spook."

"Which is why you need to follow my orders. Out of the car and the escort stands down."

"No can do."

Flynn raised his voice. "OK, guys, go through the formalities—you can't let us just leave without an escort, that's out. You can never allow that. But now you have to. I'm ordering you to stand down. Get the lead car out of the way, and do *not* follow, not even at a distance, not if you value this president's life."

Another agent came running around the corner of the building, an older guy. He looked like he was wearing a tractor tire under his tentlike suit jacket. Flynn recognized Simon Forde.

"Director! Good to see you again."

"What in holy hell is going on?"

"The president's being taken to an undisclosed location in the hope of saving his life."

"*What?*"

"Sir, I'm sorry, but you have to remain out of the loop."

"Out of the loop? Are you nuts? The President of the United States doesn't go anywhere without us. Not anywhere, sir!"

There was only one person who could stand them down. "Bill—"

"Yeah, boys, there's big dutch. Big. You stay at home." He nodded toward Flynn. "This guy—he's all I need, believe me. He's a real-life Superman."

Flynn could have cursed him to hear that. He was just as vulnerable and scared as anybody, and he had to live on the front line. But at least one thing was going in his favor right now. As long as he had the president, the president couldn't activate the football.

Aeon would know this. How long would they wait?

Forde looked into Flynn's face. It seemed a long way up. "If you get him hurt—so much as a hair on his head—or her, or that beautiful young daughter of theirs, I swear to you that I will personally see to it that you get the needle. Do you understand me?"

Flynn stared back into the desperately frightened eyes. "He's safer with me than anywhere else on the planet." And he thought, "Oh God, if only that were true."

They got in the car, Flynn driving, Bill beside him. Diana and Cissy kept Lorna, who was crying unashamedly, between them in the backseat.

As they set off, Flynn thought that this was one vehicle Aeon would not disturb, not with Bill Greene in it. But what if the implant was found and removed, and Bill came to his senses? What then?

"Where's the football?" Bill asked.

Flynn had not wanted it anywhere near them. "You can bet that the Secret Service will be following at a distance. They'll get it and bring it."

"They'd better."

The bitter finality of the president's tone worried Flynn. He had plans for the thing, that seemed obvious.

He drove on, glancing behind him from time to time, looking for tails. Soon enough, the Secret Service was there. They have two responsibilities. The first is to protect the president. The second is to obey his orders. If one contradicts the other, protection always wins.

Flynn wished that the nuclear triggering system was buried somewhere, locked away, destroyed. Anything to keep it far away from Bill Greene, and from Aeon.

CHAPTER TWENTY-ONE

THE UNITED States is a secret society with an open society floating on its surface like uneasy sea foam on a mysterious deep. The surface country, with its noisy press, its raging Internet, and its fickle, confused population, is controlled by the deep, hidden currents that are the actual power of the state.

Maybe Flynn Carroll could not have put this into so many words, but he understood it in his blood and bone, so when they arrived at the "hospital" that Diana had chosen for the MRI scans, he was not too surprised to find a dark, nondescript storefront in a Bethesda strip mall on the outside, and a glittering, multimillion-dollar diagnostic center behind the worn old doors.

It was to places like this that the very wealthy and the very powerful came for treatment, and why a rich person in America who is part of the inner circle has a life expectancy far longer than average.

As they pulled into a parking spot in front of the karate studio next door, the First Family was unsurprised. Officially, the president is treated at Walter Reed, but if he needs a tumor neutralized or his heart rebuilt, it is to a nameless, superexclusive place like this that he will come.

To all appearances, an ordinary Chrysler 300 pulled up and took a parking space. Some kids came out of karate with their parents and went off down the sidewalk toward a yogurt store. It had rained earlier, and the sidewalk gleamed. The air was touched by the sweetness and fires of autumn. Off in the dark there were storms, and leaves were racing. Flynn caught himself wondering if other beings might soon enter this place and marvel at the wealth of diagnostics here, and ask themselves if they would ever figure out all human secrets, or comprehend the meaning of mankind.

Inside, they were met by a doctor, late middle age, in a Savile Row suit. That and the watch told Flynn he was wearing an easy twenty-five thousand dollars. Money didn't mean a thing to Flynn. He had more of it than Bill Greene or the doctor or anybody he might meet. He didn't know how much, but probably well into the nine figures, maybe dancing around ten. In an expensive month, he spent ten grand. Mostly, it was a lot less. He kept his extensive charities to himself.

"We're ready," the doctor said.

They proceeded down a short hallway to a radiology unit. Inside the expansive space, Flynn could see three different MRI scanners, a PET scanner, a CT scanner, and other diagnostic equipment, all of it the newest and the best.

"Let's get you going, Bill," Flynn said.

"First, you tell me what happens if they find something."

"If it's possible to remove it safely, we do that."

"And if not?"

"We've never had any trouble. I've had two pulled. Di's had one."

They moved deeper into the facility. Unlike a hospital, it was entirely staffed with specialists. When there's unlimited money, there are also unlimited resources.

Bill was scared. Flynn could see that by his stiff, almost marching walk. Lorna, full of pills, seemed mostly interested in her distorted reflections on the looming machines all around them. Cissy's shoulders were hunched. She was deep inside herself, and Flynn knew why. If her dad was implanted, there would be an extraction, even if it was in a dangerous region of the brain. They would cure the patient, even if the patient died.

"You know," Bill said, "you put a beer in my hand and you give me a good joke to tell, and I'm doing what I was born to do. You give me these history books to read, and I get all those facts in my head but they don't stick. Close the book, and I can't tell Julius Caesar from Big Julie." He shook his head. "If this thing is in me and you can't get it out, you're gonna kill my ass, aren't you, Flynn?"

"Sir, we're ready."

"You are, damn you. I remember you back at UT. You know what people called you? The Shadow. Remember the Shadow?"

"I do not."

"'Who knows what evil lurks in the hearts of men? The Shadow knows!'" That's you, Flynn—you're the Shadow, and you will kill me as easily as you'd step on a cockroach."

"I wouldn't step on a cockroach. He's no threat to me."

"We're ready."

"Daddy, get it over with!"

"OK! Jesus!"

When Bill was lying on the narrow pallet and was about to be rolled into the scanner, Flynn noticed that he had closed his eyes, and that there were gleams at their edges. This greedy, wrongheaded, and ill-informed man was face-to-face with the devastating power of the presidency. The lives and safety of a whole world lay in his hands, and he was nothing more than a good man with a beer and a joke. At least he knew it.

So if his life had to be taken here, maybe his last thought would be "I understand."

He was deep in the scanner now, and Flynn went into the control room to watch. Lorna and Cissy sat in the back, both of them now hunched into themselves, silenced by the terror of the situation.

The scanner began recording slices of the president's brain. Flynn watched as, pass by pass, the images went deeper and deeper. He had studied brain anatomy obsessively, seeking to understand how the subtle, almost nonexistent electrical currents emitted by the implants could change thought. Through all of this there had emerged an understanding that the claustrum was the key. If a host could be physically approached, the implant would be guided into the white matter next to it. Aeon could do this without opening the skin, but the ones we implanted were inserted surgically. Implants in this position could not be removed, and it was in order to get at one of them that the Iranians had killed Albert Doxy.

Flynn was so concentrated on the imaging process that he did not instantly realize that the room was filling with people. A split second later, though, he did notice. He whirled in his chair and leaped to his feet, gun braced for action.

He found himself confronting ribbon-heavy generals, Roland Boxleitner, Director Forde, and the senator. With them were four Secret Service agents.

Forde said, "Put the gun down, Flynn."

Flynn did not move. He knew that he could probably take all four agents before they'd gotten off a shot, but the consequences would be too unpredictable.

"Mr. Carroll," Boxleitner said, "you're way off the reservation. We need you to put the gun down. You are no longer in charge here."

Flynn noticed that there was another agent lingering in the hallway. He had the football.

The gun didn't move.

One of the generals spoke. "Iran fired a Sajjil-2 missile at Israel ten minutes ago. You have to table whatever this is. The president is urgently needed."

Once again, Flynn's world lurched. What had been hours, even days, might now be only minutes. He stowed the weapon.

Aeon had outsmarted him. The football didn't matter at all. Greene wasn't the target. They had tricked the ayatollahs into triggering the war.

"Nobody's faulting you, Flynn," Forde said. "We know you're doing your duty as you see it."

"Did it reach its target?"

"It was destroyed. The Israelis have a system called Speed Wind that can intercept missiles while they're still ascending. It worked. But now they're preparing a launch, and the Iranians have no such system."

With a series of thuds, the scanner powered down. Flynn backed up, but did not take his eyes off the group. He said to the tech, "What's the story?"

"Normal brain. Nothing wrong."

Flynn took a deep, ragged breath. Another.

Diana came to him.

He looked at the stricken confusion in her expression and thought that this was the end, the last night of the human world.

Bill Greene came out of the MRI scanner. He looked from face to face, blinking when he saw the crowd. "Jesus, guys, don't tell me World War Three has broken out."

"Sir," air force chief of staff McArdle said, "I'm afraid it has."

"We need to act," Lorna said.

"Somebody fill me in."

"In the car," she said. "We've got to get back to the White House. You need to be in the Situation Room."

"Iran fired a missile at Israel," Boxleitner said.

"Did it hit?"

"It was destroyed as it was ascending. But now Israel is preparing to retaliate."

Senator Glass said, "According to their war plan, they'll raise a flight of eight missiles, all MIRVed. They will drop sixty-four hydrogen bombs on Iran's cities and critical military areas. Our analysis of their plan shows that Iran will cease to exist as a nation, and residual radiation will mean that it will not be restored in the foreseeable future."

"The Russians?" the president barked.

Boxleitner said, "They are on a war warning right now."

Bill locked eyes with Lorna, and Flynn thought he had never seen such hate as there was between them. Ice and knives.

Then it hit him, a slamming wave: It was Lorna who belonged to Aeon. Not Bill at all, but her—she was implanted, and her task was to make certain that, at some point, the U.S. launched against Russia.

Lorna said, "Don't just stand there—you need to get back and call Netanyahu. You need to reassure Putin. You need to warn the Iranians that if they don't run all of their missiles out and destroy them forthwith, their country will cease to exist." She tossed her hair out of her face. She looked around. "Where's the football?"

Simon Forde said, "We have it, ma'am."

"I want it in sight at all times."

"Yes, ma'am."

The entourage started for the door. "Boxy," she said to the DCIA, "we need to know at once if the Russians start configuring for launch."

"We're right on top of that."

Diana and Flynn stood watching them go, a thunder of footfalls in the brilliantly lit corridor.

They had been left behind. No longer needed. Their job descriptions did not include managing a nuclear conflict.

"It's like the trains in World War One," Diana said. "Once the Russians started mobilizing, the Germans had to start. When they started, the French had to start. Then came the end of the old world."

Flynn said, "We have to get into that Situation Room. They need us there."

His mouth was so dry that he could hardly speak above a whisper. So far, he'd won every battle he'd ever fought with Aeon. But this was not a battle, this was the war, and it turned out that he was hardly even a player.

Flynn saw only one way to do what needed to be done, and it needed to be carried out immediately. Lorna had to go, and he had to do it, and fast. But how?

There was a way—possibly. When he'd heard from Morris that some sort of amplifier would be needed to activate the implant, he'd looked for and found alternate means of entry to the White House. He'd dismissed the tunnels he'd found, though. Old and disused; they might or might not even be intact.

He and Diana watched the convoy disappear down the street, heading for the Beltway.

"Looks like the parade's gone by," she said.

"I need to be there."

"This is out of our hands."

He whirled toward her. For an instant, his whole body shuddered with rage. Then he stifled it. In as even a voice as he could muster, he said, "It's her. It's Lorna."

"It's the Iranians!"

"They're just the trigger. Tricked into it by Aeon because they're naive and ambitious. What Aeon needs now is escalation, and that is to be provided by Lorna Greene."

"But you don't know. You can't be certain."

"I'm certain."

"You were certain about Bill! What if it's Putin? Ever consider that?"

"It's Lorna."

The Russian system worked differently from the American. In the U.S. system, it was possible for there to be direct communication between the president and the missile command centers. Thus the football. Officially, a second person had to approve the transmission of a fire order, but in fact it could be done by just the president.

The Russians had a different system. Putin would have to transmit an order to a group of commanding generals, who would in turn transmit it to the missile command centers, where it would be sent to each individual site. It was their version of fail-safe, and it meant that an attack order from Moscow, in the absence of any sign of incoming missiles, was going to be questioned—briefly, to be sure, but questioned.

Aeon would not take a chance like that.

He was about to try to orchestrate the single most dangerous gamble in human history. Even if it worked, millions might die. But if it didn't—well, he did not dwell on a possibility so terrifying that it made it hard to do the kind of calm, logical thinking that success depended on.

They still had the Chrysler—he had been careful to keep the keys—and they headed back toward Washington. He no longer had any idea how much time they had, but he thought it must be less than an hour, and maybe only minutes. He accelerated to and through the speed limit.

"Don't go so fast."

"We need to get there as fast as possible."

"How can we even get in? We're not need to know on this in any way."

"I've been working on that." If the tunnels were intact, he thought he would probably find them guarded by some ferocious biorobots, but he didn't tell her that. Why worry her—there was nothing she could do, and he was not about to allow her to stay with him on a mission this dangerous.

She leaned toward the driver's side. "How fast are you going now?"

"It doesn't matter," he said. But it did. It mattered a lot. He needed to get stopped by a cop, or he would be stopped by Aeon.

"If you get pulled over, I'm not sure I can help."

He had to pass the convoy.

"You're going a hundred and thirty!"

"This is a presidential car."

"So what—slow down!"

At last he saw the convoy, moving discreetly along, showing no flashing lights, protecting its occupants with anonymity. To avoid being too noticeable, he passed it at about seventy. But as soon as it was out of sight, he accelerated again, once again going up to crazy speeds.

They were bound to be stopped shortly. Had better be.

His mind was a red agony. He'd been skillfully played. He'd never understood their plan, and now it was probably too late. An hour more was generous. The missiles could be rising right now.

They came into some traffic, and soon were doing forty, then thirty.

"Oh, God," she whispered. She knew the stakes just as well as he did.

The research he had done on the Washington underground would now either pay off or it wouldn't. He said, "I'm going to ditch the car in Dupont Circle and go down."

"That old trolley underpass? It doesn't lead anywhere."

"It does." There were tunnels under Embassy Row that the intelligence agencies used to set up listening devices and carry out embassy penetrations. There were tunnels between the White House and the Capitol, the Pentagon and the State Department. And these were just the new ones. There were much older tunnels, some of them predating the city, and these were the ones that Flynn had researched and that he would use.

There was one in particular that interested him. It came up right under the foundations of the White House and had a spur so deep that it was impossible to trace. Probably an early attempt to provide the building with running water, or perhaps it was an escape tunnel. After the War of 1812, a number of them had been built.

Finally, they broke out of the traffic and he floored it. The powerful car surged ahead. They were maybe ten minutes out. They went on this way for three, for five minutes, snaking through a blur of slower traffic.

A trooper pulled in behind them.

"Now you've done it, Flynn, damn you!"

He stopped on the shoulder, the Virginia State Police car close behind, its light bar flashing. The trooper got out and approached the car. Flynn slid the window down.

"License and registration, please."

"This is a stolen vehicle."

"Excuse me?"

"It's stolen. It belongs to the President of the United States and we stole it."

"Flynn, have you gone nuts?"

"Sir, you'll need to get out of the car."

Flynn opened the door and stepped out. With a quick, hard fist to the temple, he dropped the trooper. He caught him and slid him into the driver's seat.

"What in hell?"

He got into the police vehicle and killed the light bar, then started to pull out into traffic. He wasn't fast enough, though, and Diana opened the passenger door and got in before he could get onto the highway.

"What in hell is this about?"

He turned on the bar and siren, and this time when he put it up over a hundred, all he had to worry about was an occasional squawk from the radio, which he answered as briefly and noncommittally as he could.

They'd figure it out in about three minutes, he thought, but by then he would already be crossing the Anacostia Bridge.

"Flynn, please help me here. I need to know what's happening."

"What's happening is that I'm penetrating the White House without Aeon realizing it. Their eyes are still on the Chrysler. I hope."

Dupont Circle was bustling, people hurrying in the fresh breeze of autumn. As always, he especially noticed the children. Massive neutron radiation renders bodies sterile. They dry up without rotting. The great cities of the world would become a vast ocean of mummies: babies frozen in their strollers, rats in their trees, men and women and children in every posture that one could imagine, all slowly turning to dust.

He pulled into a tow-away zone and got out of the car. Diana came with him. He blocked her with his arm.

"You need somebody on your back, Flynn."

"No."

"Flynn, if you die—I don't even want to think about it. You can't blow this thing."

He turned to her—*on* her—and drew her for a moment into his arms. Her softness, her warmth—she just felt so damn, damn good. He released her.

"Don't try to follow," he said. He stepped away, moving rapidly toward the nearest opening to the old trolley tunnels. These openings were spread around the circle, almost completely unknown to the modern city. There was a group trying to turn them into an underground mall, and there were tours, but for the most part they were abandoned. The system they concealed was simple enough. Back when Washington had street rail, the tunnels had been used to pass under Dupont Circle traffic. When the trolley system had been abandoned, so had the tunnels.

So that the various groups concerned could enter easily, there was a false lock on this hatch. With a twist to the right, it could be lifted away. When it was closed the mechanism would fall back into place, and it would appear that the hatch was securely padlocked. Unless you knew just how to open it, there was no way to use it.

He drew the lock aside and lifted the heavy iron hatch. Entering, he pulled the hatch back down. From this side, you could slide the lock back into position with an iron bar. He listened as it clanked down.

Diana would be trying to stay with him, he knew, but now she could not succeed. Even if she realized where he'd gone, it would take her hours to find out how to get in. By the time that happened, if it did, this would all be over. In fact, it might already be over.

He carried an LED flashlight, a hacksaw, a small light-amplifying monocle, and his guns. Two reloads, for a total of eighteen bullets. Too bad he had no plastique but there hadn't been an opportunity to acquire any. He had a feeling that it would be useful.

There was a spiral staircase, iron and black with age, which shook on its core as he thundered down.

This was the original trolley tunnel, still with its inset tracks between the platforms. He played his light briefly around the space, which was surprisingly clean and intact; it looked as if a trolley might come rumbling by at any moment. He had no time to waste, and trotted quickly down the tracks, curving around to the next station. As he ran, he counted the long, narrow drainage openings that were inset at intervals along the track. When he reached the fourth one, he stopped.

Below it was the next tunnel he must take. This one was not on new maps. Who had built it was unknown. The earliest map he had found it noted on was from 1736, before the city even existed. What purpose it had served back then was a complete mystery. It had been integrated into the trolley tunnel's drainage system by its modern builders. To enter, you had to know exactly which of many identical openings led to it, and you had to have considerable courage, because you weren't going to be coming back the same way you'd gone in.

He lay flat against the opening and worked his way in. Here the darkness was total, no faint light from overhead vents. He let himself down to the surface, which was damp and slick. He could no longer use the flashlight—too dangerous. The electronics in the monocle worried him, too, but his decision was that it would be the lesser of two evils. In darkness this total, the eye could not adapt.

Ahead, he saw the long, beautifully mortised stonework of the gently arched tunnel. Was it only a water tunnel? Seeing it up close, he thought not. How had such sophisticated engineering been accomplished so long ago? Above all, why was it that it ended directly under the White House? What had the Founding Fathers, steeped as they were in esoteric secrets, known about the godforsaken swamp where they had chosen to locate their capital?

He peered ahead into the faint blue of the amplified light. The monocle could be enhanced with the use of infrared, but that would make him even more visible. The problem was that there was so little light to amplify that he could barely see even with the monocle. The flitting shadows that he needed to see might not show up. He could be ambushed—there was no question in his mind about that.

He listened. With infinite care, he smelled the air. Nothing but wet, cold darkness.

He could not waste time, not another moment. He had to plunge ahead, to run.

The sense of menace that surrounded him was very powerful. Instinct told him that danger was close, but it could not stop him, nor even slow him down. He charged on, running flat out into the absolute dark.

CHAPTER TWENTY-TWO

THERE WERE strange symbols on the walls, intersecting triangles and other, darker forms, flowing serpents and long, thin hands. Dominating them all, etched into the surface by an expert stonemason, was the pyramid and all-seeing eye that appears on the dollar bill.

Ahead was a hatch with a wheel in it that looked as if it belonged in a submarine. If he was right about the distance, he was directly under the subbasement of the residence. It still contained air-conditioning and dishwashing equipment, but also, now, some of the new command and control systems for the Presidential Emergency Operations Center under the East Wing. Judging from the blueprints he had seen, there was enough room in the large cable conduits for him to pass through into the communications center just adjacent to the PEOC. The president, the members of the National Security Council, and the Joint Chiefs would be in the PEOC, which was secure against all attacks save a direct hit from a nuclear warhead. Flynn didn't know if they would survive the searing wave of neutrons that would be emitted over Washington. If they did, they would wish they hadn't. That he did know.

The hatch was stuck. He threw his weight into it, dangling from it and pushing his feet against the wall of the tunnel.

Two spit-and-polish marines appeared, running up from the depths of the tunnel. Their eyes glittered like metal, a sign of stress in Aeon's biological robots.

Flynn fired and hit both of them, but they kept coming, seemingly indifferent to the bleeding craters in their chests. He'd killed many biorobots over the years, and realized at once that these had probably been modified so that their hearts were no longer in the center of the chest.

One of them leaped on him, but he threw it off ten feet along the tunnel. The other grabbed his head and twisted, trying to snap his neck. He got the barrel of his pistol tucked under its chin and fired. It flopped to the floor. But more came, some dressed as marines, some in fatigues or police uniforms or street clothes.

There were too many. Every shot would count, but he didn't have enough bullets. In the flashes from his gun, he could see them by the dozens, crowding the tunnel, and more coming up from below, their eyes gleaming like empty diamonds in the frantically questing beam of his flashlight.

They also had guns, and worse—some sort of gas that was causing him to become disoriented while not affecting them.

The firefight evolved quickly into a tumult of flashes and whining bullets, and he knew that one of them would hit him at any moment, and then this would be done.

There was a searing flash, followed by pulsating silence. Flynn knew instantly that they had detonated a stun grenade. But why? They were having more trouble with it than he was.

For an instant, in the beam of his flashlight, he saw a figure coming up the tunnel at a run.

It was impossible.

She waded in among the reeling creatures, firing into them as she came. She leaped over corpses, fisted or pistol-whipped any still moving, and descended on him like a Valkyrie.

The defenders withdrew in disarray, but he knew it would be for only a moment, just until their adaptive programming could overcome the shock that they had taken. They were programmed to take damage from bullets and knives, but clearly not from stun weapons.

"Let's do this," she said as she reached up and grabbed the hatch wheel.

"Where did you come from?"

"You left scuff marks. I followed you in."

He'd underestimated her again. Bad habit. "Glad you're here," he said.

Together, they tugged on the wheel. One of the biorobots got to its feet and Flynn blew it away.

They tugged until they were in danger of ripping their muscles from their bones. But in a situation like this, pain did not matter, damage to oneself did not matter. All that mattered was getting up into the building.

"We need something to push against!" Diana yelled.

"Keep on."

"My arms are breaking!"

"Do it."

There came a clicking sound, then another.

Then nothing.

The wheel moved. Then more. Then stopped again.

Something leaped on Diana's back. He took his right hand off the wheel, drew the gun, and fired. What looked like a sheet of skin flopped away, briefly visible in the darting beams of their flashlights. An instant later it was back, some kind of new design, a throbbing, muscular mass, vaguely rectangular. There was no head, there were no eyes, but it was covered with seething hairs, apparently its sensory apparatus. It surged up her legs faster than a snake. It was bleeding, though, from his last shot.

"God, get it off!"

"Stay still."

It had reached her face. It was enclosing her head. She got an arm free and began convulsively grabbing at the thing. Flynn took out his knife, itself a terrible weapon, a man-killer with a microscopically sharp, super-hardened blade.

Cutting into the thing was like cutting cartilage, not muscle. It was hardened against just this sort of attack. The knife was not going to be effective.

Diana went to her knees. She began to convulse. Her efforts to pull the creature off her face became disorganized. She was suffocating fast.

The only thing left to try was to get the barrel of his pistol up under it and fire, and hope that somehow broke its grip and left Diana alive.

Her light was lying on the floor, and as he thrust the gun into the thing, pressing its barrel up between her left leg and the throbbing muscle, he stepped on it and it went out.

Cursing his luck, all he could do was hope she would survive. He fired and in the flash saw two things. The first was a great, complicated chunk of the thing flying toward the ceiling. The second was a massive crowd of humanoid biorobots jamming the tunnel and coming straight toward them.

He pulled at the living mass of flesh. Pulled harder. It held tight.

Her body was now flaccid. He thought she might be dead but could not be sure. In battle, you do not linger over the dead—you keep trying on behalf of the living.

He dug his fingers into the cartilage and muscle of it and gave a last, mighty tug.

It rolled off her. He pulled out his own light and looked at it. The thing was still pulsating, and might well recover.

He fired three shots into the oncoming horde of biorobots, reloaded, and fired another five.

"Di!"

She was still. Her eyes were rolled back in her head. Her tongue lolled from her mouth.

He bent to her and gave her mouth-to-mouth. At first, nothing came back but dead air. But then she coughed, she gasped, she opened her eyes.

His love surprised him, it was like lava, a white-hot flow of sheer joy in his heart.

She cried out, again, again, scream after scream.

He held her to him. He could feel her gagging and struggling to regain her composure. His mind echoed with just one thought, repeated over and over: "There is no time, there is no time."

"OK," he said, "OK." What he had been afraid of was happening. She was slowing him down. "We need to do this."

"I know . . . please . . ."

He stood up and grasped the wheel once again. Four of the biorobots, now just a few feet away, leaped at him. He shot two of them in the face, and the other two dropped back.

He tugged at the wheel, which moved a little. She got her shaking hands on it and once again they pulled together. Perhaps it was going to give way, or perhaps the little bit of extra strength she added helped, but it finally released.

The hatch fell open. Overhead, Flynn saw parts of the frame that the floor of the equipment room was seated in.

Getting through it would take hours.

Above the next square in the grid of beams there was the outline of a hatch, but Flynn was too big to slip through the crawl space. If the hatch could somehow be opened from above, he could just make it, but that was not going to happen.

They had lost. Simple as that. The next time the biorobots rushed them or sent in some other monstrosity, they were done.

There was a strange sound. He shone his light toward it, which revealed Diana, bent double. She was vomiting. She gagged, coughed, spat, and looked up. Saying nothing, she went past him and fulcrumed herself up into the crawl space.

"It's tight," she said.

"Nobody can get through there."

"If the hatch were open, we both could."

"I know it."

She slid a little farther in.

"You'll be trapped."

"Better than being eaten."

That was true enough. His plan had always been to shoot himself if he ran out of options. For years, he'd carried cyanide capsules, but he'd stopped this practice after one had leaked in its case—leaked, or been tampered with; he could not be sure.

"Push me," she said. Her head and shoulders were in the crawl space, one arm stretched toward the hatch.

"Di, you're not coming back out, you realize that."

"Do it, and give me your knife. The latch is simple. All I need is a blade."

He pushed the knife up beside her, hilt first. "It's sharp as hell—don't even breathe on that blade."

She took it and levered her left arm under the metal grid, hissing through her teeth from the pain. She was now head and shoulders beneath the hatch. Her legs dangled down. Flynn stood watch. The biorobots edged nearer. From somewhere deep in the shaft there came the roar of some enormous beast. The biorobots began shuffling among themselves. They were making room for it, standing aside.

"Any luck?" Flynn said.

"Getting—just—just—"

Loud slithering. Enormous. He shone the light toward the sound.

"Give me back that light, goddamnit!"

It was a crocodile at least twenty feet long and it was coming fast, and it had desperately human eyes—green, staring, appalled. One of Aeon's skills was to combine species.

What would that be like, living like that, with the memories of a man and the instincts of a brutal reptile? The eyes were, of course, insane.

Flynn raised his pistol. There were now just three bullets left, and crocodiles are notoriously hard to kill.

He fired. It seemed to swallow the bullet. With another hissing roar, it lunged at him.

"Light! You damn fool, where are you?"

He fired again, this time into the brain.

It roared again, spraying a haze of blood. The eyes were all wild now, bloodshot and practically bulging out of the head.

"FLYNN, PLEASE!"

The thing latched onto his leg. He felt the teeth penetrate, then dig deep into the muscle.

Last shot. Directly into the skull, point-blank range.

The head blew apart; Flynn's devastating bullets had finally hit a vulnerable point.

The jaw dropped open and the creature began convulsing wildly, lurching all over the tunnel, momentarily blocking the way of the biorobots. But they had guns, too, and began firing past it.

With bullets whinging off the walls, Flynn shone the light up into the crawl space.

There came a clanking sound, then a metallic crash, and Diana's legs were gone. In the place of her body a glow shone down from above.

"Come on," she called.

He drew himself up. About eighteen inches of the hatch extended to the part of the floor that was directly above it, and Flynn was able to get through. She helped him pull himself into the basement.

"My God," he said. "My dear God."

Together, almost ceremonially, they closed the hatch. At once, it began shaking. The biorobots were not going to stop, and the latch that Diana had gotten through was not going to hold them back.

Flynn looked around the room. He saw large, boxy units of air-conditioning equipment and compact server farms on equipment racks, a row of twelve of them. He couldn't move the fans and compressors and dared not touch the servers.

"We can't secure the hatch," she said.

"I know it."

It began hopping on its hinges. Maybe a minute was left before they poured into the room.

"We need to get into the PEOC. Odds are they won't follow us."

"You're sure?"

"Aeon is already in that room, you can be sure. There are implanted people in there, and worse. Problem is, nobody understands this. We're a couple of intruders with a dubious agenda."

"Aeon will have support in the operational group. Somebody in there is going to be a biorobot, maybe more than one of them, and Lorna won't be the only implant."

The hatch shook so hard it felt like an earthquake. Then it stopped. The latch began to rattle.

Flynn strode along the catwalk to the heavy steel door that separated this machine room from the East Wing basement and the PEOC. He saw that the door had a locking mechanism on it that could be remotely activated. However, it was not locked—a safety measure, no doubt. It would probably be sealed only under DEFCON 5, which would not be triggered until missiles were actually in flight.

"We're good," he said. "Still good."

He pulled the door open. The corridor beyond was silent, dark, and empty. At the end was a steel door painted bright red. The entrance to the PEOC.

"Let's do it," Flynn said. As they moved toward the door, the two Secret Service agents guarding it leaped to their feet.

Flynn contemplated what was probably his greatest problem: He was out of bullets.

CHAPTER TWENTY-THREE

"STAY BEHIND me," Flynn said. "If they belong to Aeon, they're likely to open fire without warning." Hands up, he took a careful step forward.

Both agents moved to draw their pistols.

"Hey, hold it," Flynn said.

"You hold it. Stop right there."

Flynn kept walking, one step, two, three.

"Stop! Now!"

Flynn obeyed. He was not quite close enough to take them before they could pull their triggers. He needed a couple more steps.

"Please identify yourselves," one of the agents said. He was older, heavy around the edges, balding. His partner was young and vacant enough to be a biorobot.

"Maintenance," Flynn said. "There's a drainage issue."

This brought a slight smile to the face of the older agent. "Which would be why you two smell like you've been in a sewer."

Flynn took a casual step closer. "Sorry about that. Look, I don't know what's going on in there, but we need to open a valve in the men's room or they're gonna be real unhappy real soon."

"Where's your equipment?"

Flynn nodded. "Back there. Don't need it for the valve." He took another step.

The second agent's jaw clenched and his muscles tightened. His hand began moving toward his jacket. If he drew his weapon, he would certainly fire; his fixed stare, bright with menace, told that story very clearly. The older agent was still smiling.

When the younger agent started to bring his gun out of its shoulder holster, Flynn delivered a blow to his throat. He crumpled, coughing and gagging.

The older man's mouth dropped open. He looked down at his partner, then back at Flynn.

"Sorry about that," Flynn said. "No guns, please."

The agent held his hands away from his body. "No guns, OK." He regarded Flynn with the eyes of a terrified mouse.

Flynn reached down, picked up the comatose agent's gun, and slipped it into his pocket.

"Watch out," Diana said.

The older agent was going for his pistol. Flynn reached out with lightning speed, took it, and handed it to Diana.

The agent stared at his hand, then started rubbing it. "You're that weird guy that's been hanging out in the Residence at night. The alien."

"I'm not an alien."

"You still can't go in there, mister. Don't you know we're at DEFCON 4?"

"We've been buried in work, we didn't know."

"How the hell did you get in here, anyway?"

"Somebody left a grate open."

The agent frowned.

Flynn put his hand on the handle of the door. Diana braced the agent's gun at him. Hands raised, he backed up a step. "Take it easy," he said. "I know you people are on our side."

"Not him," Flynn said, indicating the fallen agent with his chin. "He's gonna wake up in three or four minutes and he's gonna come after us. You stop him, do you understand?"

"How can I stop a kid like that? Look at him."

He looked like a SEAL on steroids. Flynn could kill him easily. Break the neck right now. But he had no way to be certain of what he was, and he wasn't willing to kill an innocent human being whose only mistake was to believe that he was doing his duty.

"Get ready," Flynn said to Diana. "All hell's gonna break loose when we go in."

She came up beside him. She was silent.

The PEOC is dominated by a long room centered on a conference table. On the walls around this table are a dozen flat-screen monitors. It is at this table that the National Security Council, the president's Chief of Staff, and the Joint Chiefs sit during times of crisis, and it was here that they would be sitting now. Deeper in the facility is a communications area manned by specialists from the National Reconnaissance Office and the Joint Military Communications Command. Beyond these rooms, there is a presidential suite and a number of more spartan living facilities for aides. These, along with a communal dining area, a medical facility that is equipped with everything from Band-Aids to radiation monitoring equipment, and a wash-down decontamination unit, comprises the facility. If a nuclear warhead detonated two thousand feet over the White House, this bunker would take a severe shock, but it would survive, as would most of its inhabitants, give or take a few broken bones and shattered eardrums. Only a bunker buster, driving down through the fifty feet of concrete above it, would take it out.

Flynn opened the door and stepped inside, Diana behind him. He then closed it and twisted the lock.

Every head in the room turned toward them, but he was really only interested in one person. Lorna, who was sitting beside the president, started to leap to her feet, but then checked herself.

A voice filled the room from over the telephone in the president's hand. "We will launch in three minutes."

Flynn recognized that it was Benjamin Netanyahu.

Lorna leaned close to Bill and whispered. Flynn heard enough to know that she had counseled him to let it happen.

"Excuse me," DCIA Boxleitner said. He backed away from the table, stood, and came striding up to Flynn. The president looked over, frowned, and went back to the call.

"I want this man arrested," Boxleitner shouted. "Where's the Secret Service?" He came closer to Flynn and said more quietly, "What is this about?"

Flynn pushed past him, walking deeper into the room. Seeing the bulge in Flynn's pocket, Admiral Delaney of the Joint Chiefs came to his feet. "There's a gun," he said. His voice was shaking, but he kept his composure very well, Flynn thought. Tough guy.

"Just sit back down. Everybody stay tight here. Bill, you're going to listen to me now, not to Lorna."

The president muted the phone. "Flynn, what the hell are you doing this time?"

"OK, Bill, everybody—there's already been an alarm put in. The Secret Service is converging right now. They're going to burst through that door in about a minute. Bill, if you do one single thing wrong, you will start a chain of events that will lead to a massive worldwide nuclear exchange and the death of the human species."

Netanyahu said, "We're launching now."

"The missile will not create blast effect."

General Hamelin of the air force scoffed. "It's a hydrogen bomb! It's going to wreck the whole of Semnan Province."

"The weapon has been altered. They've all been altered. It is now something like a neutron bomb. It will emit a horrendous sheet of short half-life radiation and leave infrastructure mostly intact."

Lorna said, "All right, let it happen, then."

"The Russians will react," Boxleitner yelled. "They'll hit Israel."

"They won't," Flynn said. "This will defuse a situation that's got to be terrifying Putin, because if he launches against Israel, he has to think we'll launch against him."

"Which we will not," Bill said. "I'm not starting World War Three."

"We'll cross that bridge," Lorna muttered.

NRO Chief Henry Fielder said, "We have recon showing the Iranians are running out four more missiles."

The president said, "Get Putin on the line." Then, into the phone, "Benjamin, we have no objection to your launching against Semnan."

Netanyahu's voice boomed out into the room. "Mr. President, we launched already. We were watching them preparing four more missiles. We have also directed Speed Wind against them."

Flynn said, "Get it on satellite. Visual."

A moment later a satellite view of the Iranian missile complex appeared in detail and in color on four of the screens around the room.

Fielder said, "Russian missile silos opening. Thirty mobile units in motion."

"Bill," Lorna said, "we have to preempt."

This was exactly what Flynn had expected her to say. This was the moment that Aeon had planned for. From here, the whole terrible chain of events was supposed to start.

Homeland Security chief William Apel announced that they were moving to DEFCON 5 and warning the country.

Flynn knew that for all but a tiny handful of people in the military and the intelligence communities, the country and the world would be taken by surprise.

"Sir, prime ministers and presidents are lined up on the horn."

"Britain, France, Germany, Italy, three minutes each. The rest in a conference call," Secretary of Defense Cornyn said.

Bill Greene's cell phone began buzzing. Cissy, who was sitting behind him in the advisory line, took it. Flynn heard her talking to Bob Doxy, her voice quiet and intense. He was getting a blow-by-blow from her, one of the perks of being an eight-figure contributor.

Boxleitner said, "We have reports from the Kremlin that Putin will hit Israel."

"We must preempt," Lorna said, her voice startlingly calm and even reassuring, rich with authority.

Events were about to outrun Flynn. Lorna was winning, but if he killed her right now, he would lose anyway. He had to get them to listen to his argument, and that depended on what happened to the Israeli missile that had just launched.

"Two minutes to impact," Fielder said.

"Sir, we have the Russian president."

"Vladimir, we must be very careful here," Bill said.

Flynn was amazed at how presidential he was sounding. Was the office transforming him? The beer-and-joke guy was not present in this room, and neither was the scared, confused amateur way out of his depth. Harry Truman had risen to the challenge of the office. So had Gerald Ford and Ronald Reagan, both men seemingly poorly prepared for challenges that they turned out to handle well.

Putin's translator's voice filled the room. "We will respond carefully. The Iranians have fired first, therefore we will not fire unless the Israelis do more than destroy the missile base."

"You're running out your missiles."

"As you know, many of ours are liquid-fueled. We cannot prepare as quickly as you can."

"Run them in. This gives you a preemptive capability that we cannot tolerate."

Lorna said, "For the love of God, preempt now! He's going to hit us!"

"Vladimir, please respond to me."

Greene was pouring with sweat, his forehead gleaming, his whole face pulsing red. Would he have a stroke? A heart attack? Flynn thought that the pressure was literally unimaginable.

"We will remain in static defense," Putin said at last. "You must not fire, William."

"He's lying," Lorna practically screeched.

An enormous flash filled the room. The satellites trained on the Iranian missile site had just transmitted the explosion not of a neutron weapon, but of a conventional hydrogen bomb.

"See," Lorna said, "get that crazy man out of here!"

Bill looked toward Flynn. "I've got ten Secret Service agents on the other side of the door, Flynn. I think you and Diana had better go."

Cissy leaned forward. "Dad, she's not loyal. She's *trying* to start a war. Everything she says points to it."

Lorna turned around and slapped her hard, the smack of it like a shot, giving back ten times over what she'd gotten a few hours before.

Silence fell.

"How dare you," she said into it. "We are trying to save the United States of America and you side with this nut job and his crazy lady!" She looked around the room. "You heard the president. Get them out of here."

"I'm assuring you," Flynn said, "the other bombs will destroy infrastructure. They will not emit blast effect."

"Missile rising from Iranian region Noje."

"What in hell! Vladimir, are you seeing this?"

"We have it."

Netanyahu came back on the line. "There's a launch from outside of the Speed Wind umbrella. Unknown launch." There was a pause. "It will impact fifty miles north of Tel Aviv. We're tracking it with Iron Dome, but interception is unlikely."

"Vladimir, are you hearing this?"

"If they launch against Iran, we launch against them."

Flynn said, "This missile is off its programmed course, which was Tel Aviv. It is intended to devastate Galilee. It will NOT—I repeat, NOT—emit blast effect. There will be a short-term, extremely intense radiation emission." He raised his voice. "Mr. Netanyahu, you get your citizens in basements, in whatever shelter they can find. Prepare radiation recovery teams."

"Who is that?"

Lorna shrieked, "Somebody shoot that man!"

"Gentlemen," the president said, "if this—"

"Iron Dome launches," Fielder said. "Iron Dome detonates. No joy. Iron Dome—standby. Warhead . . . detonates. Blast effect estimate one tenth of a kiloton at altitude sixty-one thousand feet."

A voice from communications said, "Israel off-line."

"What's going on?" the president pleaded. "Vladimir, are you still there?"

"We're evaluating," he said.

Lorna said, "He's lying. They're going to launch their mobiles, Bill. For the love of all that's holy, fire Minuteman!"

At that moment, the door burst open and Secret Service agents and White House police burst in, wearing full SWAT gear and carrying automatic rifles, stun grenades, gas, you name it.

Diana, who had been standing near the door, ran to the far end of the room. Flynn took three quick shots at the upper shoulders of the three lead agents. This would graze their armor and dislocate their shoulders, but not kill them.

Putin's translator said, "We want to know what's happening."

"It's under control," Greene shouted. Then, "Stand down! All of you, stand down!"

They came on, and Flynn realized that they were not Secret Service at all, none of them. His next shot took off the head of the one nearest him. The thing reeled, then staggered forward, still alive, still attempting to manipulate its weapon.

"Look at that," Fielder yelled.

Spurting blood from the ruins of its upper body, it turned toward Fielder and fired at him, missing but causing him to fly across the table. He took Secretary of Defense Cornyn to the floor.

Total pandemonium. People fought each other to get under the table, to run deeper into the facility, to go past the attackers and out into the hall.

"Flynn," Bill shouted, "fix it, fix it!"

Cissy and another backup Flynn did not know threw themselves onto the president. The three of them disappeared beneath the table edge.

"What's happening?" Putin's translator said. "What is this, is that a coup there? President Greene, we must know."

"Military coup," Lorna shouted.

Even if Flynn had not been here, he realized, this would have happened. All along, the real plan had been to frighten Putin into firing first because he thought that the U.S. military had taken over. He would quickly see that the consequences of such a takeover would be impossible to predict, and he would launch.

So this was why all the assassination attempts against Flynn. He was probably the only person alive who could restore order in this room fast enough to stop the Russian launch.

He took out three more of the creatures with the last three bullets in the Secret Service agent's gun, then vaulted the table amid a hail of bullets and got the assault rifle from the one that had fallen first. He pulled Fielder off Secretary Cornyn.

He also knew that Lorna's cry had been intended to frighten Putin into launching, and that she would do the same thing again any moment now.

He used the weapon to clean up the rest of the intruders, who fell in a writhing heap. "They're still dangerous," he shouted. "They don't die like we do. Stay away from them." He turned to the spot where the president had been sitting. "Bill, you need to tell Putin there's no problem here."

A voice from the communications center said, "Russian missiles preparing to launch. We have launches."

"How many?" Greene shouted.

"Flight of six. Calculating impact points."

"*Bill, launch Minuteman!*" Lorna's howl tore through the air.

"Missile explodes."

The translator's voice filled the room. "An unauthorized launch," he said.

Flynn saw Greene press the mute button on the phone. "Activate Sky Dragon."

"Dragon tracking three. Tracking four. Missile explodes."

"Vladimir, we're back in the saddle," Greene said.

"Sir, I cannot understand," the translator said.

"Things are under control," Cissy said.

"Under control, yes," Bill said.

"Dragon intercepts two warheads. Detonations. Missiles neutralized."

"What do we have?"

The translator said, "We have destroyed the two of our missiles you did not. Mr. Putin says please do not launch. We are standing down."

"Russian silos closing," the NRO technician said over the intercom from the communications center.

The secretary of defense, who was covered with the reeking "blood" of a biorobot, began having convulsions. Medical personnel appeared.

"Don't touch those bodies," Flynn said. "They're going to be booby-trapped. Also, they use reptile genes to give them durability. They won't be entirely dead for hours."

The army chief of staff, who had been sitting like a stone, now came to his feet and shouted, "What is this? I want this explained! Now!"

"In good time, General," Diana said.

"NORAD report commences," the loudspeaker intoned. "This is Space Command. We have a missile warhead on track to impact due east of Minot, North Dakota. Direct hit on Malmstrom AFB."

"Get all personnel underground," Flynn said. "There will be no blast effect."

"What in hell are these bombs about?" another member of the Joint Chiefs shouted.

"They're designed to eradicate life without destroying infrastructure."

"The Russians'—"

"All of them. Ours. The Israelis'. Possibly some of the Iranians'."

"Pakistan missiles being run out. Indian missiles being run out."

"Get Islamabad on the line. Vladimir, can you hear me?"

"We're on."

"Call Delhi. Please try to spread calm."

"Yes, I will do it now." It was Putin himself. He spoke good English. As a gesture of trust, he had dispensed with his translator.

"Prime Minister Aman is on the line," one of the young people in communications said.

"Mr. Greene," the Pakistani prime minister said, "why are they doing this to us?"

"The Iranians fired a missile at Israel. I think the Indians are afraid that the conflict will widen. Mr. Putin is talking to them."

"We cannot risk this. We must destroy their missile delivery capability."

"If you fire, they fire. Your cities will be ruined."

"As will theirs! I cannot risk them firing first."

"You can respond after they fire."

"I'm not sure we will be fast enough. It's only seven minutes."

Greene looked from face to face, his eyes stopping on Flynn for just an extra moment. "Mr. Prime Minister, I tell you this in confidence: If they fire, we will take them out. No warheads will reach you."

"What is this? I know nothing of this."

"A system we have in space. It is already set to target their missiles."

There was silence on the line, then a faint click.

"He's consulting his generals," Secretary of State Costigan said.

Greene looked to Boxleitner. "Background me."

"General Nazzimuda will recommend standing down."

"You're certain?"

He held up a phone. "He just texted me."

The line clicked. "If we stand down, we want access to this system. We want to understand it so that we know it works."

NRO director Fielder had gone as pale as dead smoke. "Sir—"

"There will be time for that later," Greene said smoothly. "Right now, you can take the word of the President of the United States for it."

"You guarantee that you will explain it to us?"

"Absolutely."

"Very well, then we wait. If they do not fire, we do not."

"You won't regret this, Mr. Prime Minster. You're now a national hero; you have saved millions of Pakistani lives."

"Or thrown them away." He disconnected.

Flynn knew that Aeon would be listening to all of this. They would be hearing the apparent failure of their plan. So they would act. But how? When?

The world was still a time bomb, just ticking in a new, as-yet-undiscovered way.

"Mr. President," Fielder said, "what is this system? Is it Space Command's baby?"

"We don't have it," Air Chief Dexter said.

"Nobody has it," the president said.

Silence again, this time total. More gray faces.

"What can I say," Greene added. "I took a calculated risk."

Putin returned to the line. "The Indians see the Pakistani silos closing. They are standing down."

Greene looked around the room. "I think we've returned to stability, am I right?"

Heads were nodding. The secretary of defense said, "Permission to move to DEFCON 3 and inform the country."

Greene said to Putin, "We're going to DEFCON 3 at this time."

"We are standing our mobile units down." They were the most serious threat the Russians possessed, mobile, solid-fueled ICBMs that were difficult to track as they moved along the back roads of Siberia. "You'll see them all back at base."

"Will you please open discussions with the Iranians? They need the Supreme Leader to be gone."

"We cannot interfere like that."

"Of course not, but please do!"

There was the slightest of chuckles. "Mr. President, we must meet sometime. I have an intelligence assessment that speaks not so well of you, but I must say, I am impressed with your performance today."

"As am I with yours."

"I have some practice."

They closed the line.

One of the seconds began applauding, then another, and another. The front of the table did the same. Boxleitner went to his feet, followed by Fielder, followed by the others.

Flynn applauded, too. He had seen dopey, ill-informed, and ill-prepared Bill Greene transform into a president before his eyes. In fact, a great president. The power of the office—its magic—had found the best of the man.

Bill stood, too. After a moment, he did something a president rarely does: He lifted his right hand in salute to his team.

CHAPTER TWENTY-FOUR

AS THE PEOC was being cleared of debris and remains, and the various staffers were leaving, Flynn noticed that Lorna Greene was not present. When he asked Ginny Bowers, he was told that she was in the Residence, lying down.

Not unreasonable, but it was also true that Flynn hadn't seen her leave. He liked to know where people were, and made a note to confirm her presence in her room.

The president had been hustled out by Secret Service agents, but only after Flynn had made certain that Bill recognized each one of them personally. Later, everybody in the White House operation would be temperature-tested, and then, as part of the deeper investigation into the degree that Aeon had penetrated the government, DNA-tested as well, and scanned for implants.

In the meantime, if Flynn had his way—and he was determined that he would—the presidency would be isolated from its own support system. The only people who would have access to Bill Greene would be those he knew personally. This meant that, of the 708 staffers on the presidential roster, exactly 54 would be allowed into his presence, and then only after the full test sequence had been completed.

Now just Flynn and Diana were left in the PEOC. The bodies had been pushed up against a wall. They were waiting for a mortuary team that was coming in from Langley.

"Did you see Lorna leave?"

Diana frowned. "I'm not sure."

"Where's the football?"

"You don't think—"

"Where is it?"

"Colonel Whittier took it out with the president. That I did see."

"I'm gonna put eyes on Lorna."

"You need to get cleaned up before you go over to the Residence."

"This situation is still extremely dangerous."

"We just won! We beat Aeon. *You* did, Flynn!"

He went out into the corridor, then up the stairs that led to the East Wing. Whenever he was out of sight of others, he ran. Otherwise, he moved as fast as he could without looking like he was on the attack. Which he was. These people thought that they'd quieted a storm. They did not understand the true nature of that storm, and he had not had the chance to explain the peril to them.

As he hurried into the Residence, he was confused to hear a cheerful female voice jabbering on about the Truman portrait. A moment later, he saw a clutch of people ahead of him and realized that it had not been closed to visitors, and that tourists were being led through as they were every day. What had they done during the DEFCON 5? Were they even aware that it had been declared?

As he passed through the group, people looked up at the tall, pale man in the soiled jeans and pullover. He still stank; he could see that in their faces. A cell phone came out, but it only got a shot of his back. Otherwise he would have crushed it.

He headed for the Grand Staircase. At this point the Secret Service was no longer in his face. That was good, because he was real tired of them. They couldn't be blamed for having been infiltrated by Aeon. In fact, they'd done their job heroically, but still, he could not afford to be slowed down even a little.

There were two agents on the staircase. "Where's POTUS?" he asked.

"West Wing."

That would mean the office suite. The Oval was used mostly for ceremonial occasions—bill signings and such. Receiving damage assessments from Israel and Malmstrom, which is what he would be doing right now, was hardly that.

"And Whittier?"

"With him. Orders are to remain in sight."

That was good. As it should be. The football must remain in sight of Bill and out of sight of Lorna.

The White House was generally quiet, but there had been tourists downstairs. Up here, the silence was total. A single Secret Service agent was stationed in the Central Hall.

"Where is everybody?" Flynn asked.

"Nobody here."

"The First Lady's not up here?"

"No, sir. Nobody is."

He vaulted the stairs and headed for the Secret Service office, under the Oval. As he moved through the Residence, then into the West Wing, he noted everybody he passed. Aeon had made a mistake with the body temperature of its biologicals, but that would be corrected, and maybe it could be done remotely; Flynn could not be sure. Knowing Aeon, it might not even have been a mistake. It might have been a deception, a lie intended to hide some greater lie.

The office was crowded, and Flynn had to push his way past some unwilling people. He spotted Simon Forde and shoved his way closer.

"You've sure as hell arrived," Ford snarled.

"Clear the room."

"Excuse me?"

"Clear the room. Now!"

"OK!"

"Gentlemen, go to your stations," Flynn said. "If you don't have an assignment yet, find a hole. No clumping up—I want the whole facility covered!" He added, "I need two technicians who can work the surveillance system."

"That's classified."

"You do this! Now!"

Forde called two men back.

"I want you to roll back to when people were leaving the PEOC. Find the First Lady, then follow her. Track her to her present location."

As he waited, he realized that they were doing it in real time, which was far too slow. "Excuse me," he said to one of them. The kid turned, his eyebrows raised as if to say, "How dare you interrupt me, I'm White House." Flynn hauled him out of his chair and tossed him against the far wall. There was a rocking crash and an alarmed young cry. Flynn didn't look; he didn't have time. He took his place at the console.

"Speed it up," he said to the boy beside him.

"We can't—"

"Speed it up!"

Flynn watched the door fly open and figures go speeding out. He saw Cissy, then various officials, then Secret Service agents ahead of and behind the presidential entourage, then a flock of military brass. Then the corridor was empty. He did not see the First Lady.

He jumped up and headed for the door. On the way, he accosted Simon Forde. "You're to secure the suite right now. Nobody enters except me, nobody leaves except me. Any agent, any person whatsoever, who defies this order, you detain them. Do you understand?"

Forde's eyes were the size of plates.

Flynn shook him. "Save it! Go into shock on your own damn time."

He spluttered, gagged. "Sir—"

"Do as you're told, and do it right!"

Flynn headed down the hall and through the Oval, where a butler was carefully dusting the dusted desk. Outside, gardeners were pruning the late roses. In the distance, the maples glowed red. Between the building and the stately trees, Marine One gleamed like a jewel, waiting to speed its precious cargo to whatever safety might be found.

Flynn burst into the working suite. "Mr. President!"

He held up a hand as Vice President Milligan came over to Flynn and said, "Netanyahu's on the horn. All hell's breaking out in Israel. Galilee is a radiation zone. There's at least a hundred thousand dead and he's under siege to blow hell out of Iran. A mob's going to tear him apart unless he burns the whole country to the ground."

Bill's forehead was sheened with sweat. He crouched over the phone. "We'll do 'em. All of 'em," he said.

"We're going to decapitate the Iranian government," Milligan said calmly.

Flynn thought of Ghorbani out there on the front line, of the Special Forces operatives deep in country, of all the courage that was involved, and a feeling came into him that added pride to the determination that was the compass of his soul. If, indeed, all these people were what they seemed.

"Putin?"

"He's not going to intervene."

"The First Lady?"

Milligan shook his head.

Flynn opened his secure phone—not because it would help, but because it was what he had—and called Cissy.

"Where's your mother?"

"Don't know."

"Where are you?"

"In my room. Flynn, what can I do?"

"I'm gonna need you. I want you downstairs in thirty seconds."

He recognized Colonel Whittier by the briefcase that he carried. He went to him. "Open it."

"Sir?"

"Open it right now and run its test program."

The colonel hesitated. He had to think about this. Where was this order coming from? Flynn's gun slipped into his hand. "I'm sorry, Colonel, I just don't have time. I won't hurt you, but you can report that you did it under duress."

He opened the briefcase. Flynn saw the ancient equipment inside, that and the much newer, deeply secret quantum communicator—a dark, ominous eye half-concealed among the innocent switches and the old numerical coding apparatus.

The colonel ran it through its checks, getting green lights each time it completed a test. Then he pressed the red button that would run the system drill, and watched as each missile command center and each submarine signaled back and the relevant indicator light went from yellow to green. They all reported—all but one.

"Malmstrom?"

"Still alive, but not online. Aboveground had its day ruined. Downstairs is believed to be still operational."

Flynn deliberated. Should he stay here with the football, or locate Lorna? If he remained here, nothing she could do would enable her to activate it. But as long as she wasn't located, the danger remained.

He called Diana. She answered immediately. The PEOC was equipped with cell phone relays, even on secure systems.

"Is everything under control down there?"

"The mortuary team is trying to understand why the casualties have artificial skin and strange organs. I'm pretending to be mystified."

"I want all that material moved forthwith to the burn facility at Wright-Pat. Tell them to bag it, seal it with classified seals, and transport it at once." Outside of the presidential bubble, the press, he knew, must be in a frenzy. If word of these strange corpses got out, there was liable to be some sort of mass psychosis, starting with the news anchors.

"Got it."

"OK. Now listen up. We've lost Lorna. Fortunately, the football's safe, so that's not an immediate problem. But I need to locate her and get her off the chessboard. I want you to come up here and keep eyes on the football at all times. I've left orders that nobody enters or leaves the suite. I'm going to take Cissy with me. She knows Lorna's haunts."

"I'm in motion. What are you going to do with Lorna?"

"Get a suite ready at Walter Reed. I want the best neurosurgical team we can find standing by."

"You're going to try to save that bitch?"

"I'm gonna try to save a man's wife."

"Are you being cynical or foolish?"

"Both." He closed the secure phone and returned to the Residence. Cissy was sitting on the foot of the Grand Staircase, surrounded by excited tourists, who were listening to her tell tales of life in the White House. It was a superb performance—warm, cheerful and engaging—but nobody in the media was going to be even close to caring, not with the epochal news that must be breaking out there about now.

"Let's go," he said to Cissy. "Sorry, folks, show's over."

As he hurried her toward the private entrance, he could hear people speculating that he was a plumber.

Sort of.

"I need an ordinary car from the motor pool. Ordinary but fast. What have you got?"

"I haven't the faintest idea."

"Another question—where would your mother go if she was running for her life? If she thought the entire world had turned against her? Where would she go?"

"Home. She'd go back to Midland. We own the cops, not to mention the entire city, us and the Doxys."

"Too far. She doesn't have time."

"Then maybe Ginny's place."

The Chief Usher had appeared discreetly, and was standing nearby.

"What's the fastest car down there?" Flynn asked him.

"Miss Greene, may I call Agent Skinner?"

"No," Flynn said.

"I'm sorry?"

"Bring the car up. Do it now."

"Sir, I don't believe—"

"I don't care what you believe! Do it!"

"Please, Martin, we're on a special mission for Daddy. It's urgent."

He gave a weak smile. "Are you sure, miss, because if your mother—"

"Martin, my mother is drunk and on drugs. She's at a friend's house raising hell."

"But I thought she was here. I didn't see her leave."

"They didn't see Mamie Eisenhower, either! She used to hide in the bushes. God knows how Momma did it, but you know the drunk's skill at evasion—you've worked here for years. Under Clinton and W, for God's sake. How many times did you lose track of them?"

He called for the car, and in a few moments one of the garage attendants brought up a BMW M5. If he had to give chase or escape, this car was going to be effective.

Flynn got behind the wheel and they took off. As they drove, Cissy input Ginny's street address. "What'll you do when you find her, Flynn? Please don't hurt her, I couldn't bear that."

"I won't hurt her."

"No, just kill her."

He did not reply. As they drove, he watched and waited. They were half a mile from the White House when they reached a good location—an active street overhung by large trees. "Pull over."

"Pull over? Really?"

"Right now please."

She pulled up to the curb. He got out. Ginny's condo was now half a block away.

"Flynn?"

"Get back in the traffic stream. Keep going, then get out and go into the condo."

"Flynn, tell me what you're doing."

He couldn't tell her that he was headed back to the White House. Aeon's surveillance abilities made that too great a risk. He laid a finger against his lips, and she nodded.

He was gratified to see her do as he had asked and disappear down the street. He had noted well that Lorna had never exited the PEOC. This meant that she was under it, in the same tunnel system that he and Diana had used. She had retreated to safety among Aeon's biorobots.

Aeon would be desperate now, so Lorna wouldn't be wasting time trying to convince Bill to executed a preemptive launch. She would be seeking to gain control over the football herself.

Walking at this pace, he was going to need roughly ten minutes to get back. He was aware that the world could easily come to an end during that time. But he dared not take a cab or any other form of transportation. Worse, if he was going to avoid detection by Aeon when he got there, he was going to have to carry out a maneuver so dangerous that it might get him killed before the mission was over.

Every muscle in his body strained to break out of the crowd and use all of his swiftness to get to the White House in two minutes rather than ten. Instead, he strolled, gazing here at a pretty woman, there at a store display, stopping to look in the window of an inviting bookstore, then to seemingly chat with some people at an outdoor café. Actually, he was only asking directions he didn't need. From above, though, he would blend into the crowd, and that was what mattered.

It took what seemed like an hour, but he actually reached the White House perimeter in eight minutes. And now came the difficult part. The DEFCON 5 alert had been announced, then rescinded. As yet, the public and the press knew little of the story. They'd been told that the alert had been triggered accidentally. Later, they would be told that it had been a nuclear accident at Malmstrom involving an experimental weapon.

At this point, he could get past the guards without a problem, but that would give him away immediately. He looked up at the perimeter fence.

Since the Obama years, when numerous people had tried to scale it, some succeeding, it had been raised eighteen inches. There was no razor wire, although that had been discussed, but no average man could hope to vault it.

However, he thought he might manage it. There were horizontal bars that stiffened the verticals about two feet above the base of the fence and two feet below the spiked tips of the verticals. If he could get a grip on the top horizontal bar, he could make it over with about a quarter of an inch to spare.

He ran toward it, accelerating as he crossed Pennsylvania Avenue. Leaping up, he grasped the bar and swung his legs high over his head. For a moment, he teetered. On the sidewalk below, he saw two plainclothes officers in the process of pulling their guns. He started to fall back, right into their arms. The faster of the two was now raising his weapon. Flynn knew their orders; they had been widely publicized. One of Bill Greene's first acts as president had been to announce that, from now on, intruders breaching the White House perimeter would be shot dead.

As his body continued to angle back, he realized that he hadn't put quite enough strength into the leap. Grunting deeply from the strain, he shifted his weight as far as he could. Slowly, he felt himself crumbling. A shot whined past him.

Now his fall was uncontrollable, but it was also into the grounds, not back onto the sidewalk. An instant later he hit the ground, rolled to dissipate the energy of it, then leaped to his feet and started running for the entrance.

Four White House police uniforms were converging on him. At the entrance, he knew, there were two Secret Service suits with automatic pistols. In addition, the door was locked and reinforced. Even if he survived, entry was going to be a challenge.

Aeon would also know all this, which was why, he hoped, they would fail to identify him as who he was, and therefore would not realize that he was back in the White House.

He was a deft runner, and he was able to dodge the bullets effectively.

When he climbed the steps to the portico, the shooting behind him stopped. He was now the property of the two agents between him and the door. They had already drawn their weapons and were preparing to fire.

But they did not fire, because by this time he was known to the Secret Service. Well known. In fact, one of these men was Jim Allendale, who had been involved in the Doxy investigation and had been guarding the presidential suite when Flynn had been watching over the First Family.

"Hey, Jim," he said.

"Flynn, what in hell—"

"Just listen. You both need to fire your weapons right now. I'll go down, then you haul me in."

"I don't understand."

"Jim, you don't need to. Just do it."

The two agents opened up simultaneously, and Flynn dropped. A moment later they dragged him in.

He got up and headed for the West Wing.

"Mr. Carroll!"

Both agents trotted after him. "Sir, it's on lockdown. We can't let you—"

Lockdown meant only one thing—there was trouble again. And he was

very much afraid that he knew what it was. As he ran down the central corridor and exited toward the West Wing, the two agents dropped back.

He crossed toward the entrance. The two agents on the door watched
him uneasily. "What's going on?"

"We can't let you in."

"Please answer my question."

"There's a lockdown," one of them said. "That's all we've been told."

As Flynn pushed past them, he took both of their guns. It would be a
moment before they realized that they'd been disarmed, but he expected
to need the firepower. Voices along the corridor told him that the president and his entourage were in the Situation Room. But that wasn't what
concerned him. He was focused on just one thing, which was the location
of the football and who was near it. Of course, the Situation Room has a
fixed nuclear command post, but the fact that the president was there
wouldn't mean that the football was inoperative.

Another two agents guarded the room itself. Once again, Flynn had to
go through the lockdown drill with them. Within the past hour, Bill had
officially identified him as having a Category One clearance, which gave
him the ability to legally bypass them. But legalities take time, and that he
did not have. He dropped them both with blows to the temple that would
keep them out for a couple of minutes, and entered the room.

Diana's face flushed deep. It was relief, he knew. Seeing her again made
him feel the same. In this extreme situation anything could happen to anybody at any time. It was good to see her face.

"Where's the football?"

The president was glued to a phone, surrounded by aides. Diana pushed
her way through the dense official mass. "It's next door with Whittier, but
there's fixed base in here."

"Where exactly? Which room?"

"The Briefing Room, I believe. But—"

Flynn crossed behind the president, getting angry glares from the secretary of state and the chief of staff.

The Briefing Room was empty.

He went back to Diana. "We need to put eyes on it and keep eyes on it."

"But with the president here, how can it be activated?"

"Whoever has a valid biscuit and the DoD verifying code can simulate two-man compliance and initiate an attack." The biscuit was a plastic card containing the president's personal verification code, which would be confirmed by the secretary of defense prior to being transmitted to the National Military Command Center with whatever war plan had been decided on.

They checked the adjacent video conferencing center, which contained only the technical personnel assigned to it.

"Whittier's going to be tagged," Flynn said. He hurried around the corner to the Secret Service office. There were a dozen personnel there, watching the myriad of cameras that covered the structure and the grounds.

"Whittier," Flynn said. "I need his location."

"Whittier," said one of the technicians. This was followed by silence.

"Where?"

"Sir, I—"

"You're not seeing him?"

"No, I am." He turned, frowning. "He's in the Residence. In the First Lady's dressing room, sir."

As they headed back to the Residence, he handed Diana one of the pistols. "You'll need this."

"What's happening?"

Footsteps pounded behind them. Flynn turned to see a pale-faced Roland Boxleitner swing around the corner. "There you are! There are codes moving. Codes moving, Flynn!"

"And you don't know where they're coming from?"

His stare, woebegone, sparking with panic, was his eloquent answer.

"Go back in, tell the president to attempt verbal override."

"That won't work!"

Flynn was on him in an instance. "It might slow this down by a couple of minutes! Now go!" To Diana he muttered, "That guy is not swift."

"Flynn, please tell me what's happening?"

"Lorna's got ahold of the football. She's transmitting codes with it. Whittier is dead."

"She's—"

"—transmitting a war plan. Exactly."

"But how can she be stopped?"

"No idea. Let's go."

"Where? Where is she?"

"Residence." He said to the communications officer, "I want every man in the Residence looking for the First Lady. Every room, every closet, behind desks, under beds, in the attic. And give us buds. We need to be able to hear you guys."

The officer handed two communicators over.

Flynn and Diana went to the Residence. It was now late afternoon, and the tourists were gone. The rooms were quiet, softly lit as always. Very faintly, the sound of Washington traffic could be heard drifting in from the outside, imparting a curious sense of normality.

They were climbing the private staircase when an agent launched himself from above. Dropping down, he fired on Flynn, but not fast enough to avoid being shot dead. He tumbled in a heap and rolled onto the narrow landing.

Flynn stepped over him. "We're close," he said.

"I thought they were on our side!"

"Feel the skin. It's one of those damn biologicals."

"I thought—never mind what I thought."

When they reached the top of the stairs, Flynn emptied his pistol into the six of them that were waiting there.

"My dear God, how do you do that? I'll never come close to that level of proficiency."

"I wish I knew. They're defending the eastern side, so we'll find her—"

"Too late, Flynn." She stood in the door of her bedroom, almost lounging against the wall. "The war plan is in operation. The first flights are already launching."

Maybe they were and maybe they weren't.

"The Situation Room has been taken out of the chain of command. Shithead is talking to himself."

There was a rescind code. "When did you call the launch?"

She smiled. "It's too late for you to stop it." The smile broadened. "Kill me, Flynn. You'd love to."

He shoved her aside and entered her suite. On it, Ginny Bowers lay in a pool of blood, her severed throat a bloody grin.

Behind him Diana cried out, and another biorobot piled into him, attaching to his back with all its brutal, mechanical power. He levered himself forward at the waist, flung it off. It hurtled toward Lorna, but he killed it with a head shot before its body took her down. She groaned. "You bastard, I think you've broken my damn back."

Diana hurried past him.

He wanted to kick Lorna's head in, but there was no time for anything except the work at hand, which was to locate the football.

He said into his mike, "Colonel Whittier is down. I need somebody up here to input a rescind order into the football's communications system."

"It's in here," Diana called.

It lay in the dressing room, the worn black satchel that contained war plans in folders, codes in plastic sleeves, and the most highly classified communications equipment in the Western World.

Bill Greene came in, flanked by Secret Service officers with drawn pistols. Secretary of Defense Cornyn was with him. Staff packed the hallway.

"Bill," Flynn said, "she's activated a war plan. I don't know which one."

"Missiles are away and Russia is preparing to retaliate," Cornyn said. His voice wasn't afraid or angry, just tired. In a dull tone he said, "We've managed to transmit destruct sequences to four of them, but there are three more still rising and the rest of the war plan is about to execute."

"Rescind codes?"

"Situation Room's nonoperational."

Flynn heaved the fifty-pound satchel onto the foot of the bed.

"This is working," he said.

At once, Greene and Cornyn input their rescind codes. A moment later, the command center returned a green light, signifying that the plan would not be executed further.

"Where are we?" Greene asked.

"We have three missiles still in play. The Russians have two in play."

"Anything on ballistic trajectory yet?"

"Two minutes for us, three for them."

"Can we destruct?"

"Deflect. We've just gotten open lines on them," Cornyn said. He was listening to an earbud of his own. "Now that the war plan is rescinded, they're reachable again by telemetry."

"Get Putin on," the president said. He picked up the nearest phone. Such was the White House communications system that he was at once talking to the president of the Russian Federation. "Vladimir, we're dropping ours into the North Pacific."

"We see that."

"What's your status?"

There was a silence. After a moment, Cornyn bent double and retched. Flynn felt his own heart racing. Putin was at the other end of the line determining whether or not it was too late to abort his launch. Millions of American lives hung in the balance.

"Sir," an aide said from the corridor. "We have determined that this is their east-first wave. New York, Boston, us, plus regional command and control and CENTCOM in Florida."

"Sky Dragon?"

"Sky Dragon is expended at this time."

"Sir, we need to get you back down to the PEOC right now."

"Vladimir?"

He listened. His grip on the phone tightened. Then, very softly, he put it down.

"They have successfully aborted."

Cornyn clutched his chest. Two aides rushed to his side and took him out of the room. Bill Greene sat on the foot of the blood-soaked bed. He bent his head and covered his face with his hands. The sound that came out was a woeful, sorrowing groan, relief mixed with something deeper, Flynn thought—the terror of a man who is truly alone.

"Flynn," he said, "is this over?"

"Sir, it's over for now, but they will regroup."

"How long?"

Flynn reviewed their options, as well as he thought he might know them. "If they want to take the planet from us, it will be some time before they can come up with another plan."

As he spoke, he noted the stirring of murmurs his words brought to the room. Most of these people did not yet know about Aeon. They knew only that, for reasons that were not entirely clear, a world war had nearly started.

"What sort of a plan, Flynn?"

Flynn said nothing. This was not the place to discuss it, but Aeon had vast resources, and he thought it might be a virus, a plague of some sort. But how could he know? He could not know.

"Flynn?"

You do not remain silent when the President of the United States asks you a question, and certainly not when it is repeated. "Sir, we will get that under study at once. But I think we have bought some time. This is a very difficult, complex operation they're attempting. They won't be coming back at us tomorrow."

He grunted. "Cornyn?"

"I'm sorry, sir," the secretary said. "I thought I was having a cornonary."

"You and I are going golfing. We can save our heart attacks for the course." He glanced around. "Costigan—where's Costigan?"

The secretary of state edged into the jammed room. "Get on this right now," the president told him. "We need to get every country in the world that possesses nuclear weapons to check them and determine if they've been altered. We need those warheads pulled."

"There will be resistance to that."

Bill Greene laughed a little. "Your job. You get it done."

He stepped toward the door. As he was leaving, he stopped. Two agents had Lorna under guard. She was up against a wall, facing drawn guns.

"Get her out of the building," he said. "I don't want to see her again."

After they had hustled her away, Diana said, "Sir, she was acting under duress. That can be fixed."

"Good. Fix it. Forde! Where's Forde?"

The Secret Service chief waved from the hall and came up to the president. "She is to be placed under house arrest. Incommunicado. Put her in one of the safe houses. Any attempt at escape, shoot her."

"Sir?"

"You heard me."

Flynn watched Greene pass down the hall, heard the thunder of footsteps on the stairway as he and all who followed him returned to the Situation Room.

He and Diana found themselves alone. "A goddamn Bevo wrangler," Flynn said. He shook his head. It had been a hell of a thing to see that seeming idiot transform himself into a man of decision. But he had done it. Bill Greene was now and without question President William Greene.

"We've got a lot to do," Diana said.

"Do we?"

"Well—" She stopped.

"Time for the panthers to return to their lair," Flynn said. "Nothing more for us here."

They left the White House then, walking out among the crowds on a clear, brisk autumn evening. Diana took Flynn's hand. She said, "You're amazing, Flynn. That entire thing was amazing."

He looked back across the past ten days. "What I did is hard to understand. How it was accomplished."

"You're sort of a superman." She laughed a little. "Very impressive."

He felt a flare of anger. Surely she knew more. "Diana, what am I?"

"Basically?"

"Truthfully. What am I?"

"A small-town cop I recruited because he was obsessed with missing people. A man who does not quit."

"Perhaps I can help," said a familiar voice.

Morris was behind them.

"Jesus!" Diana said, whirling around.

More carefully, Flynn turned.

Morris had the whisper of a smile on his face. "You have saved my business," he said. "For that I am grateful."

"Your information was good, so thank you."

"Will you kill me now?"

"We're unarmed."

He nodded. "I know." He spread his arms. "As am I."

"I know."

"You're evaluating me, trying to see if you can take me physically." His hand darted out, tapped Flynn's cheek, and moved back to his side so fast Flynn had felt only the brush of the dry, cool, artificial skin, and had not seen the hand. Morris's smile widened. "Goodbye, brother," he said. He turned around and strolled off through the evening crowd.

Neither of them considered following him. They both knew it would be useless.

"He keeps calling me 'brother.' I don't understand that. I know for certain that I'm fully human."

"You are."

"But why can't they kill me? Why do I always get away?"

"All I can say is, I'm glad you do."

He took her arms and turned her toward him. "Do you know anything about me that you're not telling me, about what I am?"

"Batman? Are you Batman? Superman? An X-Man? Are such people real?"

"God, no. I'm a person." But in the back of his mind was the persistent, uneasy thought that he was not that, or not only that, and that Morris and Diana both knew some secret about him. He had sorted through his past, his DNA, his life, but he could not find anywhere an explanation for his physical skills or his uncanny ability to outwit the minds of Aeon. Maybe the means to detect what was different about him was beyond human capabilities.

She hugged him. "All I can say is, thank you."

He did not push her away, but he did not hold her, either. After a moment, she stepped back. "You think I'm lying with silence."

He nodded.

"You're a good cop from a small city in Texas. You come from a wealthy background which you're very equivocal about. Oil money. Mostly, you pretend it isn't there. You make a lot of charitable contributions from a foundation that's hidden behind an impenetrable legal firewall. Your one vice is fast cars and your best friend Mac Terrell is your moral polar opposite, a professional criminal as sleazy and dishonest as you are upright."

She wasn't from West Texas; she did not know how friendship was understood in a place that was so thinly populated. Mac's great-great-grandfather had been foreman on the Carroll ranch and Flynn's great-great-grandfather's best friend. They'd gone off to the Civil War together, walking all the way to Arkansas side by side. MacAdoo Terrell had headed south, William Carroll had joined the boys in blue. After the war, they'd both returned to the ranch and the friendship had resumed. Family legend had it that neither of them had ever mentioned the war again.

Flynn had grown up with Mac and, no matter what, would always remain his friend.

"You don't understand," he said.

"Not really."

"But there's more. There must be. I can discharge a gun so fast the eye can't see it. That's not a normal human ability, and there are others, as you know so well. You tell me the truth. Do it now or I walk away from here and you never see me again."

"You walk away? Never."

"Try me!"

"Look, we've done the same backgrounding you have. DNA, ancestry, life experience—believe me, we've covered the waterfront. Because you're the only chance we have. We need more Flynn Carrolls. When you go into the bullpen, do you know what half those people are? Genealogists, historians, neuroscientists, you name it, all trying to figure one thing out: Flynn Carroll."

"And?"

"I told you everything we know, Flynn."

Flynn understood that the law requires those who possess classified information to lie in its defense, and that he had to put his question aside, at least for now. Somewhere, though, there was an answer. He sensed it. Knew it, even. Somewhere in the vast world of the secret government, or in the ancient and mysterious reality of the universe, the truth was known.

They found a cab and returned to their house, the plan being to wash up, change, and go out to dinner.

But that's not the way it happened. Somewhere, perhaps, Abby watched her man accepting the mystery of his own soul a little more, and in so doing opening his heart at least a little to a woman who loved him deeply.

They lay together, and in their lovemaking she felt his passion, but not all of him; never that. She watched him sleeping that wary sleep of his, then fell asleep herself, listening to the quiet thunder of his heart in his powerful chest, and dreamed of melting into him and becoming his, and being welcomed there.

Very late at night, they woke up and went to the kitchen and heated some pasta and drank some wine. In one another's eyes they saw the same edge of heaven that all travelers in this life see when we find love at last, and discover that, for better or for worse, it is our destiny to journey on together.